LOVE ON THE MENU...
STEAMED

MELLANIE SZERETO

amatoria press

Love on the Menu…Steamed
Copyright © 2018 Mellanie Szereto
Published by Amatoria Press

ISBN-13: 978-1-942522-14-0
ISBN-10: 1942522142

Cover art by Dragonfly Press Design
Cover art and logos Copyright © 2018 Dragonfly Press Design

This story is a work of fiction, and any resemblance to real persons and/or events is coincidental.

BOOKS BY MELLANIE SZERETO

Love on the Menu series ~

Love Served Hot

Red Hot Pepper

Love on the Menu...Extra Hot standalones ~

Just Desserts

Iced Latté

A Little Appetizer

The Main Dish

Dressing on the Side

Flavor of the Day

Love on the Menu…Steamed trilogy ~

Egging Her On

Sweetening Her Up

Reeling Her In

Love on the Menu: Steamed Boxed Set

Death Benefits ~ A short paranormal romance

The Sextet Anthologies ~

Volume 1: Sharing

Volume 2: Dirty Dancing

Volume 3: Occupational Hazards

Volume 4: Entanglements

Volume 5: Mistletoe & Ménage

EGGING HER ON

CHAPTER 1

"No thanks." Lindie Brewster shoved the sheaf of papers at her uninvited visitor and picked up the bucket of chicken feed.

Shuffling the stack, the suit trailed her to the last of her five hen yards. "It's a very generous offer."

Lindie tossed a handful of garden scraps in a wide arc, a tangle of spinach, asparagus, and snap pea trimmings not quite missing his expensive dress shoes. Her feathered companions hesitated instead of racing for their treat like usual. "Close the gate." *With you on the other side, you pushy jackass.* "And stop rattling that stupid contract. You're scaring my chickens."

The metal latch clanked behind her. "They don't bite, do they?"

"They're chickens. They don't have teeth, unlike me." She scattered another handful for the latecomers on her way to the coop. "I have work to do. Show yourself out—without letting my flock escape."

"I'm authorized to offer more." His raised voice suggested he'd opted to wait outside the fence.

"I don't care if it's a million dollars. Tell your client I'm not interested in selling." She climbed the ramp into the henhouse before he could spout off another ridiculous number. The nest inside the doorway held her most consistent layer. "Hey, Goldie. Antisocial again, I see. Smart girl. What do you have for me today?"

With a calm cluck, the hen stood, allowing Lindie to remove the contents.

"Thank you, sweetie." She set the brown egg in her basket and fluffed the wood shavings in the nesting box. "It's beautiful."

After placing a helping of vegetable scraps in front of the hen and smoothing a hand over her soft earth-toned feathers, Lindie continued down the row, pleased with the haul from the largest of her coops. The full basket of rich brown eggs meant her customers would be satisfied and she'd have an early start on the weekend orders.

Goldie followed her out of the hen house, evidently still more content with human contact than interacting with her coop mates. The hen veered toward the gate and the unwanted visitor. Unfortunately, Lindie's best layer was more puppy than watchdog.

The lone rooster in the flock cut her off at the pass and herded her back into the center of the yard. His pointed stare toward the suit looked like a warning.

"It's okay, Red." Lindie aimed an equally unfriendly glare at the intruder. "He's leaving. Aren't you, Mr. Fielding?"

The man outside the gate pursed his lips and gave a curt nod. "For now. I'm sure we'll be speaking again soon."

"Not if I can help it." She scattered the remains of the bucket at her feet and marched toward the exit.

Her unwelcome visitor pivoted on his polished oxfords, clearly not up to arguing with her anymore today. "I'll be contacting the appropriate state and county offices to be sure you have all the proper licensing filed and up-to-date."

"Is that supposed to be a threat?" Her patience at an end, she heaved the empty bucket over the fence. It clanged against the ground no more than six inches from his feet and bounced to the right.

A chorus of squawks arose from the yard.

Fielding jumped and whirled around, his eyes wide and his mouth agape.

Satisfaction almost made her smile. "Go suck an egg, city boy. My flock is well under the five-hundred-bird max for a small-egg proces-sor. I have the required health department approval for my farmers' market sales in Ashland, Wayne, and Medina counties, and Dan came out last month for my annual inspection. Oh, that's Dan Putnam, an Ohio Department of Agriculture inspector, to you."

His she-knows-her-shit realization came in the form of a deep frown. "You tried to hit me with a bucket."

"Horseshoe champion, four years running. If I'd have been trying, you'd be out cold." She waved her hands at him in the shooing motion she used for her chickens. "It's definitely time for you to skedaddle."

His hasty retreat assured her he'd think twice before bothering her in person again. He could call her until he was blue in the face, but nothing would change. No amount of money would convince her to give up the tiny corner of the world where she'd created a peaceful life. Years of moving from place to place had brought her to this haven, and no way in hell was she giving it up for a chunk of change.

Basket in hand, she double-checked the gate as she left the fenced yard and walked as fast as her cargo allowed to the house. Her to-do list waited, and she was a good fifteen minutes behind schedule, all because some moron with too much money and an ego to match thought he could entice her into exchanging her home and her liveli-hood for a bigger bank account.

As she entered the mudroom, the flashing red light on the answering machine beckoned to her. "That better be a customer, Field-ing, or I'm auto-dialing you every hour on the hour from midnight to six in the morning for the next month."

She turned on the faucet and waited for steam to rise in the sink while the message played.

"Hello, Brewster's Roosters? This is Blaine Stockwell, your new neighbor from down the road. I was wondering if I could stop by for four eggs today. Or do I need to place an order ahead of time? You do have eggs, right? Because roosters don't lay eggs." After a few seconds of silence, he recited his number and hung up.

A disgusted sigh was all she could manage—not a snort at his obvious assumption that roosters meant male chickens or a forced laugh at his even more obvious pre-school sex education lesson.

"*Roost*-er, damn it, as in chickens roosting in the henhouse." Why did city folk think country living was the cure for their boredom? "And who buys a third of a dozen eggs?"

As she rinsed the day's collection, she tallied her standing orders and accounted for the extras two of her regular customers had requested for Friday. With her current supply, she could spare four eggs.

"Well, you lucked out, Stockwell." Instead of replaying the message, she tapped in the phone number from memory and wiped a dribble of sweat from her forehead.

After eight rings, the call went to voicemail. A generic voice recited the number and the standard request to leave a message at the tone.

"This is Lindie from Brewster's Roosters returning your call. I have four eggs available for pickup today. You'll need to stop by between three and five. Let me know if you'd like to place a standing order since I can't always guarantee I'll have extra eggs for sale. Have a nice day." The pleasantry stuck in her craw, but humoring idiots was part of running a successful business.

She sorted through the stack of damaged cartons, finally finding one with four good cells next to each other. A few cuts through the recycled fibers created a square package the perfect size for the small order. By the time the eggs were dry, she'd completed date labels and prepped enough cartons and trays for the rest of the week.

With her orders stowed in the eggs-only fridge and an hour until pick-up time, she switched to mucking boots, grabbed a pair of gloves, and hefted her cleaning tools. The flock she'd moved to the center pen greeted her with excited clucks and flapping wings as she dragged the hose toward their henhouse. Funny how they were smart enough to know Monday was housecleaning day at Coop #1. Too bad humans weren't as easy to get along with.

∽

"She said no again."

Blaine nodded, but he didn't look up from his laptop at his best friend's not-expected news. His research had warned him months ago that his new neighbor would be the last holdout. "Didn't I tell you, Erik?"

"And she threw a bucket at me. A metal one. It damn near hit me." Fielding dropped into the armchair across from him. "I deserve hazard pay for this gig."

A snort escaped. "A bucket, huh? I figured she'd be more of a warning-shot kind of woman."

Erik narrowed his eyes and jabbed an indignant finger in Blaine's direction. "You sent me in there thinking she'd *shoot* at me? God, I need new friends. You're as cracked as Lindie Brewster."

Finally glancing up from his latest financial report, Blaine rolled his eyes. "Quit being such a drama queen. *Warning* shot, not actually shoot you. I'm going over to pick up some eggs this afternoon. I want to get a better feel for her. Maybe the extra acreage from last month's deal will convince her to do a land swap."

Laughter echoed through the makeshift office Blaine had set up in his living room, but Erik's expression held no humor. "You'd give her a hundred-fifty acres of prime real estate in exchange for twenty-six acres and a hundred-sixty-five-year-old farmhouse? You *are* nuts."

"Plus the Cape Cod and its thirty-acre lot. It's called an incentive. I want that house and I'm willing to make the trade worth her while. I'll throw in moving her chickens if I have to." The ache in his gut flaring, Blaine closed his laptop and set it on the end table as he stood. "Family's always been important, but losing Bree put it in perspective. And my mom and dad aren't getting any younger. I need to get this done. The house is part of our heritage. I want my nephews to grow up in a place that's filled with family and history and good memories. Bree and I practically lived there during the summers, at least until Gram got sick. As soon as I take possession of the property, we can put my sister's house on the market."

"I get it. I really do, but you're going to be completely on your own out here." Erik leaned forward and propped his elbows on his knees. "Unless you have a girlfriend I don't know about. You planning on getting married again?"

A growl escaped before Blaine could swallow it. "One divorce was plenty, and what makes you think I can't handle being a single father? Bree and Kip trusted me enough to name me guardian of their kids if something happened. They both knew I had no intention of walking down the aisle ever again."

"I'm just trying to cover all the bases. You can hire housekeepers and babysitters, but mothers are—"

"No." The thought of sharing anything other than a meal and a night of sex with a woman made his skin crawl and his hair stand on end. "End of discussion."

Erik raised his hands as he stood. "No need to bite my head off. So what's the plan?"

"I'll let you know after I visit the egg lady. Everybody has their price, and I doubt she's an exception. It's not like she has any ties to the area. She's lived all over the state since she got her MBA."

"MBA, huh? I guess that explains why she was so pissed when I told her I planned to check her licensing."

"Bad move, dude. Maybe you should've looked over her profile like I told you to." Blaine tugged his tie loose and unbuttoned the neck of his dress shirt as he crossed to the arched doorway of his temporary office. "Help yourself to the good stuff. God knows buckets are some scary shit. I need to change into something less conspicuous than a suit."

"I'm a lawyer. I'm supposed to be conspicuous." Erik's voice carried down the hall to the master bedroom. The clink of glass against glass came with it. He wouldn't pass up a sample of eighty-year-old Scotch, bucket trauma or not. "She could've given me a concussion, you know."

Pulling a pair of shorts from the dresser, Blaine shook his head. "You'd have one if she wanted you to. All she needs to know about me is I'm a neighbor who wants to buy some eggs."

"She said the same thing. Something about horseshoes."

"Horseshoe champion, four years running. I'll say it again. You should've looked over her profile."

"Fuck you. Nothing could've prepared me for a woman like her. She's downright dangerous. Your phone's ringing."

"Is it my mom? I asked her to call if the boys had trouble adjusting to her and Dad staying with them." He tugged his tie free and tossed it on the bed with his suit coat, the possibility of an unplanned run to his sister's house pushing him to move a little faster.

"No. Local number. Not in your contacts."

"Ignore it. If it's important, they'll leave a voicemail." The cool wood floor did little to distract him from the nagging instinct to check on his nephews. He exchanged his business attire for shorts and a casual shirt and made a mental note to call his mom.

With boat shoes hooked on his fingers, he returned to the living room.

Erik held out his phone. "Voicemail and a text from your mom."

Panic worse than the first time a deal had gone sour skittered along his spine. Blaine dropped his shoes on the rug, tore the phone from his friend's grasp, and brought up the message.

"Leo and Cameron are fine. Wanted to let you know. Love you!"

His heart rate gradually slowed again, but the sudden need to see his nephews came out of nowhere. *"Thanks, Mom. I'm taking the rest of the day off. Tell them I'll be there about 3:30. Mind if I stay for supper?"*

A faint *ding* signaled her response. *"Wonderful! They'll be thrilled. You know you're always welcome."*

An involuntary smile tickled his lips. *"I know. Love you too."*

"This parenting thing agrees with you." Erik drained the last swallow of Scotch from his glass.

Blaine raised his eyebrows and pocketed his phone. "What makes you say that?"

"That worried look. Then the smile." With a smug grin, Erik shouldered his computer bag. "It wouldn't surprise me if you're taking the afternoon off to go see the kids. You make a good father."

Blaine waited for the usual proviso about being a good husband too. Thankfully, it didn't come. "They deserve my best and I like spending time with them. I'll let you know how things go with Brewster."

His friend's nod was accompanied by more of that knowing smirk. "Don't call me if she knocks you on your ass with a bucket."

"Not a chance. You're the bad guy. I'm just buying eggs from her."

"We'll see." Erik gave a half-hearted wave and headed toward the foyer. "Later."

The click of the front door eased some of the workday tension from Blaine's neck and shoulders, but impatience moved in. According to the Brewster's Roosters sign at the end of the lane, he had another thirty-five minutes before the designated pick-up hours. A listen to his voicemail confirmed it.

He carried Erik's glass to the kitchen, moved the dinette set closer to the window overlooking the backyard, and made a grocery list to kill some time. After six months of caring for a pair of young boys, his brain wanted to add peanut butter, grape jelly, and Goldfish crackers to the items he needed to stock his empty cupboards. Two weeks of vacation while he focused on the final deal had sounded like heaven, but damned if he didn't miss them already.

One night of not tucking them into bed down, thirteen to go.

It was motivation enough to step up his persuasive efforts.

He checked his watch and dug his keys from his pocket. If he drove around the block and got stuck behind a tractor, he might be only ten minutes early—and early was better than late when conducting business.

Alternating fields of ripening winter wheat and alfalfa lined both sides of the road, but a single lap yielded no harvesting equipment and brought him to the mailbox of the Brewster chicken farm at two forty-five.

A dust cloud followed him along the dirt-and-gravel lane to the familiar farmhouse from his childhood. The white clapboard structure was now pale gray with white shutters and the porch running the length of the house still invited him to sit in the shade with a cold glass of Gram's lemonade.

Home. With luck, it soon would be.

He climbed the porch stairs and knocked on the screen door. A full minute passed without a response, so he raised his fist to knock again.

Faint groaning carried from somewhere beyond the front of the house. He jogged down the steps and turned toward the corner closest to him, half expecting to find somebody sprawled out on the ground and needing a doctor.

The sound grew louder as he rounded the second corner that led to the backyard.

A naked woman stood a few feet from him with a garden hose aimed between her spread legs and her thumb plucking at the rosy tip of her left breast. The deflected spray of water landed on his feet, but her glistening skin and rapturous expression froze him in place.

She tipped her dripping-wet face toward the sky and arched her back, her taut nipples pointing right at him and a waterfall of dark hair cascading over her tanned shoulders. Another moan became a gasp. Then she cried out and rocked her hips forward, obviously in the throes of a full-blown orgasm.

A wave of lightheadedness rushed through him, every drop of blood in his veins flowing straight to his dick. Lust was a vast understatement for the feeling coursing through his body.

"Damn, that was a good one." Her gaze met his as she lowered the hose. The sunlit spray trickled down to dribbles at the nozzle and her sigh spoke of utter satisfaction.

He almost choked on his tongue at the lingering pleasure in her coffee-brown eyes. "You always shower outside?"

CHAPTER 2

"When I scrub chicken shit out of the coops in warm weather, I do. Do you always go wandering around people's private property unannounced?" Lindie perched a hand on her hip and pushed her shoulders back, flaunting her nudity in an attempt to hide her unwarranted embarrassment and make her second uninvited male guest of the day uncomfortable. The chill from the cold spray dissipated in an instant from the heat generated by his brazen leering.

The left side of his mouth curved upward, giving him a crooked but far too attractive smile. "I knocked. No one answered. I figured you were around here somewhere since your truck's parked out front." The hint of an erection behind his fly twitched and every inch of her skin tingled as he blatantly assessed her from head to toe. "You know, a lady would cover herself."

"I never claimed to be a lady. A gentleman would close his eyes or turn around."

A water droplet gleamed on his lower lip and his tongue snuck out to lick it away. "I never said I was a gentleman. What guy wouldn't watch when he catches a beautiful woman giving her clit a power wash? Do you need help getting your G-spot clean?"

Her uterus responded with an involuntary earthquake. "I'm more than capable of taking care of my G-spot. Besides, I don't sleep with men who're prettier than me."

"We wouldn't be sleeping, at least not until we were both exhausted from fucking each other senseless." His gaze left hers again, traveling downward to the parts he probably most wanted to explore. "And no man in his right mind would ever call you pretty. Gorgeous maybe, or breathtaking, but definitely not plain old pretty."

Tiring of his banter, she strutted away from him to the mudroom doorway, wiggling her bare ass more than necessary. The towel she'd left on the counter unfurled as she grabbed it. "Easy to say when you're staring at my tits and thinking about shoving your hard-on in my pussy. How about we get to the point? What do you want?"

He laughed, a low, sexy sound that bordered on an invitation to rip his clothes off him then and there. "You, but I'll settle for some eggs. Blaine Stockwell. I called."

"Mr. Stockwell, the egg-laying rooster man. Lindie Brewster. Chickens roost, including hens." A quick swipe of the bath towel soaked up most of the water on her skin. The shivers along her skin were probably from his dark eyes evaluating her ass as she bent to dry her legs. She twisted the damp cloth around her hair to form a turban. "You always come early?"

"For appointments, sometimes, but never when it counts." His amused voice seemed closer, but she didn't dare turn around to check. "Have dinner with me tomorrow and I'll prove it."

She stepped into her underwear and then snagged her bra from the pile of clean clothes, more self-conscious of the plain white cotton than her nudity. "If you want to get together for sex, fine, but I don't date."

"A no-strings hookup? I prefer that myself, even if I'm gentleman enough to feed you." His fingers nudged hers as she struggled to fasten the closure. "Allow me."

She pinched the inside of her wrist, determined not to react to the gentle brush of his fingertips against her spine. "Are you done yet? I'm expecting customers any minute, and I'm guessing Mrs. Doyle doesn't want her sixteen-year-old son seeing me get fondled by a horny voyeur."

"All trussed up." His breath tickled her neck as he smoothed the elastic band along the middle of her back. "You still haven't said if you're free for supper tomorrow."

Stepping out of his reach, she retrieved her shorts. "Tell you what. If you show up tomorrow at six thirty with a signed doctor's report telling me you don't have any sexually transmitted diseases, we'll discuss the possibility of you getting laid. I'm not interested in watching you eat."

"What if I want to eat *you*?"

"Smart ass." She removed the towel from her hair and then yanked her tank top over her head, hoping he couldn't read her body's interest in his proposition. "Wait here while I get your eggs."

The need for some physical distance getting the best of her, she stalked to the refrigerator in her bare feet instead of slipping on her flip-flops.

"What's the patch on your back for? Are you trying to quit smoking?"

Glancing over her shoulder, she rolled her eyes at the laidback way he leaned against the doorway. "I told you to wait outside. Not that it's any of your business, it's a birth control patch."

"Ah, good to know. One less question for me to ask tomorrow." His penetrating stare assured her he'd already formed a lengthy list of arguments to convince her they should screw each other until they couldn't walk.

"And it doesn't excuse you or anybody else from using a condom."

"Agreed. Good to know we're on the same page." Several strands of stylishly mussed hair had fallen across his forehead and he finger-combed them into place.

The temptation to heave the carton of eggs at him pushed to the surface, but she carried them to him instead. Her hens worked too hard to waste their labors. "Get out of here before I change my mind."

"I wouldn't want that." Amusement shone in his handsome face as he pulled a five from his wallet. "This ought to cover a standing order for four eggs once a week for a few weeks. Mondays okay?"

She nodded and took the money.

"See you tomorrow at six thirty." Without another word or ogle, Blaine Stockwell walked out of her mudroom like he didn't have a care in the world. His ego trailed after him.

Even if he was above average in the sack, her attention span would expire long before his. Wouldn't he be surprised when she kicked him out of her bed in a week or two?

The eggs stowed in his fridge and his hormones still reeling from the real-life porn scene he'd witnessed, Blaine slid into the driver's seat of his sedan. "Blunt, practical, and committed to staying unattached."

He rubbed the two-day-old beard stubble on his jaw. God, the woman was a female version of him, right down to taking the edge off her sexual appetite in the shower when necessary. It didn't bode well for his plans to buy her out, but giving up wasn't an option. He was a shrewd and resourceful businessman, and he'd find a way to make it work for both of them. If he managed a few weeks of getting to know her magnificent curves intimately, so much for the better. When he got bored, he'd walk away and she would be okay with it.

The *ding-ding-ding* of a boxing bell rang through his stereo system, signaling a call from his assistant on his cell. He tapped the Answer button on the steering wheel and turned onto the county road that led to the highway. "Yes, Mrs. Resnick?"

"You sound perturbed, Mr. Stockwell. Did the young woman refuse your offer? Or did she chase Mr. Fielding away when he showed up unannounced again?" Her snicker betrayed a fifteen-year-old sense of humor in the body of a seventy-two-year-old woman.

"Not perturbed, just thinking about options and possibilities. Erik ran to my place with his tail between his legs after she threw a bucket at him. And I wouldn't call forty young, even if she doesn't look it."

"Good for her! She's feisty like me, and I'd be careful mentioning your thoughts on forty since you're almost there yourself. Should I set up an appointment with her here at the office? She might be more receptive if you tell her why you want the property."

He adjusted the direction of the air blowing from the vent to cool the head he should've used for thinking when he stopped at Brewster's Roosters. "She won't show—if she returns your call at all."

"You don't know that unless... Oh, dear. Did you go talk to her yourself? You did, didn't you? And I bet you didn't tell her who you are." A *tsk* made her feelings on the matter clear. "If you're going to start doing business that way, you better tell me now so I can look for a new job. I don't like underhanded dealing."

"I told her my name."

"That's not the same and you know it, young man."

"Fine, I'll tell her who I am." *And probably ruin any chance of getting laid.* "I just went to buy some eggs and get a feel, um, to see if I might be able to reason with her, so no quitting."

"That's how it is, is it?" Her girlish giggle warned him she saw through his motives. "I bet she's even prettier in person than the picture I put in her profile for you."

Pretty doesn't begin to describe her. "And she's a hell of a lot more stubborn. That's for sure. Did you need something important?"

"Oh, that. Not really. Are you available for a consultation with Janda Ahlsmeyer over dinner and drinks at six o'clock today or tomorrow? I saw you blocked out three to nine today and two to nine tomorrow on your calendar. I told her you have conflicts both days, but she insisted I check with you."

Her? Hell, no. What was with his female clients thinking they could get professional and personal services from him lately? Single women had been coming out of the woodwork since he'd become an instant father. "I can meet any time between ten and one tomorrow in the office. Wait. No lunch appointment, either. Actually, tell her I'm not taking on any new projects. I already have a full load and I want to spend more time with the boys once I have the house."

"I'll convey your regrets and offer your usual referrals."

"Thanks, Mrs. Resnick. I don't know what I'd do without you."

"You'd have to turn down all those propositions yourself. See you in the morning, Mr. Stockwell." Her laughter was cut short when she ended the call.

He headed east on the interstate, more determined to limit his office hours than he had been a month ago. Working from home wasn't a problem, but reducing his client list was, not only because of his workaholic tendencies. Word had gotten around about his ability to create business plans that attracted customers and convinced wary bankers to approve loans. A lot of his success combined luck with choosing the right projects, but it still meant following through with those plans. Not many of his clients wanted to do it on their own.

Phased retirement was becoming an attractive alternative, at least until he figured out a new career to try on for size. He'd done it when he transformed himself from accountant to corporate CFO to business consultant. Another change would do him good, jumpstarting the interest and energy that tended to run dry every five or six years.

Thankfully, his interest in women didn't last that long. As intriguing as Lindie Brewster was, he wouldn't put money on more than six weeks before he was ready to return to monk-hood. Being a surrogate dad would help turn six weeks into twelve days.

I wonder if she'd be willing to have sex three or four times a day. That might earn him a year's reprieve from explaining why he wasn't interested in meeting a woman's family, going with her to her friend's wedding, or shacking up.

He'd finally met someone who didn't have diamond rings and marriage vows in her eyes. The objection to dinner bugged him a little, but he could live with nothing more than a booty call. Wasn't that every man's dream?

He flipped on his turn signal and took the exit toward Lodi. The familiar scenery sparked a feeling he'd had trouble labeling the first few times it had happened. It was similar to the anticipation of starting a new project and the satisfaction of watching his efforts unfold into accomplishments, but it was much more than that too. His heart had grown tenfold the night he'd consoled his nephews, holding them close through the endless dark hours after he'd had to tell them their parents weren't coming home—ever. He hadn't expected to have to make good on the promise he'd made to Bree when Leo was born, and again with Cameron. Nothing could've prepared him for losing her or the bond he now shared with her boys.

Half a year had dulled the pain, but seeing his mom instead of his sister sitting on the front porch with the boys brought it back to life for longer than he liked.

As soon as he shut off the engine and opened the door, Cameron wiggled free of his grandmother's lap. "Uncle Blaine!"

"Hey, Cam." Blaine scooped the boy into his arms and hugged him as tight as the squirming worm would let him. "I missed you. Are you behaving yourself for Grandma and Grandpa?"

"Yep." The four-year-old gave a vigorous nod. "We played in the sprinkler 'cause it's hot today."

"Sounds like fun." Sneaking a sideways look at his other nephew, Blaine closed his car door and walked toward the house. "Hi, Leo. Do I get a hug?"

The older boy shrugged.

Blaine stood Cameron on the top step of the porch. "Head inside with Grandma. I'll be there in a minute."

His mom's worried expression softened as she stood. "Come on, Cameron. Let's tell Grandpa Uncle Blaine's here."

"Okay!" He tugged on the storm door handle, finally pulling it open far enough to slip through.

"Thanks, Mom." Blaine kissed her cheek as she turned to go. Then he sat next to Leo, his forearms braced on his knees. "Are you feeling sad today?"

The boy nodded, but he didn't look up from his lap. "The day after tomorrow is Mommy's birthday."

"Yeah, I remember. It's okay to be sad that she isn't here to celebrate. Should we do something special? Like get some flowers for her? We can put them in the vase by her headstone."

"And a cake with a candle so we can make a wish for her?"

"Sure. You know we can't wish her alive, don't you? No matter how much we miss her, she can't come back."

Leo leaned his head against Blaine's bicep. "I know."

"But we can sing 'Happy Birthday' and blow out the candle for her. Do you know what she'd wish for?"

"Uh-uh."

"For you and your brother to remember how much she loved you, and she'd want you to try to be happy, even though it's hard sometimes." Pushing to his feet, Blaine grasped Leo's hand. "I think we need to hunt for a picture of you and your mom to add to the collage she started last Christmas. And I bet she'd want us to pick out one from your last day of kindergarten too."

"Okay." The boy rubbed the back of his hand across his cheek. "Can you stay here tonight?"

A stab of remorse nicked Blaine's heart. "I can't. I have an early meeting in Wooster in the morning. Besides, Grandma'll fuss at me for hijacking too much of her time with you. How about lunch tomorrow, just you and me?"

"Really? Just us?" Leo gazed up at him, hope shining on his tear-stained face.

Squatting in front of the boy, Blaine swallowed past the lump in his throat and hugged him close. "Yep."

"I love you, Uncle Blaine."

"I love you too, Leo."

CHAPTER 3

"Die, you son of a bitch." Giving the bucket a final swirl, Lindie dumped the contents on the three-leafed monster creeping its way up the corner fence post. "I don't care how you got here, but you're going straight back to hell where you belong."

She slung the bucket handle over her forearm and picked up her gardening tools to store in the shed until tomorrow's hoeing, hilling, and weeding session. Her next stop was the shower to scrub off the barrier cream and the top layer of her skin—after dumping her contaminated clothes in the washing machine.

"Damn poison ivy." She squeezed a generous glob of post-exposure wash onto the washcloth and rubbed until her arms and legs turned pink. A rinse, a full-body wash with dish soap, and another rinse later, she shut off the water and grabbed her towel as she stepped onto the bathmat.

Steam covered the mirror, but she dried, swiped on deodorant, and slicked a comb through her wet hair without clearing a spot to see herself. If Blaine Stockwell wanted a made-up princess, he could damn well find some other woman to get his rocks off with.

She tossed the damp towel over the shower rod and went in search of shorts and a tank top. Mostly empty dresser drawers reminded her of the laundry she had yet to put away. With a glance at her alarm clock, she hurried out of her bedroom with ten minutes to spare. Putting her household chores at the bottom of the to-do list had its disadvantages.

She bounded down the stairs, hopeful that her potential fuck buddy was as good in the sack as he seemed to think he was. Giving up celibacy for bad sex was like biting into homemade cinnamon bread and having it taste like store-bought white. As she rounded the newel post at the bottom of the steps, movement on the porch caught her attention.

"Is it just me, or do you greet all your visitors naked?" Her new neighbor stood framed by the screen door, his sunglasses hiding his eyes but not his grin. He slid the aviators upward into his windblown hair. Jeans clung to strong but not overly muscular thighs and his short-sleeved button-down shirt seemed to hint that he'd filed their tryst under dating etiquette.

Not bothering to try to cover what he'd already seen, she tapped her bare foot on the hardwood floor. "You're early again."

"I told you I like to be early for appointments. Besides, I'm horny, remember?"

She let her gaze travel to the growing lump behind his zipper and waved him inside. "Obviously. We need to go over the ground rules first. Follow me to the kitchen."

The *clunk* of the screen door preceded his footsteps behind her through the living room and into the kitchen. "Maybe you should get dressed before we discuss our agreement."

She leaned against the counter near the sink, empowered by her ability to unsettle him with a lack of clothes. "Why should I bother now? I'm comfortable. Plus, it'll save time when we're done talking."

Mirroring her pose, he leaned against the island work center across from her, seemingly amused by her audacity. "You're a cruel woman."

"Efficient. Here's the contract." She picked up the papers to her right and handed him the top one.

His eyebrows rose, but he looked toward the typewritten text instead of objecting to having to sign a legal document. "Item one. Contraception will be used every time by both parties. No excuses, no exceptions. Each partner is responsible for providing his or her own protection without financial reimbursement. Lack of contraception will call an immediate end to potential intercourse." He nodded as he glanced up at her. "Agreed."

"Good. Initial it." She tossed him a pen and waited while he did as she instructed.

"Item two. Medical proof of current sexual health must be provided prior to initiation of the contract and updated at any time by either partner's request. The acquisition of additional sexual partners by either party during the length of the contract mandates an updated professional evaluation." He fished his wallet from his jeans pocket and withdrew an envelope. His neck flushed pink against the light-blue collar of his shirt. "Here you go. It's from eight months ago, but I haven't been with anyone for over a year. Unless you have an objection, I think we should stick to a no-other-partners policy."

His admission made handing over her own report slightly less embarrassing. "Mine's from a year ago December. It's been over two years since the last time. Exclusivity is fine with me."

"Okay. I guess I wasn't overestimating how many condoms we'd need when I brought three for tonight." The foil packet he pulled from his front pocket unfolded into half a strip of Trojans. He laid them on the counter and put the pen to the paper again. "Item three. Intercourse and all related sexual activity will be referred to as sex or other appropriately worded description, not making love or any variation thereof. Works for me. Fucking, eating pussy, sucking tits, and giving a blow job are all acceptable?"

Heat spread from her lower belly to her clit. "Yes, along with ball sucking and sixty-nining."

"Good. I like dirty talk during sex."

"I got that impression yesterday. Me too."

"Item four. Absolutely no emotional entanglements are permitted. The words 'date,' 'love,' 'relationship,' 'marriage,' etc. are grounds for immediate dissolution of the contract by either party. Check. Item five. Gifts are not allowed, unless directly related to specific sexual acts or sex play. Hmm…check. Item six. No sleepovers without prior mutual consent and no clothing or personal care necessities shall be purposely left or stored at the other party's home. Check. Item seven. This contract is a private agreement and may not be discussed or shared publicly or privately with anyone not party to the contract. And check." His rapid-fire review of the last four items made her pulse beat faster.

"Anything you want to add?"

"Yeah." He leaned over the contract, writing far more than his signature on the dotted line. "All sex and related acts shall be consensual and respectful of both participants' wishes. No means no. Stop means stop. No exceptions."

"Afraid I'm going to tie you up and do kinky things to you?" An image of him blindfolded and bound to her bed popped into her head, adding to the itchy impatience to wrap up their pre-coital discussion.

"No, but you might not want me to do it to you. This means we talk and agree to terms before we do anything unconventional. We barely know each other and sex demands a certain amount of trust." He held out the pen and the paper, his eyes locking on hers. They hid something she couldn't quite put her finger on. "Initial the additions and changes, and sign on the dotted line. Then I'll take a picture of the contract and email it to myself. You can keep the original."

She read the neat block lettering he'd added to the items she'd printed from her computer. The words matched the ones he'd spoken, so she approved it and scrawled her signature at the bottom. "Done."

"Okay." He set his cell phone next to the strip of condoms and, still facing her, rested his hands on the counter at his waist. "In the interest of full disclosure, I need to tell you about an issue you might have with me."

"What? You have two cocks?" She crossed her arms under her breasts, guessing from his serious expression that the revelation would have far more troubling consequences. "Because that totally isn't a problem for me."

"No, just the one." His lips twitched, but they didn't break into a smile. "However, you might think I'm a dick for not telling you the truth yesterday. I'm the guy who wants to buy this place."

"Oh, that. I knew who you were." Handing the contract back to him, she shook her head. "I'd have to be pretty damn oblivious not to notice all the real estate changing hands lately. When a new neighbor moved into the only other house within a half mile and called me about eggs, I had a name for the invisible land baron."

"And you still want to have sex with me?"

"Hell, yes. What does one have to do with the other?" She picked up his phone and tucked it into his hand. "Take the picture. I've been looking forward to getting laid since yesterday."

Several taps on the screen yielded a pair of clicks. After a few more taps, he returned his cell to the counter and unfastened the top button of his jeans. "How much foreplay do you want?"

"I'll take care of it this time." Shoving his hands out of the way, she made quick work of the remaining buttons. A smattering of dark curls peeked out from the narrow opening, nestled around the partially visible outer curve of his cock. She slipped her fingers inside his jeans, closing around silky skin, and eased him free. A slow glide down and up transformed his semi-erect dick to a rigid boner. "Nice equipment. Let's see if you know how to use it."

His groan sent another spasm coursing through her lower belly. "Give me a condom."

"What if I want to put it on?" She snagged a foil packet.

As she tore it open, he grabbed the contents. "Maybe next time."

The wrapper dropped to the floor and he rolled the latex circle between his fingers. When it didn't unroll, he flipped it over and tried again before finally donning the protection. His biceps flexed as he lifted her onto the counter. Then he guided her knees farther apart and stepped close enough to place the head of his cock at her opening. His gaze met hers, the moment of hesitation implying an opportunity to change her mind.

"Fuck me." She braced for a wham-bam that would likely satisfy him far more than her.

He pushed inside no more than an inch, barely giving her a taste of heaven, and withdrew.

His attempt to take control of their encounter sparked her temper. "No game—"

A wicked smile carried to his eyes as he glided his dick through her folds to her clit. The brief contact triggered a breath-stealing sensation a moment before he slammed into her. Fireworks exploded behind her eyelids and a rush of euphoria shot outward from her center as he filled her. A hoarse cry clawed at her throat, giving voice to an unexpected release.

Several more forceful thrusts set off a second tremor on the heels of the first, and tingles flooded her limbs, the combination of weightlessness and the sense of sinking into quicksand too intoxicating to do more than surrender to it. "God, yes, fuck me."

A loud growl punctuated another hammering against her G-spot, flinging her higher and drawing out another surge of pleasure. Their cries echoed through the kitchen as he stiffened and the flood washed over her.

He leaned forward, resting his forehead on her shoulder and bathing her breasts in hot, panting exhales. The sound of their breathing was noisy compared to the faint chorus of birds and crickets carrying through the open windows.

Aftershocks rippled through her muscles for several minutes. They reminded her how long she'd gone without real sex and that she'd have to invest in some new and more creative toys when playtime with Blaine ended. Finding some that triggered the same reverberating shudders inside her was a top priority.

He lifted his head, but he made no move to step away or even pull out. "Keep squeezing me like that, and I'll be ready to go again in about five minutes."

Her stomach rumbled, distracting her from his intimation. "I need to eat something first. I didn't have time for supper. Too much to do."

"If you recall, I offered to feed you." His lazy grin softened his words and he stepped back, holding the condom in place as he eased out of her. "Do you have anything in mind? I'm a decent cook."

"Something with eggs, bacon, definitely cheese. Maybe spinach or asparagus since I picked some of each today. Loaded scrambled eggs?" She scooted to the edge of the counter, hoping her legs would hold her when she put her weight on them.

He grasped her by the waist and helped her to the floor. His hands lingered for the count of five before he let go. Looking like he knew where he was headed, he rounded the butcher-block island and sauntered toward the downstairs bathroom. "I'll make a frittata after I clean up."

She couldn't help but watch him walk away, with his jeans slung low on his hips and a gait that said he wasn't as steady on his feet as he wanted to be. At least she wasn't alone in the effects of their sexual chemistry.

Testing her rubbery legs, she made her way to the laundry room for a shirt. The bathroom door clicked closed ahead of her, a sure sign he'd known the exact location. *Time for a serious conversation with Mr. Blaine Stockwell.*

She stalked past the drying rack full of underwear and tugged a clean work shirt from its hanger. On the return trip to the kitchen, she rolled up the threadbare sleeves and shoved three buttons through their ragged holes. As she reached into the fridge to gather ingredients for supper, light footsteps sounded behind her.

Without casting a glance at him, she retrieved a carton of eggs and a stick of butter. "I'm curious. Why are you willing to pay over twice the fair-market value for this place?"

He was quiet while she added the rest of the supplies to her pile, but his stealthy acquisition of the properties surrounding hers suggested he wasn't keen on sharing the real reason.

With his back to her, he lifted the cutting board from its hook on the wall and slid a knife from the block of wood on the counter. "It's important to me."

The somber tone of his voice spoke louder than his no-nonsense statement, and she moved to the sink to rinse a handful of asparagus under cool water. "It's important to me too."

His shoulders tensed as he chopped four slices of cooked bacon. Then he lined up the asparagus spears next to the bacon and cut them into one-inch lengths, with only the rhythmic *tap, tap, tap* of the knife against the cutting board breaking the silence. Fresh parsley from her flowerbed herb garden went under the knife and came out as a bright green pile of chopped leaves. "You live on part of the original homestead my great-great-great-great grandfather owned. He and his brothers and sons built this house."

Family. It figures. "Who's the suit? A cousin?"

"Erik Fielding is a friend of mine. He's my representative in legal matters and sometimes business dealings. For the past few months, he's been handling my land purchases in this area, including all the acreage that belonged to my grandparents. My grandfather had to sell it off in chunks to pay my grandma's medical bills."

A twinge of sympathy pinched her conscience, but she shook it off and unwrapped the half moon of Colby cheese a customer had given her in trade for a dozen eggs and a few spring vegetables.

"It belongs back with the family." He opened the upper cupboard door in front of him and pulled out a bowl like he lived here. He'd clearly spent as much time in this house as he had his own while he was growing up.

She raked the chunk of cheese down the coarse side of the grater. "You do realize no amount of sex is going to talk me into selling, right? I'm willing to give you first right of refusal if I ever decide to sell or if I die before you, but I don't plan on giving it up any time soon. I've worked my ass off to grow my flocks and make a peaceful place to live the rest of my life."

CHAPTER 4

Blaine grabbed the whisk from the crock of cooking utensils and took out his frustration on the eggs in the bowl. He added the parsley, a couple shakes of salt, and a few twists of black pepper from the grinder to the frothy bubbles.

The woman was stubborn and unsympathetic when someone else's wants were pitted against her own—more like him than he cared to admit.

"How much cheese do you need?" She dumped an orange pile into a bowl and snitched the strands still clinging to the grater. "Never mind. There's no such thing as too much cheese. Whatever you don't use, I'll put on top."

"It's just right, unless you keep eating it." He sorted through the pans in the lower cabinet for an iron skillet the right size for a two-serving frittata to keep from sneaking a handful for himself.

"Would you stop doing that?" The annoyance in her voice matched a small part of his mood.

"Stop what?" He set the pan on the stove to preheat.

"Finding stuff on the first try. It's creepy." The hem of her nearly see-through white shirt shifted on her thighs as she removed plates and glasses from the dishwasher, revealing a hint of her exceptional ass.

"I remember my grandma's kitchen. You put everything where she had it." The butter sizzled and melted into a pale-yellow puddle in the skillet. He added the asparagus, still debating the advantages and disadvantages of the proposal he'd run by Erik. "Would you be willing to trade if I offered you and your chickens another property not far from here?"

She paused in her task of setting the table. "I'm willing to listen. I won't promise any more than that."

Better than a flat-out no. After the addition of the bacon, he stirred the contents of the pan and then transferred a generous helping of grated Colby to the eggs. "Do you want toast?"

"Yeah. Seedless rye better be okay. It's all I have."

"Perfect." He dumped the egg-and-cheese mixture over the asparagus and bacon, a little taken aback by the lengthening list of likes and dislikes they had in common. *Back to business, damn it.* "I picked up an extra hundred-fifty acres with the Cape Cod up the road from the ranch I moved into, most of it farmable, but some woods too. I'm willing to exchange that house and the acreage to the north—one-eighty in all—for this house and the twenty-six acres you bought four years ago in an even trade."

Pursed lips drew his attention to her mouth, the mouth he'd forgotten to taste during their quickie. Her responses while he was inside her had consumed him. Next time, he'd have to remember to kiss those full lips and enjoy more of her amazing body.

"I'll think about it."

"Hm?" *Head in the game.* He lowered the flame under the pan and turned the oven knob to Broil. "Okay. I'll throw in moving costs, including your chickens."

"What about my coops and fencing? And my garden? I'll lose roughly a third of my egg output until the flocks get resettled, and I can't abandon this year's crops, not to mention I'm finally at full harvest on my asparagus. Hell, it'll be another three to four years before it's established enough again. And the orchard. I have customer contracts to fulfill and others expecting my produce at the local farmers' markets all summer and into fall." She dropped two slices of bread into the toaster. "You have no idea how much time and money I've put into my business."

Her reasons for refusing his offer made financial sense, but an earlier remark stood out in his mind. *"...a peaceful place to live the rest of my life."* He should've requested more than the college-education, work-history, and current-situation research of Mrs. Resnick's profile on Lindie Brewster. Personal details might explain her need for peace in her life.

"Maybe we can work out an arrangement to minimize the impact." The eggs jiggled under the gooey surface when he shook the pan, signaling another two to three minutes before the frittata needed to go in the oven. "Since your garden and the orchard are part of your livelihood, I'd be happy to allow you access here until the off-season and provide whatever resources you need to prep new spaces at the other house. What about moving your coops one at a time?"

"It sounds like a lot of unnecessary work." She turned toward him, nothing in her expression exposing any emotion. "I understand why you want the property, but I think we're at a standoff. This is my home and my livelihood we're talking about."

Although he had hoped for a quick resolution, he'd expected a challenge—and relished the opportunity to spar with a worthy adversary. Her use of the term "home" was, without a doubt, connected to the peace she found vital to her existence. He'd have to get damn creative to convince her she could make a new one somewhere else.

He transferred the skillet from the burner to the oven and set the timer. "You're right. It's a stalemate, at least for now. Supper'll be ready in about three minutes."

"Good. I'm starving." Her apparent willingness to let the subject drop wasn't typical of the women he knew, but she wasn't like them in most other ways, either.

"If you handle the toaster, I'll take care of drinks."

"Okay." She moved the butter closer to her area of the counter, putting her back toward him again. "There's milk, water, juice, iced tea, and beer. I'll have orange juice. Please."

"Me too." As tasty as a cold beer sounded, alcohol didn't mix with business or sex in his chosen context. Having a clear head kept him from making careless mistakes, like giving a woman the impression he might be interested in anything beyond temporary sexual encounters. It had served him well for the past twelve years.

The lack of conversation as he filled their glasses, topped the cooked frittata with more cheese, and served their supper bothered him, even though it shouldn't have. Only a few select people were allowed inside his circle, and a sexy chicken farmer wasn't one of them.

She guided a bite of cheese-smothered eggs between her lips and groaned. "No going out, but you can cook for me any time."

With his fork halfway to his mouth, he paused. "You still want to have sex with me?"

"Of course. Why wouldn't I?" The next mouthful was followed by a bite of toast.

Did he dare tiptoe through what would normally be a landmine?

The worst that could happen was she'd send him home without round two or round three and tell him to go screw himself. *Blunt, practical, and committed to staying unattached.* "I don't know many people who can separate their emotions from business."

She took a long swallow of juice and then set her glass on the table. "I learned to compartmentalize a long time ago. Whether or not we do real-estate business has nothing to do with our agreement to fuck each other. I'm sure as hell not going to punish myself because you and I don't see eye-to-eye on my farm."

My farm. He could only chuckle at her last jab as he cut into the wedge of frittata on his plate. "Glad to hear it. Let's finish eating so we can use the rest of the condoms I brought."

Her attention to the food in front of her was as focused as her concentration on sex had been, giving him insight into a deceptively complex personality. She might be straightforward and down-to-earth, but she wasn't uncomplicated. Discovering her motivations would lead him to the resolution he wanted.

By the time he ate the smaller portion he'd plated for himself, she was pushing her chair away from the table. "Since you know your way around the house, go upstairs and strip while I rinse the dishes. First bedroom on the left. And no snooping."

"I'll be naked and waiting." He pocketed the pair of remaining foil packets from the center island as he headed to the living room.

A quick study of the mantle above the fireplace, walls, and tables offered no information about the woman who'd bought his grandparents' house—no decorations, no magazines, no framed photos. Even the rocking chair in the corner was missing the personal touch of an afghan or a quilt. Without the details, the room seemed empty, like someone had partially furnished it and been interrupted. He'd change that as soon as he moved in.

He climbed the stairs, flooded by images from his childhood. The memory-triggered scent of Grandpa's liniment hit him at the doorway to the master bedroom. Grams had rubbed it on his aching muscles after hard days of planting crops, bailing hay, and repairing fences. Then she'd laugh at something he said and they'd share a passionate kiss before they caught Bree and him watching their intimate moment.

His grandparents had been lucky, as had his sister—and his parents still were. Blaine had tried to find the kind of love they shared, but a single error in judgment put an end to that hope. It was the only part of his life where he couldn't trust his instincts. The fallout from that mistake had left him with plenty of regrets and a lesson he wouldn't forget. Revenge was a dish best not served at all.

It's done. History.

Lindie's expectations were the same as his—physical satisfaction with no entanglements, no commitments, and no chance of getting screwed over.

He tossed the condoms on the nightstand and kicked off his shoes by the end of the bed. A gentle breeze caught the collar of his shirt as he unbuttoned it, drawing him to the open window. The roof of the old bank barn was visible above the oak trees and five white chicken coops stood out against patches of grass closer to the house. Beyond the hen yards stood a large rectangle of ground with neat rows of green plants surrounded by a fence. Colorful bunches of flowers dotted the landscape here and there, and the orchard still stood where it had when he was a kid.

Home. He'd sell his soul to wake up to that view every morning.

"You're not naked."

Or use whatever means necessary to get Lindie to hand it over. He shrugged out of his shirt, letting it fall to the floor, and then went to work on his fly as he turned away from the window. "Neither are you."

She yanked the well-worn cover-up over her head, revealing every delectable inch to him. "You were saying?"

"You should never wear clothes." With the last button free, he shoved his pants down his legs and tugged them off with his feet. "Better?"

Her gaze drifted lower. "Much."

The invisible caress of her eyes sent a welcome pulse of hunger through his dick. He crawled across the bed and leaned against the pillows at the headboard, the need to be inside her only marginally less urgent than when he'd arrived. "I want to touch and taste you everywhere."

"I think you can talk dirtier than that." Her graceful cat-like movements seduced him further as she straddled his hips and skimmed her neatly trimmed nails along his abs. She stopped short of his cock and grinned. "A lot dirtier."

"I'm going to start with your mouth and work my way to your toes. I'll get dirty as I go."

She guided his hands to her jaw. "My mouth can be pretty filthy."

"I'm counting on it." He sat up to meet her lips, not bothering with any of the finesse he usually employed with a new lover.

Her tongue molded around his, every bit as aggressive as he'd imagined her kisses would be. She held nothing back. Each powerful glide demanded he hand over control to her, but it wasn't in his nature. He slid his fingers into the damp hair at the nape of her neck and sucked on her tongue.

She groaned, nipping at his lip as she withdrew. The sting from her teasing bite fueled his lust instead of cooling it. Then she licked the spot, like she might not have meant to hurt him. Her husky growl said otherwise. Somehow, the woman knew all the right buttons to push to make sure he was far from bored.

He opened for her, inviting her inside again as he pulled her closer. Her nipples tightened to hard buds against his chest and she ground her pussy into the base of his erection. He was tempted to forget exploring her body. Scarier still was the temptation to say to hell with using a condom and bury himself inside her with nothing between them.

Smothering the irresponsible impulse, he focused on the kiss and eased her sideways onto the mattress. She rolled him toward the middle of the bed, her connection with his mouth never weakening. Momentum carried her on top of him, and the combination of soft skin and her lower belly laying on his cock tried to derail his plans again.

He finally had to break free for a breath before the lack of oxygen made him do something stupid. "Are you always this energetic during sex?"

"Yeah. Is that a problem?" Her teeth scraped his ear lobe, pushing him toward a total lack of self-discipline. She was a challenge, one that promised his interest would wane later rather than sooner.

"No." He dragged her upward so he could nibble a path down her neck to her collarbone. Then he inhaled the fruity scent clinging to the still-damp hair hanging past her shoulder. "I like a woman who can keep up with me."

Another shift brought her higher, and the maddening friction of her pubic bone moving up the swollen vein of his dick was worth having her breasts even with his mouth. The weight of her body on him antagonized the disenchanted wish for the happily-ever-after he'd witnessed growing up. *Sex doesn't signify love.*

He licked a circle around her areola and then sucked her nipple between his lips to distract his thoughts. It puckered against his tongue, tightening to the same enticing bud it had during her outdoor masturbation session.

She arched toward him, pressing against his cock. "More."

He flicked his tongue over the tip before switching to the other side for another taste of her silky skin. Drawing more of her flesh into his mouth, he savored her moans and pelvic grinding. Her responsiveness sent an unexpected jolt to his balls.

Before he could kiss a path across her ribs to her belly button, she straightened and knee-walked up his body, pausing when she straddled his chest. "Eat my pussy."

The intoxicating smell of her arousal drugged his brain and fanned the flames already threatening to burn him. "Suck my cock."

Her gaze locked on his, showing exactly what he expected to see—intensity, strength, and candor. "If I suck you, you'll come."

He didn't doubt her statement. "I'll never complain about you giving me a blow job."

"You won't get much of one if you don't make my clit happy." She repositioned herself above him, giving him a close-up view of her shapely ass.

A tug on her hips brought her within licking distance, but he dipped his thumb into her folds and let her slickness guide him to the apex of her pussy lips. The bundle of nerves responded to his touch, swelling under his fingertip. "You mean this clit?"

She gasped and her body trembled. "Yeah, that one."

"It'll be ecstatic by the time I'm done." He pressed a chaste kiss to the soft skin covering her sweet spot and then went in search of it with his tongue. Salty-tart flavor coated his taste buds with the first lick, welcoming him to the dessert course. The treat at the top made no effort to hide from him.

"Right there."

"Mm-hm." He glided over and around her clitoris, pleased with the tremors his attention caused.

Her breathy sigh caressed his dick. "You're pretty good at that."

"Mm-hm." Twelve years of avoiding relationships had taught him a lot about how to please a woman sexually. Women, on the other hand, had seldom been content with only the perks of his carnal knowledge.

"I might actually miss this when you're gone." She rubbed her face down his cock and her hair trailed after it. Her mouth closed around his right ball, sucking it into the warm, wet recess.

The reference to their fleeting association was lost in the sensations that swept over him. She loosened her hold, only to draw both testicles inside. Each firm pull on his sac amplified the tightness in his cock and tried to distract him from actively participating.

He plunged his tongue into her vaginal opening as he ran a finger down the valley between her ass cheeks. Her puckered anus slowed his progress, but a wiggle and moan seemed to indicate she had no problem with his exploration.

Then she mimicked the motion, triggering an unexpected contraction in his abs and sending a shiver through his already rock-hard erection. The release of his balls was followed by a slow lick up his length. "Pussy juice makes great lube."

She nudged his chin out of the way and slid two fingers into her vagina. Instead of rubbing the lubrication over herself, she touched her fingertips to his anus.

Panic blossomed with the realization of her intent, and he smothered the automatic instinct to cite the item he'd added to the end of her contract. "Be gentle. I'm a virgin."

"Good to know. I'm not, but gentle is still good."

Her lips closed around the head of his cock with a hint of pressure to his hole. A finger slipped past the outer ring of muscle, causing no pain, and halted long enough for him to acclimate to the new sensation.

After helping himself to her lube, he eased a slick finger into her, stopping at the first knuckle. A wiggle of her hips came across as permission to proceed. As he pushed in another inch, he parted her pussy lips and licked a path to her clit again. A groan implied experience had taught her how to enjoy the kind of play he'd rarely been encouraged to engage in, let alone be a recipient of.

"Yeah, just like that. A little bit at a time." She sucked more of his dick between her lips and then sank her finger deeper inside him.

The distraction proved effective, enough that he didn't give a damn if she got impatient and finished her penetration with a single motion. Her mouth was pure heaven, every draw and lick stealing his concentration. Then she caressed a spot inside him that promised an orgasm like no other.

"Fuck, that feels good."

"Prostate massage." She rubbed over it again. "Supposed to be equivalent to the female G-spot."

"Don't stop." Even as he focused on her tasty pussy and delectable ass, she dragged half his attention to his own combination of internal and external stimulation.

A steady flick on her clit and an easy in-and-out glide of his finger brought more sexy noises, adding to the building pleasure in his cock. The swollen bud hardened with a firm suck. She bucked against his mouth and gave his balls a squeeze with her free hand as she cried out.

Her continuing pressure on his prostate amplified the sensuality and decadence of her lips and tongue. A burst of heat shot up his length in a rolling surge of ecstasy, drawn out by her massage. He released the growl in his throat as his orgasm went on and on, stronger and far longer than usual. Every ounce of energy drained from him into her.

She collapsed on top of him, her unsteady breaths caressing his thigh. "You passed the test. I'll be ready to go again in twenty minutes."

CHAPTER 5

Blaine sipped his coffee and clicked on the first link Mrs. Resnick had emailed to him before he'd arrived at his office. A newspaper headline popped up in the window, the kind most people read with morbid curiosity. *Toddler Dies; Parents Charged.* The article was dated nearly thirty-five years ago. A sick feeling settled over him, but he skimmed the four-paragraph story.

The next report had been published months later. *Guilty Verdict for Local Couple in Toddler Death.* His roiling stomach warned him the story would expose parts of Lindie's life she tried to forget on a daily basis. The two-columns of newsprint confirmed it.

He leaned back and closed his eyes, his gut aching on her behalf. The pain of losing a sister was fresh for him, but she'd experienced it as a child. She'd been blamed for it by her neglectful parents and sentenced to three years of being passed from relative to relative, ten years as a ward of the state, and a lifetime of trusting no one. Her parents had gotten off easy with a slap on the wrist and by losing custody of their surviving daughter.

Her wish for a peaceful place was understandable. He even admired her remorseless determination to hold onto the home she'd found. She was genuine in a way the majority of people he knew weren't.

A knock on the door brought him upright. "Yes?"

It swung inward and Erik stepped into his office. "Any progress with the Brewster woman?"

"No." Technically, his answer wasn't a lie since she hadn't agreed to sell. His sexual relationship with her and the details of her childhood weren't open for discussion.

Erik sank into the chair on the opposite side of the desk. "I have a possible solution."

"Oh? Let's hear it." Raising his mug, Blaine nodded toward the coffeemaker. "Want a cup?"

Erik's right eyebrow quirked upward and the crooked set of his grimace signaled something enlightening had suddenly unraveled in his head. "No progress, my ass. You slept with her, didn't you? Since when are you so reckless that you screw the enemy?"

"I wouldn't call her 'the enemy' just because we're on opposite sides. And who I have sex with is none of your business. No, that isn't an admission."

"You don't have to admit it. It's written all over that my-dick-is-happy-so-I'm-happy look on your lying face." His nosy friend pushed up from the chair. "I'll get my own coffee. You'd probably poison me so I can't tell anybody you have a girlfriend."

"What's your solution?" Blaine tipped up his cup and willed Erik to let the subject of his exceptional sex life drop.

After blowing across the top of his coffee and taking a sip, Erik stepped toward the window. "You're not going to like it, but it would definitely solve the issue. Your obvious compatibility with Ms. Brewster might make it more bearable, though."

"Spit it out, Fielding."

Erik turned toward him, his pause in the conversation lasting long enough to make Blaine dread the advice. "Marry her."

Blaine's lungs seized for several seconds as horror swept through him. "Are you out of your fucking mind?"

Raucous laughter sent a splash of coffee sailing over the rim of

Erik's cup and onto the windowsill. He wiped it away with a napkin from the sideboard. "And you call *me* a drama queen? Think about it. You can live in your grandparents' house. The boys will have a mother figure during their formative years—plus no more single parenting for you. She's smart and financially independent. Did you know she paid cash for the homestead? And here's the bonus. Every night, you go to bed with a woman who evidently knows how to satisfy you and is aging pretty damn well, in case you haven't noticed."

A snarl threatened to crawl out of Blaine at his friend's blatant appreciation of her body. He swallowed it with a gulp of coffee and hoped the hot brew singed the surge of possessiveness the comment had sparked.

"But I wouldn't worry too much about her temper. If she's anything like you, a steady diet of sex will improve her disposition. I'll throw in a pre-nup for free."

Blaine set his mug on the coaster. "Have you considered that my disposition is directly related to how much you annoy me? And Lindie just tells it like it is. No unnecessary bullshit."

"See? You like her. When was the last time you defended a woman you were dating?"

"We're not dating." That much was true.

"So you don't deny liking her?" Erik's smirk disappeared behind his cup. "Good. You should like your future wife. Anything specific you want me to include?"

"Include in what?"

"The pre-nup. Can't you keep up? All that wild-monkey sex must be slowing down your brain." After another sip of coffee, Erik sat. "A hundred bucks says you're a goner within two weeks. I'll wait for payment until you realize you can't live without her. I bet she's going to be madder than one of her wet hens when you tell her you're in love with her."

Blaine's tie tightened into a noose around his neck at the prospect of love and marriage. His cock, however, responded to the unbidden image of wet-and-wild Lindie hosing down her clit in the backyard.

"No wedding, no pre-nup, and sure as hell no falling in love. Why don't *you* go find a wife?"

"Hey, at least I'm trying. I have a date with"—Erik withdrew his phone from the chest pocket of his suit coat and thumbed the screen—"Regina the environmental geologist tonight. We're going to see the RubberDucks."

"Does she know it's baseball and not actual rubber ducks? Like one of those duck races on the canal? Mrs. Resnick's taking her great grandkids tonight."

"Well, um, maybe? Hell, I don't know." Concern dampened his friend's optimistic expression. "With my luck, she has no clue I meant a baseball game. Seriously, why does this shit always happen to me?"

"To remind me why dating sucks." The buzz of the desk phone announced the arrival of his ten o'clock appointment. "Got to work. You want to grab lunch today?"

Erik took his mug with him as he headed toward the door. "Can't. I have back-to-back meetings from ten fifteen to twelve thirty. Then I'm headed to my mom's to mow grass and go car shopping with her before my date. How about tomorrow?"

"Sounds good." Pleased with his narrow escape, Blaine stood to greet one of the few clients he'd truly miss when he moved on to his next career. The phone buzzed again, setting off a warning in his head. "Yes, Mrs. Resnick?"

"Your ten o'clock is here. Mr. Wannemacher was double-booked, so he sent his daughter." His assistant's eye-roll came through loud and clear with every word.

Son of a bitch. I need to revise my retirement timetable. "Thank you. Send her in."

Tracie Wannemacher strutted past Erik into his office, her low-cut blouse and skin-tight skirt showing more breasts and legs than they covered. Her puffy lips curved into a predatory smile. "Blaine, it's so good to see you again. We really need to get together for drinks and a chat sometime soon."

Only if soon means never. He dodged her attempt at a hug with a firm handshake and then gestured toward the chair Erik had vacated.

"Have a seat and we'll go over your father's updated business plan."
*And have you out of my office before you get any crazy ideas about
sinking your claws into me.*

His phone vibrated in his pocket. A glance at the text message as he
rounded the desk added to his exasperation.

"Marry Brewster and your woman problems are over. LOL"

The drive from his office to Lodi gave Blaine a few minutes to
mull over his career options. Nothing jumped out at him, but the
sooner he moved on to something new, the better.

Maybe Lindie had the right idea. The best nights' sleep of his life
had come after days of bailing hay and stacking it in the barn loft with
his grandpa. Being a farmer had been on his list of life goals as a
teenager, standing in line behind making a shitload of money.

He'd succeeded at hoarding nearly every dime he'd earned and his
investment choices had created a respectable nest egg. Acquiring the
last part of the farm was the only obstacle preventing him from real-
izing his dream.

Erik's advice echoed in his head. It made financial sense and
wouldn't be a terrible decision from a business standpoint, but a
second marriage wasn't part of plan A, B, C, or D. He still had options,
limited though they were, and he wasn't desperate enough to make a
lifetime commitment that probably wouldn't last a month. Mind-
blowing sex didn't make a good foundation for marriage.

With flowers and a cake on his shopping list, he took a slight right
toward downtown. A brightly painted sign greeted him as he entered
the business district, announcing the local farmers' market and
directing him toward parking. Although it didn't open for another five
minutes, he followed the arrows to the square, careful of the early
birds, and pulled into the first empty space.

The afternoon sun beat down on him as he walked toward the
gazebo, giving him another reason to get rid of his businessman image.

He could make money in an old pair of jeans or shorts as easily as a suit. Success was about skills and attitude, not clothes.

A scan of the vendors sent him to the left and the aroma of freshly baked rolls lured him to the bakery booth near the middle of the row. He weaved through the customers who'd had the foresight to arrive before him.

"Blaine! How's the best consultant in Ohio?" The gray-haired woman behind the makeshift counter beamed at him. "Pick whatever you want. It's on the house."

He shook his head and grimaced. "Margie, we talked about this when we updated your business plan last year. Free samples are okay, but no giving away the merchandise unless you're donating to a good cause. I'm not a good cause."

"Baloney. But I guess I have to follow your rules."

"I'm just trying to protect your financial interests." A scan of her wares revealed a selection of cookies, petit fours, and her signature cinnamon rolls. "Do you have any cakes today?"

"I sure do. Is it a special occasion?"

"Leo and Cameron want to celebrate Bree's birthday." The words weren't any easier to say today. He hated the thought of spending the day—and the rest of his life—without his sister.

"Oh, you're such a good man to take care of those two precious boys. I can't imagine how hard this has been for your family." Margie pulled a square box from the wheeled cart to her right and set it on the table. "German chocolate with coconut-pecan icing. It was her favorite."

"Perfect. Thanks." He handed her a twenty. "Keep the change."

"Blaine Stockwell, you know I can't do that. I don't even like that you insist on paying."

"Tell you what, Margie. Earn the difference by pointing me toward somebody selling flowers."

She pursed her lips at him. "Stubborn man. Head down to the booth at the end of the row. Lindie's got some beautiful flowers today."

"Lindie?" A tickle in his belly caught him off guard.

"Lindie Brewster. Such a nice girl. She sells eggs, fruit and vegetables, flowers and plants. Good stuff. Always fresh." Margie winked at him. "I hear she's single."

"Is she now?" He picked up the box and cast a glance over shoulder in the direction his client had indicated. "I'll be sure to tell Erik."

"You're hopeless. One of these days, though... You just wait."

"I'm content waiting." Waving with his free hand, he set off at a brisk pace to escape the older woman's matchmaking attempt. "Have a great day, Margie."

Her sigh carried over the chatter surrounding him. "You too, Blaine dear."

He dodged small groups of customers gathered at each booth, careful to keep the cake level. Nearly a dozen people stood at his destination, so he took his place at the end of the line.

A woman with two young kids stepped up to the table. The baby reached for Lindie as the older child gave her a sparkly trinket. She hooked the present on the collar of her sleeveless shirt, smiling like she'd been gifted a priceless heirloom. A graceful one-armed scoop ended with the giggling little boy cradled in the crook of her arm. With her free hand, she thumbed the screen of her phone and then held it out for the woman to swipe her credit card. After they loaded the purchases in the bag with the help of the toddler, she handed the girl a flower and returned the baby to his mother.

Blaine stomped on the warm, fuzzy feeling in his chest. *So she's good with kids. That doesn't mean I should marry her.*

The line moved forward with efficiency he could admire, without compromising service or interaction, and finally putting him directly behind her current customer. Her eyebrows rose as she met his gaze over the elderly woman's head, but she continued the transaction as if they hadn't fucked each other like rabbits last night.

She motioned to a teenage boy in the next booth. "Caleb, would you please help Mrs. Bauer get home? She has too much to carry by herself."

The young man nodded and rushed to take a bag of produce from

Lindie. Then he offered his arm to her customer. They set off at a slow but steady pace.

Stepping up to the table, Blaine lowered his voice and focused his attention on the flowers in the water-filled buckets. "You have clothes on this time."

She snorted, a barely audible sound. "Yeah, and you're wearing a suit, like your buddy Fielding. What can I help you with, Mr. Stockwell?"

The professional persona she donned toward him stung a bit, although he shouldn't have been surprised by it, considering their agreement. "I need a bouquet."

"Large or small bunch? Any particular colors?" She pointed to the sample next to a tub of asparagus. "I can customize it for you."

"Large. A mix of colors is fine. Something bright and cheerful."

As he slid his wallet from his jacket pocket, she plucked several flowers from one bucket and more from another. "Special occasion?"

The edge in her question hinted at a minor case of jealousy, which pleased him more than it should have, but the answer chased the elation away. Or maybe she was pissed because she thought he planned to give them to her at their appointment in her bed later. "My sister's birthday."

"That's thoughtful of you." She wrapped the stems in a damp paper towel and tucked the bouquet into a plastic sleeve. "You'll want to put these in water as soon as possible to keep them fresh."

"She would've been thirty-five today. She died in January." If he hadn't been watching for a reaction, he might have missed the there-and-gone flash of anguish in her eyes.

"I'm so sorry for your loss." She ducked her head, hiding whatever emotion had escaped. When she looked up again, her generic expression had returned. "Cash or credit?"

"Credit."

Her hand shook as she took the card from him and swiped it through the device on her phone. "If you'd like a receipt, you'll need to enter your email."

"I trust you." He returned his card to his wallet, not sure where the words had come from. She was practically a stranger, not someone who was part of his inner circle of family and friends. *I trust her not to overcharge me or cry when I say the fun's over.* "Thanks for making the bouquet."

She laid the flowers on top of the cake box and cleared her throat. "Seven?"

The slight huskiness in her question was the only hint that she'd referred to their meeting tonight.

A nod was all he could manage before he walked toward the gazebo. *Fuck you for planting stupid ideas in my head, Erik.*

CHAPTER 6

The dark sky promised rain and the forecast had predicted thunder and lightning to go with it, but Lindie hefted her hammer and pounded another nail into the ramp of Coop #2. She tested the boards with a vigorous jump before reattaching it to the side of the henhouse.

As she hooked the hammer in her work belt, noisy crowing came from behind her. "Yes, Rocky, I fixed it. Thanks for cheering me on."

She turned to leave the fenced yard, but the rooster blocked her path. He flapped his wings and splayed his speckled tail feathers, his wattle jiggling with the show.

"Fine." She frowned at the beggar and dropped the last snap pea from her pre-supper snack at his feet. "You're welcome."

He pecked at his reward, clearly happy to relinquish his guard-chicken status for a treat.

A raindrop landed on her shoulder, sending her hurrying to the gate. A distant rumble of thunder joined several larger drips.

She mentally skipped down her to-do list to tallying her income from today's Lodi market sales as she quickened her pace. Her stomach flip-flopped again like it had when Blaine had shown up at her booth earlier. She shouldn't have been disappointed that the purchase was for someone else. His reason for buying flowers was none of her business, even if he meant to give them to another woman. He was allowed to date, so long as he didn't have sex without informing her first. Exclusivity had been his idea, not hers.

She also shouldn't have made small talk with him like she did with her regulars. Finding out the bouquet was for his dead sister had been worse, bringing back memories she preferred to leave buried.

Why had he shared a personal detail with her? In another week or so, they'd be nothing more than casual acquaintances who'd engaged in a temporary no-strings affair.

After a quick stop at the tool shed, she continued to the house, hoping to put him out of her head.

Halfway to the mudroom entrance, the sky let loose, drenching her from head to toe in the half minute she needed to reach the door and duck inside. Grabbing a hand towel from the shelf above the sink, she sighed. "At least I don't have to water the garden or shower."

She stripped out of her soaked clothes, all too aware of Blaine's imminent arrival and that every time he'd knocked on her door she'd been naked and wet—and not always in the good way. She rubbed most of the moisture from her hair and wiped her skin dry. The phone blinked at her as she hurried to the laundry room to toss her shirt and shorts in the dryer and dress. After the remark he'd made earlier, having clothes on when he arrived was more important than a missed call, even if she'd have to take them right back off.

With five minutes to spare, she pulled on a tank top to go with her cutoffs. Her stomach rumbled at her, but she detoured to the answering machine.

"Hi, Lindie. It's Blaine. I might be a little late. How do you feel about a sleepover tonight? I'm stopping to pick up food and beer." The gruffness in his voice suggested his mood was anything but cheerful, not surprising since the day was a reminder of his sister's death.

She shook her head at the obvious attempt at bribery and cursed his choice of bait on her walk through the kitchen and down the hall. No hungry woman in her right mind would refuse his offer, although all-night sex was a worthy enticement to allow him to stay—no matter his mood.

Headlights in the lane and the sound of pouring rain met her at the front door. She plopped into the closest rocker on the front porch to wait for her visitor.

The car stopped near the garage, its wiper blades going from high speed to off. After what seemed like forever, the driver's side door swung open and Blaine made a mad dash through the downpour. He hugged a carryout bag close to his chest, but the duffle bag hooked over his shoulder obviously ranked lower than supper.

Water dripped from his hair and clothes as he bounded up the porch steps. His shirt clung to his torso, outlining the defined but not overly muscular pecs and abs. The dark hair below the hem of his shorts was plastered to his skin. A puddle formed at his feet, spreading across the plank flooring.

He set his cargo beyond the expanding pool and kicked off his sandals. His shirt landed on his shoes seconds later. Struggling to unbutton his saturated shorts, he huffed out a noisy breath. "Are you just going to sit there and watch me undress?"

She used her bare toes to set the chair rocking, the scent of slow-cooked beef adding to her contentment. "Yep. I kind of like the view."

"Then take off your clothes and let me fuck you." His order was full of desperation instead of horniness and teasing.

As she halted the motion of the rocker by standing, she tugged her tank top over her head. Her shorts and underwear puddled around her ankles with a push and a wiggle.

His gaze dropped, presumably to her braless breasts, and he withdrew a condom from his pocket. Then he shoved the rest of his clothes down his legs and stepped free. His cock bobbed toward her, already hard enough to execute the fuck he wanted. He rolled the latex into place. "Come here."

She closed the distance between them and was welcomed with a searing kiss. His tongue sparred with hers as he lifted her against him, taking all that she gave and demanding more. Fairly certain neither of them had any interest in foreplay, she wrapped her thighs around his hips and hooked her ankles at his back. With his hands cradling her ass, he guided her pussy up and over his erection.

She sank onto him, letting his cock fill her. The snug fit sent spasms rippling through her inner muscles and goose bumps spreading across her skin. If she lived to be a hundred, she'd never forget sex with Blaine Stockwell.

He pressed her shoulder blades to the column at the top of the porch stairs, planting him deeper inside her. Stray drips landed on her skin, but they didn't cool the steamy heat of his body connecting with hers. His groan vibrated through her jaw, the sound barely audible over the torrential rain.

She gasped with his first thrust against her G-spot, and his mouth claimed hers again before she could take a full breath. The damp hair on his chest teased her nipples with every powerful rock of his hips, adding to a quickly approaching wave of gratification.

His rough kisses and rougher pace spoke of a man who'd lost control and meant to take her with him into oblivion, whether she was ready or not.

I'm ready. She tightened her hold on him, certain she'd float away if she didn't. Every uncontrolled thrust brought an almost-there bout of lightheadedness and ripples of endless pleasure.

He tensed and jerked his head back. His roar sent her tumbling past the edge, even though his release seemed more about finding an escape from reality than sex. She surrendered to the free fall, caught up in the rush of weightlessness and rapture. It left her drifting in a mindless cloud, allowing her own temporary escape from a past that would never change.

The world faded beyond the downpour, ceasing to exist. They were alone, together in the only place that mattered—somewhere away from real life and memories.

Only the pouring rain and his ragged breathing trespassed on her brief respite, except they didn't seem like intrusions. Both were comforting, or at least they would be until the euphoria wore off. Then his heartbeat would return to normal and she'd have to pretend she didn't understand his pain. A momentary wish for more than she'd bargained for brought the bliss to an abrupt end.

Her muscles fighting her all the way, she maneuvered herself higher to let his cock slip free. "Time for food."

He lowered her feet to the porch floor. "Help yourself. Am I allowed to bring in my overnight bag?"

Surprised by his lack of presumption regarding the sleepover, she picked up the carryout sack. "Yeah. Breakfast is at six fifteen. You need to be gone by seven so I can get my chores done. I have deliveries and another farmers' market tomorrow afternoon."

"Okay. Can I throw my wet clothes in the dryer?"

"Sure. Put them in with mine. They've only been in there for a few minutes, so I doubt if they're dry yet." She picked up her discarded clothing, grabbed their supper, and held the door open for him. The aroma of yeast rolls surrounded her, its enticing smell reminding her how long ago lunch had been. "You know the way."

His curt nod triggered a twinge of guilt she had no business feeling. With a handful of wet clothes and his bag hanging at his side, he lumbered into the living room, looking like the weight of the world rested on his shoulders. The bag thudded on the rug at the foot of the stairs as he walked toward the kitchen.

She stopped at the table, but her gaze was trained on his bare ass until he disappeared around the corner to the laundry room. His problems were none of her business. Sympathy and empathy had no place in their short-lived association.

After emptying the carryout bag, she retrieved two beer glasses from the cupboard. Although he didn't seem like the kind of man to mix alcohol with wheeling and dealing or sex, she could hardly blame him for needing something to take the edge off his pain.

Palpable grief announced his presence as much as his footsteps behind her. "I bought a pot roast platter with mashed potatoes and gravy, onion rings, and a roll. Comfort food. I figured we could share."

She handed him a serving of dark-brown ale, sure he needed a gulp or two to dull the ache before he sat. "Smells great. If you're worried about having enough food, I can contribute pickled beets and eggs."

His sorrow-filled haze lifted with a hint of a smile and a subtle change in his eyes. "My grandma made pickled eggs for my grandpa. They were his favorite. I liked them because it was like having Easter eggs all year round."

Relieved to have prompted a positive memory, she padded to the fridge for the quart jar she'd refilled last weekend. At the table, she fished out a reddish-purple egg with a slotted spoon and rolled it into the lid of the onion ring box. Then she served up a spoonful of small round beets. "Help yourself to more. I have an almost endless supply of eggs."

He pulled her down onto his lap and nuzzled her ear. "I want to help myself to more of you."

Shivery tingles raced along her skin at his touch. She fed him a bite of onion ring and shifted until her clit lay nestled against his hairy thigh. "We could eat and play at the same time. Food and sex are both nourishing and satisfying."

He touched a beet on her bottom lip and then licked away the juice before sharing the pickled flavor with her in a slow kiss. "Tasty too."

"Mm-hm." She helped herself to the beet as she stood. "If we're going to eat without clothes on, you better go get a condom."

A lingering caress along her hip sent her insides somersaulting. "You must not have found the one I put in the beer carrier. I thought it might come in handy."

A quick search of the remaining holes in the carton yielded a blue foil package. "Very clever. Expecting to get laid in the kitchen again?"

"Hoping, not expecting. I can't be disappointed if I don't have expectations." He turned her toward him and guided her down to his lap again, her legs straddling him this time. His dick showed visible signs of recovery as she snuggled against his balls. "Of course, anywhere you want is fine with me."

She placed her palms on his pecs and nibbled a path from the base of his neck to his chin. The faint smell of shaving cream invited her to continue along his jaw. "Feed me while I make sure you're ready to suit up."

His nipples hardened against her thumbs, matching his growing boner below. Whether his desire to be screwed was a distraction from his mood or not, his libido didn't seem to care.

Impressed with his recovery time, she rolled the latex down his length. "Okay, so just feed me then."

The forkful of mashed potatoes he brought to her mouth dripped onto her chest, sending a drop of warm gravy trickling along the valley between her breasts. After he delivered the bite, he followed the droplet, lifting her to her feet as his tongue skimmed lower. A leisurely circuit around her belly button triggered a current of electricity through her vaginal muscles.

Then he guided her onto his sheathed cock. Lust clouded the anguish in his hypnotizing gaze. "Got it."

Goose bumps skittered up her arms with his inch-by-inch impalement. Every hard bulge and curve molded to her body, filling her. She tightened her pussy around him and was rewarded with a groan and a pulse of his erection. "Yep."

"You feel amazing." He opened for a bite, sucking her fingers into his mouth with the helping of pot roast. As he licked each of her fingers clean, he rocked his hips forward and back. The gentle but firm caress of his cock against her G-spot promised as much pleasure as the frantic pace of their porch fuck. Then his thumb found her clit, moving in the same easy motion. "I want to watch you come again."

The combination of his words and breath-stealing strokes pushed her to the edge faster than she would've thought possible. "Just like that. Oh, yeah. Touch me. Fuck me."

His lips parted and a groan accompanied the hardening of his dick inside her. He lowered his mouth to her breast and fluttered across her nipple.

A quake shuddered through her uterus and she let it carry her into oblivion as he continued his slow fuck. It dragged her on and on, with orgasm after orgasm as he slipped in and out of the elusive spot most men never found. Her throat prickled from the almost endless cries.

He gripped her ass tighter and quickened his pace. A feral growl followed seconds later, his muscles spasming beneath and inside her.

She melted into a boneless, breathless puddle against his chest and hoped she didn't pass out.

Boredom wasn't even a remote possibility for at least a month.

Unable to ignore her internal alarm, Lindie turned toward the nightstand to check the clock as she yawned. The dim light of the rising sun shone in the bedroom windows, casting shadows on the face of the man beside her. Emotion still darkened his eyes, but the grief seemed to have faded a little. If the sex they'd had couldn't fix it, nothing could.

Blaine hooked his hand at her waist and pulled her to him. "Thanks for letting me stay."

"I had ulterior motives." She snuggled against his mostly flaccid dick, glad she hadn't lost interest in it—or him—yet.

"It's been a rougher week than I expected. Losing a sister is pure hell." His even tone calmed the stitch of pain his admission incited. "We were really close."

"Time doesn't heal all wounds. Some scab over for a while and then rip open again with the right trigger." Personal experience had taught her that lesson—over and over.

"But how do you get to the point where it doesn't knock you on your ass for days at a time?"

"Compartmentalization. Years of practice. Working sixteen-hour days."

His laugh held no amusement. "I'm done working sixteen-hour days and I don't have thirty-five years of experience putting my feelings in a box."

She jerked out of his hold, the statement hitting too close to home. "What the hell is that supposed to mean?"

"Shit." The expletive gave away whatever cover he'd meant to hide behind, but a noisy sigh followed rather than an apology. "I know about your sister."

The loss squeezed her heart, but she focused on his betrayal. "That's none of your business."

"It was in the newspaper. Anybody who knows how to use Google could find it." His attempt to justify his actions added to her outrage.

"I don't believe this. You Googled my life?" She scrambled off the bed, kicking at the tangled sheet every inch of the way. His violation stung, not nearly as much as her parents', but certainly enough to rationalize her accusation. "How dare you invade my privacy like that?"

CHAPTER 7

L indie's anger was justified, but Blaine refused to apologize for finding out what made her tick. "I wanted to understand your motivation so we could come to an agreement."

"You mean, so you could try to use my personal life to manipulate me into selling." The glare she aimed at him should've hard-boiled his balls.

He swung his legs over the side of the bed as he sat. "It might have crossed my mind at first, but... God, Lindie, I won't take anything else from you. You—"

"And don't you dare treat me like some fragile flower who needs somebody to make life easier for her. I survived—on my own—and I don't want or need your sympathy." Her voice rose with every word, and the fire in her eyes added to her beauty as much as it conveyed her fury. She grabbed her tank top and yanked it over her head as she faced the window. "Consider this your official notice that I'm terminating our contract."

He climbed out of her bed and picked up his clothes, relieved she'd been the one to end their sex-only deal. It made his difficult decision that much simpler. "Thanks for saving me the trouble. Now we can solve the problem of who has the rightful claim to this house."

"What problem? It's mine and I refuse to sell."

"I don't want you to sell."

She jerked her head around, finally meeting his gaze. The wariness in her eyes said she suspected him of foul play and hidden motives—rightly so, but he didn't have a choice.

Braced against the door to his own past, he swallowed the panic trying to tunnel through his chest. The answer was right in front of him. He only had to say the words. "Marry me. We share the house and—"

The color drained from her anger-reddened cheeks. "Are you out of your fucking mind?"

He barely contained a laugh at the identical reaction he'd had when Erik had suggested it. If he could adjust to the idea, she could too. "We can do this. It's no different from a business arrangement."

"With lying and fighting and cheating." She crossed her arms in front of her chest, pushing her gorgeous breasts higher. "No thanks."

"Marriage doesn't have to be like that."

"Really? Did your research tell you how my parents fought all the time? How they lied to each other—and me? What about my parents' infidelity? Did you find out if my little sister was actually my sister? Because nobody could ever tell me. I'd be surprised if anybody knew, including my mother. What do you know about marriage?" The question sounded like an indictment.

His throat constricted, threatening to cut off the words he had to say, even though he should be more horrified by her childhood than a closed chapter from his own life. "I'm divorced. I know firsthand what can go wrong. My ex-wife cheated with a friend of mine. Instead of letting it—and both of them—go by walking away, I got my revenge by telling his wife...and convincing her to sleep with me. It got ugly. Really ugly. Two bitter divorces. I lost two friendships I valued. They had a nasty custody battle over their kids, especially since my ex-wife was pregnant with his baby. I may not have been completely blameless, but I shouldn't have lost everything, including my self-respect."

Her stony expression gave nothing away. "You just proved my point."

"One example of failure doesn't mean all marriages are doomed. My grandparents were happily married for fifty-seven years before my grandma died. My mom and dad celebrated their forty-second anniversary last month. I grew up thinking marriage was supposed to be easy because of them. I won't make that mistake again."

She paced to the nightstand, pivoted, and returned to the foot of the bed, staying well out of his reach. "It doesn't matter. I won't. I can't. Absolutely not."

"You have to admit the sex is pretty damn remarkable, and a little bit of arguing isn't the end of the world. It means we can have make-up sex. The only time I've broken my monogamy rule was when two people I trusted stabbed me in the back." Desperate to convince her she could depend on him, he offered the only thing she wouldn't say no to. "If I cheat on you, the house and property are yours without a fight. I'll have Erik put it in a pre-nup."

"This was probably his idea. I should've knocked some sense into him when I had the chance." The sun rising through the trees cast shadows over her, silhouetting her bare shoulders and raised chin against the morning sky. Not a hint of vulnerability showed in her posture, but he didn't have to see it to know it was there. Her doubts mirrored his.

"It *was* his idea, but I wouldn't have suggested it if the idea didn't have merit." He pulled on his shorts and then slipped his shirt over his head. On his way to the hallway, he picked up his shoes and overnight bag. "I'm asking you to consider it. You're the only woman since my divorce who's made me consider having a long-term relationship."

"You're not allowed to use that word." Light footsteps followed him into the hall.

Without looking back, he scuttled down the staircase. Right now, they needed space and time away from each other to allow for some perspective. "You terminated our agreement. I can say whatever the hell I want, including asking you out on a date, saying I want a relationship with you, proposing marriage, and calling what we've been doing making love."

"Like hell you can. Where do you think you're going?" Her question drowned out the squeak of the screen door. "You can't leave in the middle of a discussion."

Walking out took more determination than he'd planned on, but she'd probably take a swing at him if he admitted he was scared shitless too. She wasn't alone. Taking a chance on something he couldn't control was his worst nightmare.

He paused at the bottom step of the porch, crossing his fingers he'd made the right decision. "There's nothing left to discuss. Think about it. Call me when you're ready to say yes."

~

L indie's eyes stung, but she squeezed them shut.

Blaine Stockwell wasn't worthy of tears, a stuffy nose, and puffy, bloodshot eyes. He'd violated their agreement, violated her privacy. Then he'd forced her to put an end to their sexual relationship before she was ready.

No, not a relationship.

Booty call? Fuck fest?

"Don't hold your breath." She slammed the front door shut, not interested in watching his departure. If he wanted to give up perfectly good sex with her, so be it. That was his problem. She'd return to the self-service variety for the rest of her life—because no dick would ever convince her to come out to play again.

After a stop in the laundry room for underwear, shorts, and boots, she stalked out of the mudroom exit and to the barn. The pile of logs below the loft had been waiting for her to split them into firewood for three weeks, but keeping up with her daily chores and tending her garden had taken all but the hours she ate and slept—at least until she'd decided to screw the neighborhood stray. He'd disrupted her routine for half a week, putting her farther behind.

No more.

The sliding doors rattled open with her vigorous shove, flooding the interior with light from the rising sun. It touched the corner and reflected off the long-handled axe hanging on the wall.

She stood a piece of poplar on end and hefted the axe. A *thwack* rang through the rafters and vibrated through her fingers and wrists to her elbows with the first blow. A pair of half-round logs dropped to the floor. As she prepared to cleave a piece into smaller wedges, movement outside the barn caught her attention.

"Goldie, are you trying to move into the house with me again?" She abandoned her task and meandered toward the wide doorway, careful not to spook the hen.

Goldie answered with a disgruntled squawk and several cackles. Then she pecked at the loose gravel littering the ground.

"I'm sorry, sweetie." With a weary sigh, Lindie sat cross-legged on the dirt floor. "Men can be such a pain in the ass, Red included. They always try to make you think they know what's best for you, but it's usually all about keeping their dicks and their egos happy."

More pecking brought Goldie closer, and Lindie extended her hand. The hen stretched toward it, rubbing her neck against Lindie's fingers. Then Goldie toddled into the space between her folded legs. After a soft cluck and a fluff of her wings, the chicken settled into the makeshift nest.

"Why couldn't he have been satisfied with awesome sex and the occasional blow job? Most guys would've been thrilled with a temporary no-strings affair." Lindie ran her palm along the silky feathers of her favorite layer, her anger morphing into disappointment. "I wasn't even bored yet, and he had to go and ruin it. If he thinks I'll change my mind, he's going to have a hell of a long wait."

A rumbling coo suggested the hen disagreed.

"I'm not getting married. Ever."

Goldie looked up at her and tilted her head to the side, as if to question the truth of the statement.

"I'm not, no matter how good he is in bed. Or that he can cook. Besides, he only wants me to marry him to get his hands on this place. I don't want to share it. You've seen how bitchy I get when I have to be around people too much."

With a gentle flap of her wings, Goldie hopped out of Lindie's lap nest and tottered toward the closest support post.

"I wasn't talking about you." Lindie scooted on her bottom, following her best friend across the barn floor. "Where are you going?"

The hen stopped at the twelve-by-twelve and scratched the dirt at its base. Then she pecked and scratched some more.

"You digging for buried treasure?"

Her beak produced a hollow *twang* with the next peck.

Lindie lifted Goldie into her lap again and tapped the spot with her knuckles. The same muffled sound sparked her curiosity. "What did you find? Wait over there while I find the edges and dig it out."

As she set the hen aside, a narrow shaft of light hit the base of the post, illuminating a carved arrow in the wood. It pointed straight down to the location of whatever was buried. With her luck, it was probably a body.

A matted edge of burlap came loose with a few swipes of her fingers. She tugged on it, hoping her surprise find would pull free. After a few alternating yanks of the burlap, a corner loosened, allowing her to pry the rest of the bundled rectangle from the packed ground.

"What have we here?" She pulled a mostly disintegrated length of twine and the wrapping from a metal cookie tin. Bits of rust lined the edges, but the container was in fairly good condition considering the number of years it had likely been buried.

Time capsule? Box in hand, she pushed to her feet. "Come on, Goldie. Feeding time."

The hen trailed after her, waiting patiently while Lindie closed the barn doors, and then through the gate. The rest of the flock clucked and scurried to greet them, obviously ready for their morning meal.

The sun hovered partway below the tree line at the woods, gradually brightening the long shadows as Lindie made her rounds to the coops and headed to the house to wash off the dust. She would've preferred another round of sex with Blaine before breakfast, but she'd settle for looking at the contents of the tin. Multiple manmade orgasms in a twelve-hour period were better than the usual one she gave herself.

Sitting on the rug at the foot of her bed, she tapped the heel of her hand along the edges to loosen the rusty lid. It popped off with the third try, revealing a square of the local newspaper from twenty-five years ago. A black-and-white photo of a boy holding several ribbons filled the center of the newsprint. His teasing smile and air of confidence belonged to the man she'd kicked out of her bed at sunrise.

Disappointment made her insides squirm, and she wavered between tossing the box out the window and snooping through what were probably his personal belongings. Hadn't he nosed into her childhood, delving into things he had no business knowing about her?

She removed the newspaper clipping and set it aside. A ticket stub from a Cleveland Indians game rested against a signed baseball. Several arrowheads lay nestled in a narrow strip of bubble wrap beside a stack of photographs. A report card and a Boy Scout pin partially covered a faded blue envelope at the bottom of the tin.

None of it seemed anywhere near as private as the information he'd gathered about her—and she had no intention of using it to convince him to marry her.

The top photograph spoke loud and clear about his perfect childhood. He and the girl in the picture wore wide smiles. They had to be brother and sister by the similarity of their facial structure and hair color. *His sister who died.*

The next picture was a teenage Blaine and probably his grandfather, the man who'd had to sell his farm to pay his wife's doctor bills. They sat in the hayloft, their legs dangling over the edge, as they grinned down at the person with the camera. The writing on the back confirmed her guess.

The rest of the stack showed more of the same happiness and intimacy—the kind of life she'd never known. Blaine's family would undoubtedly welcome her into their world if she accepted his offer, but trusting another person with her wellbeing was equivalent to jumping out of an airplane without a parachute and expecting someone on the ground to catch her. Not even a Boy Scout could manage that. Did he have any idea how lucky he was to have grown up with a loving family?

She removed the pin and the grade card, more curious about the envelope than anything else. The message on it matched Blaine's block-style handwriting from their contract. "'Open in 25 years.' It does belong to him."

The flap might have originally been sealed, but time had rendered the glue useless, allowing her to slide a folded sheet of notebook paper from the envelope. Familiar handwriting listed numerous ages and goals for each. His life plan closely mirrored hers, with the exception of marriage. A divorce had marred his well-laid plans, but she'd bet he hadn't veered off track otherwise, based on his resolve to acquire her property.

The last two items on the list had been underlined with repetitive strokes of the pencil.

"Make lots of money so I can afford to keep the farm in the family. I want Grandpa and Grandma to be able to relax on the front porch and not have to worry about taking care of the land when they get older. That'll be my job."

"Failure isn't an option."

She slumped against the footboard, wishing she'd tossed the box out the window.

CHAPTER 8

Plunking the bucket down beside the last tomato plant in the row, Lindie tried once again to exile Blaine from her thoughts. Two long days and two longer nights had passed since he'd given her the ultimatum. Marriage had never been on her to-do list, much less with a man she'd known for less than a week. She'd far underestimated his determination to get his hands on what had been his grandparents' farm—and the means by which he'd try to accomplish it.

She stowed the fishtail weeder in her back pocket as she straightened and wielded the *hori hori*. Its knife-like blade and wicked edges made it the perfect tool for releasing her frustrations with him and her stupid conscience. Even her usually logical brain had come up with excuses for accepting his offer.

A vicious stab into the soil did nothing to chase away the ridiculous hope that he might actually like her in a romantic rather than a sexual way. She'd been a handy diversion, something to keep him from thinking about his dead sister. From a tactical perspective, his research into her past was no worse than conducting a background check on a business rival or a potential employee. She probably would've done the same if the circumstances had been reversed.

But I shouldn't miss him. Conversation wasn't her favorite pastime, no matter how easy it had been with him.

The newly sprouted dandelion popped free, ending yet another chore she'd finished early during her twenty-hour workdays since he'd left. Her fruiting tomatoes and peppers were weed-free and they promised a bumper crop for her market sales, special orders, and canning supply. The coops were clean, the grass mowed, and all the logs split and stacked in the barn.

She tossed her victim into the bucket, along with the dirt-covered weapon. "Let that be a lesson to all you nasty weeds."

"Maybe now isn't a good time to talk."

Her insides scrambled at the voice she'd dreamed about during the short spurts of sleep she'd managed since Thursday. She picked up the bucket and headed to the gate. Walking past him to put her tools in the shed and dump the bucketful of weeds on the waste pile was harder than she expected. "I didn't call you."

"I know." The disappointment in Blaine's voice had to be her stupid imagination. "There's something else I need to tell you. It might influence your decision."

She closed the garden shed and finally turned toward him, hoping the detached expression she'd perfected decades ago didn't fail her. "Forgive me if I doubt the possibility that you're pregnant. Damn biology and health classes."

He frowned. "Lindie, please. This is important."

Rolling her eyes, she crossed her arms in front of her chest. "Fine."

The dark smudges beneath his eyes said he hadn't slept any more than she had since their falling out, but he was still as handsome as the day he'd caught her showering in the backyard. The loss of his sister clearly hadn't gotten any easier, either. "I'm the legal guardian of my nephews. We're a package deal."

His revelation forced the breath from her lungs. "But... What about their father? You're raising... How many boys?"

"Bree's husband died in the car accident too. Leo and Cameron are six and four. Besides working on a deal to buy the house, I knew this week would be too rough on me to focus on the boys, so my mom and dad have been staying with them to give me a break. They're in the car if—"

Squawks and clucks drowned out the rest of his sentence.

"Shit." He sprinted toward the noise, his wingtips and suit pants not hindering his speed.

Recognizing Red's and Goldie's cackling, Lindie cut through the orchard instead of trailing after him. As she ran along the fencing behind the coop, she caught sight of a child at the gate and another smaller one sitting in the hen yard with Goldie on his lap. The rooster paced a circle around them.

She cupped her hands to her mouth as she continued the trek to the gate. "Bedtime!"

Red stopped mid step and glanced toward her. His obvious confusion only lasted until she reached the opening in the fence.

"You heard me, Red. In the coop." The older boy's eyes widened as she hurried into the yard. "Leo or Cameron?"

"I'm Leo. Are you Lindie?"

"Yep. Can you make sure the gate's latched please?" Still staring the rooster down instead of analyzing why Blaine would've told his nephews her name, she marched straight at Red. Now standing between her guard chicken and the hen, she waved at the boy in the dirt. "Hey, Cameron. Goldie's a great cuddler, isn't she?"

His giggle was as mischievous as it was endearing. Without a doubt, Blaine had his hands full fathering his younger nephew. "She likes me."

"She sure does. Red likes her too and he gets kind of grumpy when she pays attention to people." She pulled one of the snap peas she'd planned on adding to her supper from her shirt pocket and handed half to the boy. "I give him treats so he's friendlier. Can you toss it to him?"

Cameron heaved the pod in Red's direction and squealed when the rooster chased after it. "He's like a dog, only with feathers!"

"Yeah, but you have to keep a treat for him in your pocket if you come in the pen, in case he's in a bad mood. Otherwise, he may decide to peck *you*." Lindie handed him the remaining half of the pea pod. "I think Goldie deserves some too, don't you?"

"Mm-hm. She's a good chicken."

"My best layer. Lay her treat on the ground, and she'll climb out of your nest." As soon as Goldie was occupied, Lindie held out her hand to Cameron. "Want to go to the house to see some of her eggs? They're brown."

He jumped up and dragged her toward the gate. "Is it 'cause they're dirty? The eggs at the grocery store are white."

"No, it's because different kinds of chickens lay different colors of eggs. Some even lay green eggs."

"Wow. I want to see one of those." Her escort lifted the latch and skipped through the opening.

"I don't have the right kind of chickens yet. Now you have to make sure the gate is closed up tight so my flock can't get out."

Cameron jiggled it until the latch dropped into place and then raced ahead.

"Ring the bell and sit on the step." Her pulse had returned to normal, but she kept an eye on him to be sure he followed her instructions as she tagged along after him.

With a glance toward his uncle, Leo ran after his brother. The bell rang a second later.

Blaine fell into step beside her, looking like he'd had the scare of his life. "Thanks."

The urge to hug him almost overwhelmed her. "You're welcome. Curious little guy."

"Yeah. They're good kids."

An awkward silence filled the space between them, only becoming slightly less pronounced while she showed the boys her supply of eggs and the many shades of brown her hens produced. Then, at Leo's insistence, she walked with them to the front of the house.

Blaine met her gaze over the roof of the car, his expression giving her no indication what he was thinking. "Climb in, guys. I told Grandma we'd be home for supper."

As he checked the belt on Cameron's car seat, the older boy slid in next to his brother on the opposite side. "Lindie, are you going to marry Uncle Blaine?"

Her heart hiccupped, assuring her it wasn't any closer to an answer than her brain. "I don't know."

～

"*I* *don't know.*"

At least she didn't say no. Blaine shifted into Park, but he didn't shut off the engine. Leo's question to Lindie was nothing compared to the one he'd asked Blaine on the drive to Lodi. It had been stuck on repeat in his head the rest of the trip there, through supper, and all the way back to his temporary residence. He was almost certain of the answer, even if it put him inches from a full-fledged panic attack.

The standard ring of a telephone sang through his speakers and the push of a button answered the call. *Perfect timing.* "I need you to do me a favor, Erik."

"A favor, huh? What do I get in return?"

He braced for the thorough razzing he had coming to him. "The hundred bucks I owe you."

"What hun— No way." Raucous laughter filled the interior of the car. "You've gotta be bullshitting me. What's it been? A week?"

"Five days." *Since Monday afternoon.* "I know it's crazy, but… there it is. And she's gonna kill me when I tell her."

"That's got to be a world record. You know what. Keep the money. You'll need it to buy another bottle of Scotch. What can I do for you, buddy?"

Gripping the gearshift, Blaine fought the impulse to hit the highway and drive until he ran out of road. The only thing stopping him was the possibility that he'd never see Lindie and the boys again. "I want you to revise whatever you were planning to put in the pre-nup. The property stays solely in her name and passes to Leo and Cam."

"That's it? No mention of separate bank accounts, businesses, and investments?"

"No. I want it simple and straightforward. Can you have it ready in ten minutes?"

For the first time in their twenty-year friendship, Erik didn't have an immediate comeback. "Okay. Damn, you must have it bad."

"You have no fucking idea." Blaine leaned against the headrest and let out a slow exhale. "How did this happen?"

"I'd be rich—and married—if I knew. Check your email in five minutes. Oh, and go tell her how you feel."

"That's the plan." A slight case of lightheadedness passed with another measured breath. "You called me. What's up?"

"I was going to see if you wanted to go out for a beer, but asking the woman you love to marry you tops that."

Love. Could he say the word? "I already asked her."

"Then why aren't you flaunting an engagement in my face? Flowers, a ring, and a declaration of love. On one knee is a nice touch too. Do it right or go home. Your choice. Call me when you need a best man."

The line disconnected, leaving Blaine alone with a feeling he'd never experienced before. Two days without her had turned him into a walking zombie. He hadn't been able to sleep, eat, or concentrate for thinking of her and counting the minutes since he'd proposed a solution to their standoff. He'd missed her sense of humor, her lack of pretense, and, of course, the unequaled sex. What he hadn't expected was that he would miss waking up next to her and talking to her.

He missed *her.*

Today's visit to inform her of the parenting responsibilities she would have to take on had been a convenient excuse to see her. He hadn't recognized it at the time, but watching her rescue Cam from her territorial rooster had triggered a possessive instinct of his own. Once the adrenaline had worn off, a new rush had hit him twice as hard. Leo's question kept him from denying the truth.

He turned off the engine and climbed out of the car. His business mind weighed the advantages and disadvantages of admitting his feelings to her as he headed for the printer in his living room. In his experience, a half-assed commitment to a project yielded half-assed results.

If he married Lindie Brewster, he owed himself—and her—a hundred-percent effort.

The premarital agreement folded and tucked into his shirt pocket, he rose from the desk chair and forced his legs to carry him past the Scotch without pausing for a fortifying shot. It wouldn't improve his odds with a woman who likely didn't trust him. Why would she when he'd used subversive tactics from day one?

He detoured through the kitchen and out the sliding door, Erik's advice sending him in search of the items on his do-it-right list. The white and purple flowers at the edge of the field drew his attention as he stepped onto the deck. He picked a bunch and added some other colorful wildflowers to his handful, their simple beauty more like Lindie than a clichéd dozen roses.

Ring. Returning to the kitchen for a glass to hold the bouquet, he racked his brain for a reasonable substitute since finding an open jewelry store would require too much time. His key ring was round, but at least two of her fingers would fit inside it. He could bend a paperclip into a close copy of a circle—if he found any in a search through his computer bag. With so much of his business now digital, that wasn't likely.

With the flowers in a beer glass, he turned the faucet to cold. A spray of water squirted sideways from the spigot, shooting him in the belly. He jumped back and slammed the handle down to shut off the water. "Damn it!"

He twisted the aerator from the faucet, hoping the fix was as easy as installing a new O-ring. The misshapen rubber seal fell into his palm. Thankful for a trip to the garage rather than a call to a plumber, he set aside the filter pieces and filled his makeshift vase.

Loosening his tie, he hurried to the bedroom to change clothes. A suit wouldn't impress Lindie anyway. She wasn't the superficial type who had to have fancy clothes, an expensive car, or a diamond the size of Mt. Everest. Maybe he'd find a piece of string when he got an O-ring from his toolbox.

O-ring.

Ring.

Problem solved. He could live without an aerator on his faucet, but going empty-handed to propose for real was part of the go-home option.

Five minutes later, he buckled his seat belt and did a final check of the items he needed for the do-it-right version. The short drive from his ranch house to the farmhouse gave him time to adopt his business mindset, a somewhat comforting approach to the most important deal of his life.

Unfortunately, seeing her on her hands and knees at the front flowerbed with her ass in the air obliterated every thought in his brain.

CHAPTER 9

"I didn't call you. Again." Lindie snipped several stems of parsley from her personal herb garden and dropped them in the basket beside her. Maybe if she didn't look at Blaine, she'd have the strength to tell him the answer that made the most sense.

"I know, but I wanted to thank you for how you handled Cam messing with your chickens. Most people wouldn't have been that patient or understanding."

"He's four. Four-year-olds are curious. Besides, Goldie loves the attention." She dared a glance and a scowl at him over her shoulder. "You didn't yell at him for not staying in the car, did you? Or blame Leo for not keeping an eye on his brother? You're the parent. It's your responsibility to make sure they're safe."

"No yelling or blaming. It was my fault. I should've brought them with me to talk to you." He held out a vase filled with wildflowers, apparently unfazed by her accusatory tone. "For you."

Turning back to her task, she steeled herself against the flutter in her belly that promised telling him no would be damn near impossible if she faced him. "You don't owe me anything for teaching Cameron a lesson about territorial roosters."

"The flowers have nothing to do with the boys." He moved closer, now standing within her peripheral vision. "Can you take a break long enough to look at me?"

"It's best if I don't. And you should go." A pang of regret accompanied the words, even though they were true.

"As much as I appreciate your beautiful ass, I'd rather see your face. Don't you think I deserve that much?" He sounded more amused than impatient by her rudeness.

Thankful for her stubborn streak, she continued clipping herbs to take to the kitchen. "My answer isn't going to change. I like Leo and Cam, and I won't risk causing them more hurt if things don't work out. What happens when you meet somebody and decide you want a real marriage?"

"I have met someone."

His revelation cut through her soul, but she blinked back stinging tears. When had she given him the power to make her cry? Why didn't he leave instead of tearing out her heart and stomping all over it?

"I'm in love with her, but she doesn't know." He set the bouquet on the ground and knelt beside her. The brush of his leg against hers ignited the same sparks that woke her hormones every time he was near. "Actually, *I* didn't know until a couple hours ago. Love whacked me over the head while I wasn't looking."

"Then I guess it's a good thing I didn't call you and say yes." She pushed to her feet, desperate to get away before he saw how much his admission hurt her.

"Lindie, it's you. I love *you*."

"*Me?*" Relief, panic, and rage trampled disappointment in a race to define her emotions, but she continued toward the porch. As usual, her temper trounced the competition. "I never would've expected you to stoop to lying about something like that to get your hands on my farm. You pathetic son of a—"

"I'm not lying, and I can prove it." He waved a folded paper in front of her as he cut off her retreat at the foot of the stairs. "I had Erik draft a prenuptial agreement. The house and property will be in just your name. Leo and Cameron will be the sole heirs, even if I'm still their legal guardian. I'll never own or be part owner of the homestead. It's yours and it stays yours."

She unfolded the document and skimmed the lines of text through tear-blurred vision. The legal terms matched his simplified account, but allowing him to be more than a temporary sex partner meant taking a risk she'd never anticipated.

"Erik offered to witness our signatures and keep a copy in his records. Now will you let me do this the right way?" He dropped to one knee in the grass and handed her the unpretentious mix of Queen Anne's lace, chicory, red clover, and fleabane. His other hand opened, revealing a black circlet resting in the middle of his palm. "I love you. Will you marry me? For real?"

She could only stare at him, his declaration and question stunning her into silence. *Love?* His willingness to give up any claim to the Stockwell homestead had to signify something. *What if he's telling the truth?*

"Oh, and the boys couldn't stop talking about you. Cam wants to be an egg farmer when he grows up and Leo thinks you're a chicken whisperer." He slid the ring onto her finger. "Please say yes."

A closer look at his gift brought more tears. "Oh my God. You gave me an O-ring."

~

Cursing his unreliable instincts, Blaine rose from the ground and shoved his hands in his pockets. He'd screwed up the most important moment of his life. "I should've found something nicer, but it's all I had and I didn't want to put it off until tomorrow. With all the work you do in your garden and with your chickens, I didn't think you'd want—"

"It's perfect." Lindie rubbed her forearm across her flushed cheeks and sniffled. "If it breaks or I lose it, you're not out thousands of dollars. I can get a gross of them at the hardware store for less than a cup of fancy coffee."

"Yeah, it's very practical. Does that mean you'll marry me?" Her comment suggested an affirmative response, but he waited for her answer, knowing it would be as straightforward as she was.

"I never thought I'd... Shit, this is hard." She set the improvised vase on the porch railing, the shaking flowers a good indication of her state of mind.

Her hesitation allowed his nerves to calm and his pulse to return to normal. If she'd meant to say no, she damn well would've done it the same way she'd rip off a Band-Aid.

"I know." Grasping her elbow, he guided her down onto the second step. "Do you need a drink of water? Or maybe a shot of whiskey?"

She shook her head, looking as stunned as he'd felt an hour ago. "How did this happen?"

With a shrug, he sat beside her, careful not to invade her space. "I don't have a clue."

"You're no help."

He stifled the urge to smile at her retort. "You still haven't answered. It kind of makes me wonder if I'm going to have to beg."

"Just give me a minute, will you?"

"Take all the time you need."

She rolled the narrow band of rubber back and forth on her finger for the count of sixty-nine, each successive number giving him more reason to hope for the answer he wanted. Her unsteady exhale gave him the sign he needed. "Okay, I'll marry you, but I've never said the L-word to anyone except my sister, and no one has ever said it to me."

Happiness and affection eased the tension from his back and neck muscles. "You're overdue then. I promise I won't push you to say it. People say the words all the time without meaning them. The feeling is all that matters."

"I'm not sure I like it yet, either. It's... God, I can't even describe it." Her tone was much closer to her normal bluntness, suggesting his promise not to pressure her was sufficient to relieve some of the stress of falling in love for the first time. "I suppose you want to know when and where and all that stuff now that I said yes."

He scooted closer and rubbed his leg against hers. "I can take care of the details if you want me to. I'm good with a justice of the peace right here on the porch whenever you have fifteen or twenty minutes free. No fancy clothes or big to-do. Just the boys, my mom and dad, and Erik. Anybody you want to invite?"

"Not that I can think of, but thinking isn't going great at the moment."

Finally allowing himself a grin, he lifted her chin and met her gaze. "Maybe we should go have sex and talk about it later."

She popped up and darted to the screen door. "No maybe about it. Bed. Now."

Not risking her changing her mind, he followed her into the house and up the stairs. Her tank top landed on his head halfway to the landing and her bra hit him in the chest as she reached the doorway. He snagged both items of clothing and held them to his nose. Instead of a cloud of unnecessary perfume, her natural scent surrounded and seduced him. It was one of the many things he loved about her.

At the bedroom doorway, she shoved her shorts and underwear to her ankles, leaving nothing but a Lindie version of a farmer's tan. "We still need to work on your undressing speed."

He climbed the remaining steps and closed the distance between them. The length of dark hair falling over her breast invited him to fuck her against the wall, but he backed her into the bedroom instead. "You distracted me."

"You've been distracting me all week." Her fists closed around the hem of his shirt, and she tugged it up and over his head without unbuttoning it. It sailed toward the dresser as she attacked the button and zipper on his shorts.

"I'm not sorry." He worked them down his legs as he toed off his shoes. Stepping out of the last of his clothes, he brushed his lips against hers. The featherlight caress sparked the same sense of urgency he'd experienced when sexual hunger had led him down the path of temptation. "Are you?"

"No regrets. Yet." Her tongue glided along his with something more tentative than the passion of their previous kisses, but each stroke grew bolder than the last. This was the Lindie he'd fallen for, the woman who lived life on her own terms and didn't back down from a challenge. She wouldn't lie to him or cheat on him. It wasn't in her nature. She valued truth and loyalty above all else.

He eased her down onto the bed, savoring the feel of her body against his for the first time in what seemed like weeks instead of days. She wrapped her legs around his hips, holding him close as she pulled in a ragged breath. The desire burning in her eyes and the heat of her skin—everything about her—called to him.

Why hadn't he recognized the significance of his attraction to her from the beginning? It had been instantaneous and intense, unrelenting and undeniable. Sex had been merely the beginning, no matter how determined he'd been to avoid a deeper bond.

He braced himself on his elbows and cradled her face in his hands, astonished by the depth of his feelings for her. "Can we make love this time?"

She pursed her kiss-swollen lips and raised one eyebrow. "I should've known the only man to add rules to my contract would end up breaking half of them. Using words like marriage, relationship, and making love. And now emotional entanglements and gifts. Plus talking to your lawyer friend about me. What am I going to do with you?"

"I have plenty of ideas." He pressed his erection against the soft folds hiding her clit, probably torturing himself as much as her. "We can start by making love and do the rest over the next fifty years."

"Fifty years is a long time."

"Not when you love someone."

Her left hand crept under the closest pillow and reappeared with a foil packet. "We're going to need more of these. You forgot this one the other morning."

The lack of acknowledgment to his reference of loving her didn't surprise him. She'd accept their fate when she convinced herself they had no other option, just as he had.

"Left, not forgot. I was hoping it would make you think about how good we are together and motivate you to say yes. Walking out was about the hardest thing I've ever done." He adjusted his position with a downward slide along her slick pussy. "Unfortunately, I didn't take into account your willingness and inclination to take care of yourself. Most people are much more susceptible to redirection."

"Mm. You mean manipulation." She nipped at his chin, but he dodged the attempt and nuzzled her ear.

"Manipulation implies negative intent. I created a solution that would benefit both of us. It wasn't about just me."

"So the Boy Scout tries to play fair."

"Mm-hm."

"That reminds me. I want to show you something I found later."

"Later." A trail of nibbles brought him to her mouth. He dropped several teasing pecks on her lips, pulling away every time she tried to deepen the kiss. "And having a challenging adversary was a huge turn-on."

She placed a hand on his chest and pushed. "Why aren't you prepared, Boy Scout? You should already be inside me, and I'm getting impatient."

"You missed me then?" He snagged the condom and sat back on his heels.

"No more than you missed me, so wipe that smug grin off your face." Lust gleamed in her eyes, ruining the delivery of her command.

"Of course not." He tugged on her legs to line up his sheathed cock with her pussy. Inch-by-inch progress finally seated him in the hollow leading to her G-spot. Lifting her against him, he let gravity guide him deeper. "You couldn't possibly have missed me as much as I missed you. Every minute away from you was pure hell. I couldn't stop thinking about you and what it would be like to wake up next to you for the rest of my life. Once wasn't enough."

The catch in her breath signaled he'd hit his target. "Yeah, well, I've been working twenty-hour days to get you out of my head and it didn't work, damn it."

"Good." He thrust upward, too caught up in being surrounded by her to care if she argued with him over which of them had suffered the most. "Because that means you love me."

A spasm squeezed his cock and she groaned. Her hips rocked

toward him, generating more friction along his length and pressure in his balls. "Don't put words in my mouth."

"I can think of better things to do with your mouth. Besides, coercion isn't my style." He licked her bottom lip and greeted her tongue with a leisurely glide when she opened for him.

She fought him for control, but he ignored the confrontation and countered by rotating his lap in a circular motion, regaining the give-and-take balance neither of them had much experience with. A melodic sigh replaced her grumbling protest, and she settled into a smooth-and-easy rhythm of slow-dancing tongues and bodies. Each of her movements complemented his, letting him focus on the emotion he wanted to share with her.

A necessary breath interrupted their kiss, allowing him to watch her succumb to the beginnings of an orgasm. Her uninhibited cries and euphoric expression pulled him along with her. Heat and tightness flared in his dick as she arched against him and pulsed around him.

Her breasts and belly aligned with his and she bathed his neck in warmth and humidity with her panting breaths. Another contraction gripped him as she cried out again, propelling him toward the edge. "Come."

Unable to resist her plea, he gave in to the rush of pleasure and clung to her through the release. Her strength grounded him, even as he soared with the clouds. He embraced the loss of his heart to the woman who trusted him with hers and vowed to earn that kind of trust from her.

She dragged him down to the pillows without loosening her hold on him. Then she kissed his neck. "I love you."

The whispered words carried him higher than the crest he'd reached moments ago. He smiled against her cheek. "Good thing I didn't have to tease you for being too chicken to tell me."

SWEETENING HER UP

CHAPTER 1

"You're late."

The accusation came from behind Erik Fielding as he collapsed his wet umbrella and stepped toward the hostess stand. He faced the heart surgeon he'd contacted through the new dating website he'd joined last month. "I know. I'm sorry. I had to stop at my mom's on the way here."

Her flawless makeup couldn't hide the frown lines on her forehead and between the symmetrical eyebrows numerous shades darker than the almost-white haystack on her head. The photo on the site—and her natural hair color—had obviously been retouched, unlike his. Only her piercing blue eyes were the same. "Good God, not another mama's boy. I suppose you live with her, too. What are you? Thirty-five? Thirty-six?"

"Forty. It was in my profile, and not since I was an undergrad." He pasted on a smile to prevent the scowl dying to show itself, but her disapproving expression didn't change. *Being polite to a rude stranger doesn't cost a damn thing, except maybe a few wasted seconds.* "I picked up a prescription for her so she wouldn't have to go out in the rain, even though it was out of my way. It's the least I can do for the woman who gave birth to me and taught me to treat people with kindness and respect."

Color flushed her cheeks, but her silence and narrowed eyes clearly indicated she didn't plan to apologize.

Anger? Seriously? She deserved the damn scowl. Erik fished his keys from his coat pocket, too disgusted to share a meal and conversation with a woman he had no intention of asking for a second date, let alone marry. "I think it's best if you remove me from your list of possible matches."

Not waiting for a response or bothering with his umbrella, he headed out into the mid-October drizzle again. Rain landed on his hair and dripped past his collar, but the chill was no worse than he'd gotten from the cardiologist with no heart. She'd ruined his craving for female company, along with any desire to find a wife through an online service. Why did they all have to be so superficial?

Muffled music sang out as he ducked into his car. The familiar tune offered him the opportunity to vent—with no narrow-eyed stares or disapproving frowns. He switched to speaker as he set his phone in the cup holder. "Hey, Blaine. What do you want?"

"I thought you had a lunch date. I was just going to leave a message about a contract I need drawn up."

"I'm on my way back to the office to cancel that idiotic membership you suggested. She was pissed off because I was six minutes late. Six. Fucking. Minutes. She didn't remember how old I am, even though it was in the first section of my profile, right under my name. *And* she called me a mama's boy for taking care of my mother. I've had it with this shit. Did you know she's my forty-third failed first date this year? We didn't even make it to the table. Maybe it's time to pretend I'm only interested in getting laid and staying single. I still can't believe it worked for you."

His best friend's raucous laughter added to Erik's disgruntled mood. "I wasn't pretending. You know, you're not exactly the kind of guy to have sex with a woman for physical gratification alone, and Lindie wasn't interested in a relationship any more than I was. Good luck finding another woman like her."

"I don't want a woman who uses lawyers as target practice for her horseshoe-throwing skills. Hell, I can't even find someone who wants to marry me for my stinking money. Speaking of money, what kind of contract do you need?" Erik slid the dripping umbrella onto the floor in front of the passenger seat and buckled his seatbelt.

"Residential lease agreement. Somebody called about the Cape Cod yesterday. Not sure who told her I was planning to look for a renter, but it saves me the trouble of running an ad. Plus, I'd rather make money from the property than leave it sitting empty any longer. I'm showing it to her this afternoon, although I got the impression she's already decided to sign. I'd like to have a standard open-ended contract ready for her to look over by five today."

"Not a problem. Text me the specific terms of the lease, deposit, and monthly rent, and I'll have it done in less than an hour."

"Perfect. I'm meeting her at the house at one thirty. How about supper tonight? The boys have been asking when Uncle Erik's coming to visit again. We're having vegetable soup, homemade rolls, and peanut butter cookies."

"No thanks. I'm not in the mood to watch you and Lindie sneak foreplay while I eat. It's kind of nauseating and not even a little bit subtle."

"If you're staying home to pout, at least find some good online porn and jack off. Lack of sex is turning you into a whiner."

"I hope your dick falls off from overuse. Check your email at twelve forty-five." A tap of the screen ended the call, but the ability to be blunt with his friend left him a little less irritable.

After shoving his phone in the inside pocket of his suit coat and starting the engine, Erik backed out of his parking spot. Blaine was right about one thing. Abstinence sucked. The third-date rule Erik had put into place four years ago meant sex was in shorter supply than eligible women he liked, and his hand was no match for the snug fit of a pussy around his cock. Hands were made for cradling a woman's breasts and ass while they took each other to heaven.

Damn, I need to get laid.

As he merged onto the highway with a cheap burger and fries,

Blaine's ringtone cut off the mellow jazz coming through the stereo. Erik pressed the Answer button on the steering wheel after a brief temptation to let the call go to his voicemail. "What now?"

"I need a favor." The sound of running water almost drowned out his friend's words.

"I'm already doing you a favor."

"Cam's sick. Stomach bug. No preschool for him this afternoon, and Lindie's out on deliveries until two. Can you meet with the renter for me? Give her a tour of the house and go over the details of the lease?"

"Poor kid. Sure, I can cover for you. What if she wants to sign right away? Do you want me to drop off the rental agreement or email it?"

"Unless you want to catch preschool plague, you better email it or leave it in the mailbox. I need to tell Lindie to pick up a gallon of disinfectant while she's out. Kid germs mutate and make everybody else twice as sick."

I'll take a sick-as-a-dog kid and a busy wife over being alone any day. Erik signaled to take the next exit. "I'll scan and email it. Does your renter have a name?"

"Um, Cross maybe? I think that's what Mrs. Resnick said. The initial call came to the office, and she set up the appointment."

"No problem. An emergency came up before I left for lunch, and Mrs. R is taking the rest of the day off to babysit her great-granddaughter. I'll get the details at the house. Let me know if you need anything else."

"Thanks, buddy. I owe you. Name the favor, and it's done."

Erik snorted. "You can't give me what I want."

"Hey, you already told me you don't want my help finding you a woman. I'd do it if you'd let me."

"I have zero interest in dating your pre-marriage groupies. Go take care of Cam. I'll call you later." Erik disconnected before Blaine could offer another helpful suggestion that scored him a longer string of disastrous dinners, excruciating evenings, and miserable meet-ups.

Silence and an empty reception area greeted him in the office space he and his best friend had shared for nearly seven years. Contract law and business consultations had seemed a good fit back then. Side-by-side offices and a shared administrative assistant who kept them both in line had been a wise investment, saving them money and time.

He didn't blame Blaine for choosing to focus on raising his nephews and keeping his wife happy over working fifty to sixty hours a week. Unfortunately, working a day or two a week from home had evolved into three or four since he'd married Lindie. Erik had never expected to be the one left behind in their longstanding friendship.

A confirmed bachelor...with a wife and kids.

He didn't want it and I can't get past a first date.

Settling behind his desk, he powered on his laptop.

Maybe I need to be less picky.

He replayed the scene from today's catastrophe in his head. *Not a chance.*

A quick search of his files yielded the residential lease template he'd used for his and Blaine's clients over the years. As he copied and pasted the Cape Cod's address into the form, his cell phone buzzed.

"Sorry for the delay. Cam missed the bucket. Had to change sheets and start laundry. Still have the extra set of keys?"

He cringed at Blaine's text. *"Keys and the security code. Thanks. I'll let you know how it goes. And you're not getting any sympathy from me."*

The next message contained all the information Blaine had promised.

Erik typed in the details, did a thorough read-through while he ate his lunch, and then renamed and saved the document. By the time he printed two copies and stowed them in his computer bag with the house keys, the better part of an hour had passed.

On his way out of the office, he made a stop in the restroom to brush his teeth and check for evidence of lunch on his suit and tie. The rain had turned his usually controlled waves into unruly curls, reminding him he was overdue for a haircut. No wonder both dates in the last week had been disasters. Women didn't take him seriously when he looked more like a twenty-something beach bum in a business suit than a forty-year-old lawyer, especially when he'd specified a preference for a professional woman with a matching appearance.

As he dodged raindrops on the way to his car, he made a mental note to call for an appointment after his meeting with Blaine's renter. Even if he chose to pursue a casual hookup, a professional hairstyle was part of his persona—one he'd adopted and been comfortable with since law school.

The clouds continued spitting at him until he turned into the gravel drive less than half a mile from his best friend's house and Brewster's Roosters chicken farm. Lindie may have agreed to change her last name to Stockwell, but Blaine had insisted she keep the name of her business and retain sole ownership of the property that had once belonged to at least four generations of his ancestors. How the two of them had managed to fall in love was still a mystery to Erik.

Love was a mystery to him.

He parked in the wide turnaround with six minutes to spare. As he picked up his computer bag and retrieved the house keys, the sun cut through the overcast sky, lighting up the pale-yellow house and renewing his first impression that it was meant for a family—husband, wife, a couple kids, a dog. He'd even toyed with the idea of buying it from Blaine, but what was the point of living in it all by himself? Moving his mom into the mother-in-law suite would only make the heartless surgeon's assertion true.

All the same, when he stepped into the welcoming foyer, the urge hit him again. The panel on the wall blinked a red warning light at him until he entered the final digit of the security code, distracting him from the ongoing daydream for a few seconds. Then he meandered from room to room, flipping on lights and imagining a simple life with a woman he loved and their two-point-five children.

Hell, at this point he'd be happy with a wife and one kid. *Or just a wife.*

A sharp three-rap knock echoed through the empty house, accompanied by a feminine voice. "Hello? Is anybody here?"

Pulled from his fantasy, Erik shook off the unrealistic expectations and followed the banister to the stairs. "Be right there."

"Sorry I'm late. A semi took an on-ramp too fast and overturned. Traffic was backed up for miles."

"Not a problem. An emergency came up, and Blaine asked me to cover for him. I'm Erik—" As he rounded the newel post, she flipped the hood of her long red cape toward her back, revealing a perfectly shaped bald head. *Okay, not completely bald, but definitely as short as a classic buzz cut. Still beautiful.* He caught himself a moment after his chin dropped and left his mouth hanging open like an idiot.

Her eyes widened. "Erik Fielding? Oh my God, it *is* you. You haven't changed a bit. Well, except you cut off most of those gorgeous curls. I loved running my fingers through them while we"—she let out a soft sigh—"entertained ourselves."

The only woman who'd ever played in his boyish hair had thick, dark waves that reached almost to her waist. Blaine's renter couldn't be the girl he'd shared a bed with for most of the last month of his pre-law degree. Could she?

"You do remember me, don't you?" Her familiar coy smile sent his pulse hammering and his blood surging to his dick like it always had, from the first time he'd seen her shelving books in the library to the day he'd moved across the state to attend law school.

How could I forget you? Disappointment budded with another glance at her barely there hair, but the tension unwound as he remembered the impact she'd had on him. The red cape might imply innocence and naivety, but the big, bad wolf—or any unsuspecting male—was in for a big surprise.

Maybe a change of pace was what he needed in his life.

"Layla Krause."

CHAPTER 2

A nonchalant peek at Erik's left hand told Layla everything she needed to know about his marital status. While divorce was a possibility, it was highly improbable. Her former lover was a loyal, ring-wearing, for-better-or-worse kind of guy, which meant he'd more than likely never been married. Spotting his type was a useful skill in her line of work.

She crossed the cheery foyer with her gaze locked on his, thrilled at the unexpected perk in her plan. It certainly would improve her stay. "You sound uncertain. Do I need to prove it? With a kiss perhaps?"

A hint of hunger glinted and disappeared in his puppy-brown eyes, but his lips parted ever so slightly. His brain clearly thought to refuse her invitation, but his body wasn't willing to go along without a fight.

Just like old times. Rising to her tiptoes, she pressed her mouth to his and then slipped her tongue past the tiny opening. The minty flavor of toothpaste was no surprise, but his hand at her neck, pulling her closer, caught her off-guard.

He deepened the kiss, his tongue gliding along hers and exploring every recess. The same surge of desire that had drowned her in college hit with a vengeance. Although his approach was no less gentle than eighteen years ago, the sense of limited experience was gone and a much hotter fire burned in the urgency of his touch.

She closed the inches between them, ecstatic when the hard length of an erection met her lower belly. They'd always been in tune, always ready to give to and take from each other. Pretending they needed to waste precious hours with dinner, a movie, or a study date hadn't been necessary.

Dragging her mouth from his, she sucked in a breath. "Condom?"

His single nod brought relief and joy, even if substituting mutual oral stimulation for intercourse was an easy and acceptable option. "Sorry, no furniture. Upstairs? The bedrooms have window seats."

She smiled at his gentlemanly apology and offer of an option that promised more privacy, if not necessarily comfort. As she unfastened his suit pants, his abs twitched beneath her fingertips. "Upstairs is too far away."

He unhooked her cape, hesitating for a split second before spreading it over the carpeted stairs. Then he fumbled with his wallet and withdrew a blue foil packet.

"Unzip and put it on. We can take off our clothes next time." She bunched her prairie skirt around her hips and shoved her underwear past her right boot.

Shaky hands completed the tasks she'd given him, and his sheathed cock bobbed toward her in a graceful bow.

Conquering his control empowered her. It always had, preparing her for sex better than any amount of foreplay could. Part of their attraction was based on her ability to liberate the animal in him. What he did with that freedom made up the rest. "I want to be fucked by you. Right now."

He guided her leg around his waist, pressing his hard length against her clit. His lips caressed her neck as he lowered her to the steps and lined up with her opening. In a single smooth movement, he was inside her, filling her, touching a deeper part of her than any other man had.

Goosebumps skittered along her skin and warning tremors radiated outward to every nerve ending. Burying her hands in what remained of his curls, she wallowed in the friction his rough in-and-out motion created. Then his mouth was on hers again, seeking and demanding her attention. His groan vibrated through her jaw, letting her know he was close to reaching the ultimate pleasure sooner than he liked.

The animal still lives.

She rocked her hips upward to meet his frenzied thrusts, so close to flying apart she could taste it. The next collision of body against body flung her into a weightless, euphoric world, with an orgasm more carnal and absolute than her memories attested to.

He growled and stiffened, joining her on the wild flight at the last possible second like he always had. His lips released hers, but his hold tightened, keeping her from floating away without him. Steamy puffs of air warmed her neck, and she closed her eyes to block out reality for a few more precious minutes.

Their ragged breathing and motionless connection distracted her from the chaos, giving her a safe place to land, like their stint together two decades ago had done for him. Crossing paths with Erik again couldn't have come at a better time.

He rested his forehead against her brow and pressed his sex-softened lips to hers. Then he pushed upward, disengaging in the same careful way as dozens of other times. "I need to get rid of—"

As she pushed up on her elbows, a dribble of warm fluid trickled down her panty line to her bare bottom. "It seems we had a blowout."

"Son of a…" He spun away from her and rushed around the corner. "Don't move."

"You do realize holding still doesn't prevent pregnancy, don't you?" She dug in the purse still slung across her torso for a tissue to the *whoosh* of running water. Her search yielded a candy wrapper and three gas station receipts, none of which was particularly soft or absorbent.

"This is my fault. I'm sorry." His brittle acceptance of blame triggered the urge to smack him upside the head. He returned from his errand with a roll of toilet paper in one hand and a handful of wet paper towels in the other. "I should've checked the condom before I put it on. I was too…zealous."

The animal is caged again. She grabbed the toilet paper and yanked off a handful of squares. "The package looked brand new, and I don't want to have sex with the uptight version of you. Would you mind giving me a little privacy while I wipe your cum off my ass?"

A frown marred his handsome face. "That's a better place for it than where I put it."

"Mr. Fielding, are you suggesting we engage in anal sex in the future? Because, while I'm game, I'm not sure you can handle it." With exaggerated slowness, she stroked the folded toilet paper from her clit to her anus. "You're welcome to any part of me you want. All you have to do is say so. Or beg. Begging might be fun."

His jaw tensed, selling out his buried desire to be more than a boring, uninspired lover. Half the excitement of having sex with him was pushing his buttons to see how he would react. He was so much more man than he let himself be, in and out of bed.

With a huffy sigh, he finally turned his back to her. "When you're done cleaning up, I'll show you around."

"Avoidance is an effective, if temporary, coping mechanism." With the majority of the mishap taken care of, she pulled up her underwear and lowered her skirt. "Where's the closest bathroom?"

"Follow me." Spine more rigid than the hardwood floor they walked on, he led her past a closet on the left and then gestured to the next doorway. "Downstairs half bath. Meet me in the foyer when you're finished."

His post-orgasm demeanor hadn't evolved an iota since they'd parted ways all those years ago. The aloof, not-quite-rude but far-from-personable act made her itch to manipulate his repressed emotions back to the surface. Arguing beat the hell out of having a civilized conversation with him, especially considering his definition of civilized.

She grimaced at herself in the mirror as she washed her hands. Why did she have to be sexually attracted to somebody like Erik Fielding? Egging him on challenged her mischievous mind, but he lacked a sense of humor and probably had never stopped to smell the roses or any other flowers in his entire life.

At least I don't have to worry about him breaking my heart. She snorted and shook the water from her hands. No man had a chance of doing that, not after watching all her mother had gone through.

Her heart smarting at the reminder of why she was here, Layla exited the bathroom and retraced her steps to the foyer.

"I'm sorry about the condom." Erik handed her a business card, glancing toward the front door and then the room beyond the stairway instead of looking at her. "I accept full responsibility if there are… consequences. Not that I have any diseases. I don't. Just if… Child support won't be a problem. I can set up a trust so you'll continue to receive payments in the event I'm unable to make them. And I'll pay for any medical expenses related to the pregnancy. I'd appreciate shared custody and am willing to discuss sole custody, depending on your needs. I'll be glad to put it in writing if you'd like."

She fished her own card out of her purse and tucked it in the chest pocket of his suit coat. "In writing is always preferable, especially since an oral agreement with no witnesses wouldn't hold up in court."

His head jerked upward, and he finally met her gaze. "You've done this before?"

The temptation to get his goat was appealing on so many levels after the assumption he'd obviously made. "I have lots of experience."

The color drained from his face. "Lots?"

"Yep." She retrieved her business card and stuffed it into his flexing and un-flexing fingers. "Read it while I take myself on a self-guided tour of the house."

The urge to wipe the disapproval from his horror-stricken expression sent her fleeing upstairs. The stuffed-shirt professional she could deal with, but the judgmental snob would lure her straight to an assault charge.

At the top of the stairs, she stomped into what seemed to be the master bedroom, its beige walls a bit sedate for her tastes, but a view of the backyard through the French doors made up for the bland color. A dozen or so young maples stood scattered across the landscaped expanse, their sparse mix of yellow, orange, and red leaves no match for the thick woods beyond. The balcony invited her outside to enjoy the whole experience, even if it meant a few minutes of goose bumps and chattering teeth.

The floor creaked behind her as she stepped onto the wood decking. Moments later, footsteps suggested Erik now blocked her escape.

She smothered the urge to order him back downstairs so she could savor the beauty in peace. Her plan depended on living in this house long enough to find out the truth. Who knew how much influence he had on Blaine Stockwell?

"This is my favorite room." His words were a whisper, as if he too saw the need for reverence.

She bit her lower lip against the delicious shivers his voice prompted, even though she could easily blame the chilly weather. He didn't deserve a reaction or a response. Content to freeze rather than push her way past him into the bedroom, she rested her forearms on the railing and focused on the *drip, drip, drip* from the rain gutters and the tiny reflections of filtered sunlight in the wet grass, hoping he'd get the message.

"You were a psychology major. What made you switch to law?"

So much for that idea. "I didn't."

"So you went back later?"

"No." *Open your mind, Erik. I did both.*

The damp air seeped through the thin cotton of her blouse, so she imagined curling up in a comfy chair in front of a roaring fire to fool her senses.

"Look, I said I was sorry. I'm trying to do the right thing. What more do you—"

His abrupt silence tested her willpower not to react. Her neck muscles fought to turn her head toward him and her feet strained against her mind's control to pivot.

"Your hair. I didn't realize. Can you even get pregnant?" His hand curved around her waist. "Please tell me it isn't terminal."

She spun out of his reach, inadvertently trapping herself in the corner. "Terminal? What are you talking about? Of course I can get pregnant."

He scraped his fingers through his curls, frowning at something above her. "You don't have cancer? But your hair…"

The one word she didn't ever want to hear again brought a swell of anger and resentment, but she took advantage of his bewilderment, ducking past him into the bedroom. God, she had to squelch the sudden need to cry. "Not everyone who's nearly bald has cancer."

"Then why did you shave your head?" He followed her into the room and closed out the cold. "I've heard of people doing it to honor someone they lost to the disease."

Why did he have to be so damn insistent about knowing the reason?

Nothing about their past or present association gave him permission to venture into her private life. So what if they'd hooked up right after his dad passed away and the timing of their reconnection had coincided with a loss of her own?

He had no right to ask such a personal question. Sex was the extent and context of their relationship—nothing more, nothing less. His willingness to do everything but make an honest woman of her was evidence of that truth, not that she would ever agree to marry him.

The master bathroom to her right offered an opportunity to slam the door on his inquisition, and she took it, well aware of the psychological reasons for the wall she'd built. With a twist of the lock, she put all her weight into forcing the door shut.

It stalled less than an inch from latching and widened faster than she could close the gap.

"Layla, open the door. Tell me what happened." He wedged his polished wingtip into the increasing space. "We're not discussing the lease until—"

"How dare you blackmail me?" She jumped back from the doorway, ready to funnel her roiling emotions into her fists and pummel his body until she couldn't move.

A slow inward swing revealed Erik, standing straight and tall, unaffected by her rage. "I can help. Talk to me. Tell me who died."

Her throat tightened, cutting off her ability to speak, but not the threatening tears. She wrapped her arms around her middle and whirled away from him.

"Your husband?" His shadow overtook hers on the floor. "No, you wouldn't have seduced me if—"

Anger rose inside her again, pushing aside the heartache. "*Seduced*? You misogynistic, chauvinistic—"

"Seduced. You kissed me, and you know damn well I can't be in the same room with you without wanting to touch you." He clasped her shoulders and pulled her against him. An erection every bit as hard as the one she'd discovered earlier was nestled in the valley between her butt cheeks. "You do that to me. You've always done that to me. Now tell me who you're mourning so we can find another condom—hopefully, a stronger one than last time. I'll make you forget for a little while."

Pressing her ear to his chest, she let the steady *thump-thump, thump-thump* of his heartbeat soothe her rage and grief. His ability to provoke her temper was expert-level, but the way he made the world disappear equaled it.

Needing that escape more than she needed to breathe, she forced the words from her aching throat and let his shirt soak up the tears that escaped. "I made my mom a wig from my hair and told her I'd grow it back as soon as she didn't need mine anymore. She was supposed to get well, not die."

"Aw, Layla. I'm so sorry. I don't think we're meant to understand why some people are taken from us. Just know that I'm here for you as long as you need me." He lifted her into his arms and kissed her forehead. "For whatever you need me for."

CHAPTER 3

Cradling his distraught lover, Erik sat on the window seat adjacent to the French doors. Tears weren't something he would've expected from Layla. She was strong, sexy, and smart-mouthed. He wouldn't have described her as emotional, based on her easy agreement that finishing their degrees took precedence over a temporary sexual relationship. The death of her mother had evidently broken her in the way losing his dad had done to him. Not much could alleviate that kind of pain.

Their roles might be reversed, but the basic attraction between them hadn't changed. Eighteen years seemed like eighteen hours with the intensity of her impact on him. The fact that he wasn't supposed to be a hormone-driven college student anymore clearly didn't matter.

She peered up at him through long, dark eyelashes. The tears were gone, but the palpable sadness remained. "Make me forget."

"I think I have some condoms in the gym bag in my car. Will you be okay for—"

A low rumble accompanied a flicker of the ceiling light. Then Blaine's muffled ringtone punctuated the end of the thunder.

You owe me big for this interruption, Stockwell. "Sorry. I need to answer that." At her nod, Erik worked his phone free of the inside pocket of his suit coat. "Yeah?"

"False alarm. The monster snuck off with a dozen of the cookies we whipped up after breakfast and made himself sick. Why don't you and Ms. Cross stop by when you're done with the tour? We can go ahead and finalize the lease then. Signatures, deposit, keys. It seemed like she was in a hurry to move in."

"She got stuck in traffic, and we're just now doing a walk-through." Erik met Layla's gaze, desperate to reassure her of his intention to put her needs before anything else. "If the rain holds off, we might have a look around outside, too. We should be there in about an hour."

"No hurry. Lindie says to invite our new tenant to supper and that she isn't taking no for an answer from you."

"I'll ask her. See you later." He disconnected before his friend could put his tenacious wife on the line. A refusal would only result in her bringing supper to him or some other retaliatory action.

The tip of Layla's tongue snuck out to wet her lips. "Ask me what? The owner's not thinking of backing out of the deal, is he?"

Her apparent worry stopped him from taking a taste of her lips himself. "No, he wants to take care of the lease in person and mentioned getting the keys to you today. His wife invited you to supper. They live just up the road. A short drive. Maybe half a mile."

Her muscles tensed beneath his fingertips and she frowned. "You'll be there, won't you?"

Surprised by her expectation, he paused to weigh the advisability of viewing a shared meal at a friend's house as a dinner date. In all probability, she simply wanted a familiar face to help her through a difficult time in her life. "Yeah. Do you remember Blaine Stockwell, my college roommate? He and his wife, Lindie, own the house, and he and I share office space and an assistant."

She groaned. "I'm not sure I can do this."

"You have nothing to be embarrassed about. He doesn't know anything about us. I never told him back then, and he doesn't need to know about us now. This is between you and me." His promise didn't seem to ease her concern, so he gave in to the temptation to kiss her, determined to take full advantage of the hour they had alone together.

She responded to the gentle nudge of his tongue against her lips by opening to him and greeting him with an aggressive invasion. Drugged by desire, he followed her lead, ready to give her everything he had. The enticing sweetness of her mouth contradicted the unforgiving attack on his hormones, but the blend drew him deeper into lust.

Her shaky inhale as she pulled away said she was still as affected by his kiss as he was by hers. "Go get those condoms while I undress."

Not giving himself a chance to change his mind, he stood and lowered her to her feet. "The family room's carpeted. Come on. I'll show you where it's at on my way to the car."

She made no move to break free of his hold when he grasped her hand. The fit of their interlocked fingers reminded him of the hours they'd spent discovering every possible means of pleasuring each other. That exploration had kept him from saying to hell with his studies. Finishing his degree had seemed insignificant in the wake of his dad's death, but she'd saved him from his grief and let him go without a fight when he'd needed to move on.

At the bottom of the steps, he led her past the bathroom and into the kitchen. "Family room is to the left. I'll be back in a minute."

Doubts tried to crowd into his thoughts on the trip to his car, but he concentrated on his task. Even if Layla ended up pregnant or he somehow became more attached to her than he should, his personal life couldn't get any worse than what it had been for the last few years. Unplanned fatherhood had changed Blaine for the better, and feeling more than casual affection for a woman had been Erik's goal since he and his friend had settled into their referral-based partnership. For once, he was comfortable enjoying the ride instead of thinking about the destination.

He pocketed the half strip of foil packets from his bag and grabbed the blanket he'd tossed in the car last weekend during his winterization activities. As he closed the trunk, a raindrop pelted him on the head, sending him jogging to the house.

A black ankle boot rested on its side a few feet inside the front door. Its mate stood not far into the hall leading past the half bath. Wool socks too small to cover more than two-thirds of his foot lured him into the eat-in area of the kitchen. Her skirt, blouse, and tank top lay scattered across the tile, a clear invitation to follow her to the family room.

Bra and underwear left.

A scrap of black lace landed at the edge of the carpet less than a step away from him. The familiar tickle in his stomach and uptick in his pulse tested his patience. Her summons—that last piece of clothing —would likely land at his feet as soon as he entered the room. He wouldn't resist, *couldn't* resist. His earlier admission was the truth. She was an irresistible craving he hadn't realized he had, and controlling his reaction to her was impossible.

He removed his shoes and socks, leaving them on the tile, and padded into the family room. The plush carpet promised a softer bed than the stairway, but not as welcoming as the exquisite woman walking toward him with more black lace dangling from her fingertips. The sway of her hips matched the hypnotic movement of her breasts, each mound of flesh fuller than those from his memories. Her tapered waist drew his gaze downward to the apex of her sexy legs, legs he wanted wrapped around him while he buried himself inside her.

She stopped in front of him and hooked the tangle of elastic straps behind his neck. A gentle tug urged him closer and her breath warmed his chin. "Did you find what we need?"

"Three of them. I thought the blanket might come in handy too." He dropped his armful, intent on exploring every inch of this breathtakingly beautiful, more mature version of his unforgettable lover.

Before he could manage a caress along the smooth curve of her ass, she pushed his suit coat from his shoulders and down his arms. It fell to the floor behind him with a little encouragement from his hands.

"Mr. Armani isn't invited to this party. Just you and me." She worked his tie back and forth twice and then slid the knot along the narrower end of silk. It unfurled as fast as his dick had gone from interested to fully engaged with her teasing.

He resisted taking over unfastening the buttons on his dress shirt and hurrying to remove his pants. Undressing him had been her favorite part of foreplay, proving to him over and over that she wasn't the mild-mannered female most people thought she was. A sensuous, curious, and intelligent woman hid behind the easygoing personality and eccentric clothes.

Her fingers grazed his nipples, likely on purpose, triggering a jolt through his pecs to his balls as she removed his shirt. Then she pressed her lips to one sensitive tip. "Lean and muscular. Still a runner?"

He nodded, too caught up in her uninhibited examination to speak.

She dragged her fingertips through his chest hair and down his abs, stopping at the fabric between his cock and her hand. "I'm glad to see you haven't succumbed to the man-scaping craze. Men are supposed to be a little furry."

Unable to stop himself, he leaned into her touch, close enough to make contact with her breasts. The buds tightened against his skin, but she backed away instead of moving closer.

"Not until you're undressed. I want all of you." Her hand brushed his erection as she unzipped his pants, sending another pulse of electricity racing through his body. Then she hooked her thumbs in the waistband of his underwear and maneuvered both layers past the obstruction.

His cock finally free, he tugged off the tangle of clothing at his knees and kicked it aside. "I'm undressed."

Her slow visual assessment was a lingering caress, stoking the fire she'd already lit. "We need to make the bed."

He unfolded the blanket and spread it on the floor, with the condoms a few inches from the edge. Only her merciless tendency to prolong their contact-free foreplay stood between them now. "Let me make you feel good. I want to touch and taste you everywhere."

She gave an almost imperceptible nod and walked into his open arms. The silkiness of her skin against him filled part of the void that had plagued him during his unsuccessful search for someone to share his life with. Whether lack of sex or lack of love was to blame, he couldn't say, but she satisfied a basic need that had gone unfulfilled for too long.

He cupped her ass, lifting her to her toes and lining up her breasts to his chest. With his cock nestled against her belly, he lowered his mouth to hers, narrowly holding on to the control she'd stripped from him time and time again. She deserved better than the wham-bam he'd given her earlier.

Her tongue slid along his, dancing instead of sparring, moving slower but with no less intensity than usual. She threaded a hand through his hair and the other inched its way from his shoulder blades to his spine, following it until she mirrored his hold on her. Each motion elicited a positive memory from the dark period of his life when she'd been the only flicker of light. Everything about her was familiar and easy.

He broke the kiss as he lowered her to the blanket. Her whimper became a moan when he nibbled a path to her ear and palmed her breast. "God, I've missed going down on you. Will you let me eat your pussy?"

Her breath hitched as he traced a circle around her nipple, and she trembled beneath him. "Mm-hm. I love it when you talk dirty. Want me to suck your balls while you play with my clit?"

"Uh-uh. This orgasm is all about you." He flicked his tongue across her earlobe, disappointment making an unexpected appearance when her hair didn't tickle his nose or inadvertently find its way into his mouth. The crew cut suited her personality, but he preferred the long, dark waves he could bury his face and hands in while he lost himself inside her.

"I guess that means we're going to have to get together again." She leaned her head to the side, giving him better access to her neck.

The pale stretch of skin invited him to travel its length with his lips. At the spot where her neck met her collarbone, a slow inhale rewarded him with the delectable scent of cinnamon and apples. He nuzzled the hollow at the base of her throat, still breathing in the spicy goodness. "Not a problem, especially if you always smell so edible. Is that apple pie perfume?"

She giggled, sending tiny vibrations through his lips. "I made apple butter at my mom's house this morning while the movers were packing and loading next door at mine."

"Yum." Progressing lower, he closed his mouth over her nipple and gave it an unhurried lick. The puckered bud tightened against his tongue as he alternated between fluttering and sucking.

She moaned and arched toward him, but he savored her assault on his senses instead of rushing through the flavor, scent, and softness of her breasts. Every sound she made was a step farther from the loss she'd suffered, from the pain that went with it, from reality.

He shifted to the other side, content to ignore his aching cock and focus on evoking the reactions he wanted. A light stroke over her belly and along her hip yielded a soft coo, and she wiggled beneath his touch. Her impatience was evident in the sudden sting in his scalp, where her fingers still tangled in his hair, and the tilt of her pelvis toward his hand. In college, he would've given her what she asked for without a moment's hesitation, but experience had taught him to prolong the good things as long as possible—if he could maintain control.

"Eat my pussy, so you can fuck me."

He snorted against her ribs as he kissed the outline of each one. "Still bossy. We have about thirty-five minutes until we have to go, and I'm taking advantage of every second."

"I'll need at least fifteen minutes to recover and get dressed, and I want to see the rest of the house. That leaves fifteen minutes, give or take a minute or two, unless you need more time to get ready than I do."

Shimmying down her body another few inches, he shook his head. "I bet you don't lose in court very often."

"I prefer to negotiate instead of taking my chances with a judge." Her hold on his hair loosened and she gave his shoulder a downward push. "You can have all the time you want tonight if you settle for immediate gratification now. I'll even share my apple butter with you."

"I want the *whole* night, and I'll make breakfast for us tomorrow if you supply the apple butter." He feathered his thumb along her inner thigh in an effort to sway her judgment.

She stretched, obviously trying to guide his hand closer to its target. "Okay. Let's shake on it."

He maneuvered over her leg and settled on his stomach between her knees. Her clit now within reach of his mouth, he levered up on his elbows and licked his lips. "How about if I make you shake?"

CHAPTER 4

The gleam in Erik's eyes warned Layla he planned to give her exactly what she wanted and hold her to their bargain. He'd evidently learned to lay his demands on the table and use false compromise to get what he wanted, not that she cared in this instance. She had as much to gain from their deal as he did—multiple orgasms, sooner *and* later, and breakfast consisting of more than a granola bar on the go. Considering their lack of clothing and his proximity to her pussy, he could've insisted on much more.

"Put this on if you're not going to let me play." She tossed a condom at him. It bounced off her thigh and landed on the blanket.

"You can do anything you want tonight." After a close inspection, he tore open the package. His examination continued to the circle of latex as he rolled sideways.

"I'll take that as a contractual promise."

He repositioned himself, threading his arms under her legs and reaching toward her breasts. His eyebrows rose as he made contact. "Anything we've done before. New things with consent."

With the first roll of her nipples between his thumbs and forefingers, a current zipped to every other erogenous zone in her body. "Mm. Too late. You said anything."

"Maybe." His mouth closed over her labia and his tongue swept through the folds, finding her clit on the first attempt.

Several rapid flicks, accompanied by another roll of her nipples, and then a forceful suck triggered a jolt through her entire body. She clutched at the blanket as a rough cry escaped her throat. Spots danced in her vision, the colors intensifying when he hooked his arms under knees and slid inside her.

He rose above her, touching his lips to her cheeks, her forehead, her eyelids while he rocked into her. Each steady thrust kept her adrift with a massage of her G-spot and rhythmic pulses through her muscles. Even the pleasant weight of his body didn't ground her. It only added to the sensations drawing her into another release.

His cock swelled inside her, growing harder against her inner walls and pushing into the cleft that promised pure bliss. Rough panting breaths matched her own as his pace turned erratic.

"Fuck, fuck, fuck." He tensed and gave a low, rumbling growl, the combination finally liberating the rush of pleasure and sending her to paradise again.

Tingles flooded her fingers and toes, sapping every bit of energy from her, and contraction after contraction fluttered through her belly. She melted into the blanket, sated and trembling like she hadn't experienced in a long, long time.

He unhooked her legs and rolled to his back, taking her partway with him. His deflating erection slipped free, but he guided her head to his chest. His racing pulse drummed in her ear and he placed his palm on her quivering abdomen. "You're shaking. Deal. Maybe...next time...I can last...longer."

She rubbed her cheek against the smattering of coarse hair as her heart rate and breathing slowly returned to normal. "Nothing wrong with quickies. Quality versus quantity has never been an issue for us. It's always both."

"You're easy to please and good at pleasing." He smoothed his hand along her waist and pulled her closer still. "Damn, I want to just lay here for an hour or two."

Her rubbery muscles concurred. "You could text my landlord and say I had car trouble."

"Not sure I can move far enough to get my phone. Besides, his wife would want to come over to fix whatever's wrong. She's a little pushy that way."

A dash of trepidation skittered up her spine. "You sound like you don't get along with her."

His bark of laughter vibrated through her bones. "I'd say it's more that I respect her. She has kind of a...strong personality, but Blaine's happier than I've ever seen him. She's an excellent mother. Protective. Loving. And stubborn as hell. Self-reliant. She threw a bucket at me when I was trying to convince her to sell the farm."

She jerked her head up to look at him. The friendly woman she'd met at the farmers' market two days ago hadn't seemed the type to have a violent temper. "A *bucket*? What did you do?"

A wide grin lit up his eyes and set off another spasm in her lower belly. "I underestimated her business sense and made the mistake of trying to use it against her—not something I'll do again. She's the most honest and forthright person I know. What you see is what you get. You'll know right away if she doesn't like you."

She levered up onto her elbow, nervousness hitting harder than ever. *Better get this over with. And I'm going to have to be damn careful about the questions I ask.* "We should start getting ready to go. I don't want to be late."

His smile dimmed, but he pushed to his feet and offered her a hand up. He released her as soon as she straightened. "You can use the bathroom off the foyer. I'll meet you at the bottom of the stairs when you're done."

Looks like the uptight Erik is back. She picked up her bra and underwear as she headed to the kitchen, annoyed with herself for letting him lull her into casual post-sex pillow talk. The real Erik Fielding never failed to reappear the moment the afterglow faded. Agreeing to spend a whole night with him was more than foolish. Sexual escape didn't require actually sleeping with him, and waking alone beat an awkward morning-after decision about not repeating the mistake.

The need for solitude beat out collecting the shoe she'd left near the front door. Ducking into the half bath, she locked the door behind her and flipped on the lights. At least the condom hadn't failed this time, even if her common sense had. Why had she given in to an attraction—and distraction—that promised complications she didn't want, especially now?

Grief was no excuse for recklessness.

A few trips to buy produce from Lindie Stockwell should've sufficed. Proof, beyond a reasonable doubt, was as simple as a few brief conversations and a little more research. A dying mother's last request shouldn't require upheaval in her daughter's life. Wasn't saying goodbye sacrifice enough?

She splashed cool water on her face to relieve the stinging in her eyes. Tears wouldn't bring back her mom, nor would they satisfy the promise she'd made.

A month. Each piece of clothing she put on gave her more time to consider all the possible things that could go wrong during the next thirty days. Subterfuge wasn't her style, not even in divorce, custody, and paternity cases.

She fastened the final button on her blouse and knotted the fabric ties at her waist. A check in the mirror revealed the same woman who'd looked back at her this morning, except for the hint of color in her cheeks. Orgasms, anger, and anxiety were all to blame. She preferred pale, mourning Layla.

Her right boot in hand, she opened the door and braced for more of Erik's rigid disposition since he was, no doubt, ready and impatiently waiting for her. Hot-and-sour soup had nothing on the man's temperament.

He glanced up from his seat on the third step as she entered the foyer, his forearms on his knees and her missing boot in his hands. He zipped and unzipped the side closure in an uncharacteristically insecure motion that was at odds with the suit and tie he wore so well. "I won't hold you to our agreement since it was under duress. I just thought you might appreciate a distraction from what you're going through."

Hot's definitely gone again.

Swapping the boot for the computer bag beside him, he stood. "You don't have to come to dinner at Blaine and Lindie's, either, if you don't want to. I'll tell them you had another appointment. I have the paperwork. You can sign it and give me a check, and I'll have one of them drop off your copy once you're moved in. You can have my set of keys since I won't need them anymore."

She had an out for everything but the promise. Why, then, did his willingness to let her off the hook seem like a list of concessions instead of a blow-off?

"Take your time looking around. I'll wait in the kitchen." His bottled emotions invaded her personal space as he walked past her, but they were different somehow—more moody than control-happy.

Brooding.

She pitched her boot toward the stairs and marched after him, her gaze glued to his scrumptious backside until he stopped at the breakfast bar. A poke between his shoulder blades brought him face to face with her. She jabbed him in his conservative black-and-gray tie. "Did I say I wanted out of our agreement? I'm the one who invited you back for more. If you're not interested, fine, but don't try to make it my fault. And I'll eat supper wherever I damn well please. That includes accepting an invitation from my sis—" *Shit!* "Sincerely nice landlord."

The lines around his mouth softened. "Okay."

"You better keep those keys too. I'm expecting the same deal I gave you. Sex. Whenever I want it. No questions asked. For as long as I decide." She brushed her palm down his tie, erasing the indentation from her finger.

"They're going to know we're sleeping together. Nothing gets past Lindie." A blush crept past his snowy white collar.

"So?"

"I don't want you to be uncomfortable."

"Uncomfortable was having a step in my tailbone while you fucked me, but it was worth it. I don't care if they speculate."

His lips relaxed into a genuine-looking half smile. "I owe you a back rub. When does your bed get here?"

"About an hour after I text the movers. The owner is a very grateful former client. If we leave the patio doors in the family room unlocked, they can unload while we're taking care of the lease and eating supper." Satisfied with the resolution of their latest clash, she headed to the staircase to find her phone.

Her cape and her purse hung from the newel post, keeping her shoes company. Erik's penchant for neatness had probably intimidated the boot she'd tossed toward the stairs into landing next to its mate. Why couldn't it have rebelled and landed on the step above or below? Or knocked the other one over?

She shoved them to the floor as she sat to type in a go-ahead message.

Her on-again, off-again fuckbuddy winced at the clunk and thud of heels on the hardwood floor a few feet from her, almost precisely in the spot she'd occupied during his attempt to nullify their deal. "Would you like to ride with me? We can put your car in the garage so the moving truck has more room to maneuver."

Confused by his polite suggestion, she paused mid-sentence in her text and then continued instead of trying to make sense of his roller-coaster attitude. She nudged her purse toward him with her knee. "Sure. Keys are in the zipper pocket on top."

He stepped closer and retrieved her keys. "I'll hook the opener on the driver's side visor."

She tapped Send. "You might as well put the other one in your car. No reason to leave it sitting out all night."

His nod followed two jingles of her keys and a blink. Then he disappeared around the corner. "You're right."

Of course I am. And men bitch about not understanding women. She grabbed the closest boot and pulled it on. Facing her purpose for choosing this house was far more palatable than trying to figure out his moods. He wasn't the reason she was here and they'd go their separate ways again when she left.

Her phone buzzed as she slipped on her other boot, confirming delivery of her belongings within the hour. She swung the cape around her shoulders and flipped up the hood. *I wouldn't do this for anyone but you, Mom.*

The faint hum of the garage door greeted her as she passed through the kitchen on her way to the family room. No sign of her tryst with Erik remained, but ghost feelings of his body connected to hers triggered recurrent shivers as she crossed to the patio doors. Sexual compatibility was their strength, the common denominator in their strange attraction. In every other aspect, they were night and day.

Movement beyond the sheer curtains prompted her to push them aside. Erik closed the trunk of his car, and two long strides carried him to the driver's side. He lifted his phone to his ear as he set his computer bag in the backseat. The charcoal-gray suit shifted with each efficient motion, hinting at the lean, muscular man beneath.

After swinging the door closed, he leaned against the rear fender in an unexpectedly casual stance, crossing one ankle over the other. Easy confidence, with a helping of humility and kindness, emanated from him until his gaze seemed to catch hers. He gave a curt nod and ended the call as he straightened.

She dropped the curtain into place, not sure how to take his abrupt change in demeanor. Unless her ability to read people had stopped working, the chance of him having a girlfriend and screwing around with a former sex partner was zero. He could've been talking to Blaine, but he clearly was at ease with whoever it was.

What does it matter?

Erik stood near the front door when she returned to the foyer. "Did you hear back from the movers?"

"Yes. They'll be here shortly. Ready to go?" She adjusted her purse strap across her body and squared her shoulders.

"If you are. You seem nervous."

"Just anxious to get moved in." Hoping he didn't question her excuse, she crossed to the entrance. "French doors are unlocked. Let's go."

He led her to his car, offering his arm and then opening the car door for her. His gentlemanly behavior came as no surprise, but it served as an amusing diversion from the commitment she was about to make. He cast a glance in her direction as he settled behind the steering wheel. "What do you want me to say if they ask about us?'

"You could tell them it's none of their business." She snickered at the speed at which his eyebrows rose. "You worry too much about what other people think. We're both old enough to have sex without anyone else's knowledge or permission."

His noncommittal hum was barely audible over the crunch of gravel beneath the tires. At the end of the driveway, he flipped on his turn signal and turned right. "I need to run home for a change of clothes and stop to check on my mom after supper."

"Not a problem. You can drop me off first. The guys'll put the bed together, but I need to unpack sheets and blankets. Is your mom sick?" She tried to keep her tone light, but the thought of anyone's mother being ill made her insides cramp.

"Sinus infection. She's on a second round of antibiotics."

"You're a good son to check on her. You never know when..." No more words would form in her brain or her mouth.

"Yeah." He caressed her hand as he switched on his turn signal again. Trees lined the lane to the inviting gray farmhouse and he stopped beside a flashy yellow Mustang in the parking lot-sized turn-around. "We're here."

Muffled laughter carried from somewhere beyond the living room as Erik held the screen door open for Layla. Cam's high-pitched chortle dominated his older brother's more reserved laugh, Lindie's snort, and another familiar chuckle—one Erik hadn't heard since Blaine's wedding in June. The poorly hidden smirk on Blaine's face was all but an admission of a setup.

Cross, my ass. You knew, you sneaky bastard. Chances were damn good his friend had known more than the correct last name of the Cape Cod's new tenant. That he'd invited Russ Novotny, their other college roommate, to dinner was a sure sign they were well aware of his previous association with her. Those secret trysts had evidently never been secret.

"Come on in." Blaine ushered them inside. "Coats can go on the hooks by the door. Erik, do you have the lease?"

"Yeah." Erik reached for Layla's cape as she tossed back the hood. "I'll hang it up for you. Layla, you remember Blaine Stockwell, don't you? Ladies' man of Collier Hall?"

His friend's wide grin said he didn't consider the moniker an insult. "Good to see you again, Layla. How do you like the house? In case you didn't notice, we stocked a few things in the kitchen for you. Eggs, of course, and winter squash, potatoes, carrots. My wife's planning on digging leeks tomorrow. Just let her know if you want some."

Layla looked toward the kitchen, where the voices had likely come from, and back toward Blaine. The curling and uncurling of her fingers on her purse betrayed her outward composure, leaving Erik to guess she wasn't as aloof about being judged as she'd implied. "Thank you. That's very generous. The house is lovely."

"Okay, then let's get the paperwork out of the way so you can meet Lindie and the boys." Blaine gestured in the direction of the study.

Halfway to grasping Layla's hand, Erik stopped himself. She didn't need—or probably want—his reassurance, at least not in a social setting. "This way."

At the doorway, Blaine groaned. "Ignore the basket of laundry. I had to check something for a client while I was taking care of the cookie thief. I should've made him wash his own sheets."

She finally smiled. "The emergency?"

"Yeah. I can almost guarantee the little monster won't make himself sick on cookies again for at least six months. It's a good thing Erik was available to meet you at the house." He rounded the desk and held the chair. "Have a seat."

Another of his smirks flashed as Layla sat and pulled a pair of reading glasses from her purse. She looked over her shoulder toward him, her apparent nervousness now masked behind an impassive expression. "I hope you don't mind if I look over the contract first. Work habit that should be everybody's habit."

"Oh? What do you do for a living?"

"I'm an attorney. Mostly family and estate law. Some elder law."

"Looks like you and Fielding have something in common, except he's contract law." Blaine's cocky grin turned thoughtful as he sauntered out from behind the desk. "You handle adoptions and guardianships?"

She took the papers Erik handed her and unfolded her glasses. "Mm-hm."

"Excellent. I'd like to engage your services."

"I'll give you my card when we're done here." Her tone left no doubt she preferred to concentrate on the contract in front of her at the moment. With the glasses perched on her nose, she ran her finger back and forth across the first paragraph, line by line.

Erik forced an easy inhale and exhale to slow the sudden uptick in his pulse. Seeing her in professional mode, especially with the touch of nerdy intellectual, warmed his blood and sent it flowing to his dick.

Waving for Erik to follow him, Blaine crossed to the bookshelf on the opposite side of the room. He slid a book partway from its shelf and leaned closer to Erik. His voice was a low whisper. "You're welcome."

"Fuck you." The hissed response didn't seem to carry to Layla, unless she chose to ignore their hushed conversation.

"Save that for Ms. *Cross*. I'm sure she'll appreciate it more." Blaine's throat-clearing cough was a poor disguise for his laugh.

Erik rolled his eyes and poked his elbow into his friend's ribs. "Razz me all you want, but you better not embarrass her. Russ needs to watch his mouth too."

"Give me some credit, dude. And Russ has his own problems. He'd be an idiot to harass you when Sasha just dumped him. She moved out while he was away on business last month."

"You're shitting me. They've been living together for what, seven or eight years? Weren't they planning to get married next spring?"

"Not anymore. At least he was smart enough to take my advice about separate bank accounts. She could've cleaned him out instead of just taking his car. The poor guy's talking about quitting his job. He came up here to check out some prospects this week." Blaine returned the book to its place on the shelf. "You know anybody looking to hire an IT genius who'd rather work from home than be around people right now?"

"Not offhand, but I'll ask around. She took his *car*?"

"I'm ready to sign if you two are done gossiping." The amused tone in Layla's voice took the bite out of her allegation.

With a shrug, Blaine returned to the desk. "There's plenty to gossip about, don't you think, Fielding? Of course, trying to help a friend isn't really butting into somebody else's business."

Erik grunted and joined them to finalize the contract. "It depends on whether you're the one being helped. You didn't like it so much when I told you getting married would solve your problems."

"Yeah, well, I eventually listened, didn't I?" He scrawled his signature beneath his tenant's on both copies of the lease and shoved them at Erik to witness. Then he exchanged a set of keys for her check and a business card. "No more business today. Come meet the crew."

Layla seemed to focus on finding a spot in her purse for the keys, almost hiding the tension in her neck and shoulders. When she stood, a fake smile confirmed what Erik suspected. She wasn't happy to be in a situation where his two closest friends knew about their sexual relationship—past and present.

And the more I try to make her feel better about it, the more obvious it'll become. He let Blaine lead her toward the kitchen, wishing they could go back to the house and keep their secrets private.

"Uncle Erik!" Cam plowed into him at the kitchen doorway, his uninhibited enthusiasm brightening Erik's mood. "I got to collect eggs and feed the chickens this morning. And Red and Rocky didn't even chase me!"

Erik hefted the four-year-old into the air for a hug. "Cool. It looks like you've been eating lots of those eggs too. You've grown at least a foot since the last time I saw you."

A contagious giggle filled the room. "You're 'xaggerating. I'd be taller than Leo!"

"It looks like he's grown too." Erik wrapped his free arm around Cam's brother. "Hey, Leo. Want to go for a run with me on Saturday? Maybe out at Hubbard Valley?"

The older boy squeezed him around the waist. "That'd be awesome."

Cam grabbed Erik's jaw with both hands and turned his head until they were face to face. "What about me?"

"Sorry, but I can only handle one of you guys at a time. Lindie would strangle me if you fell in the lake or got lost in the woods."

"Darn right, I would." Dropping a kiss on Leo's head, Lindie handed him a mug. "Can you hold that until Uncle Erik has a free hand? Cam, I need you to peek at the rolls to see if they're ready to go in the oven. Remember, just peeking. No poking."

"Okay." Erik's armload dashed past her as soon as he set the boy on his feet.

Erik accepted the mug from Leo and grinned at his former nemesis. "Thanks for the save."

"You're welcome. Leo, will you preheat the oven please?" Lindie looked past Erik, curiosity evident in her attention to the person behind him. "Since my husband hasn't yet seen fit to introduce me to our renter, would you mind?"

Geesh, did he tell everybody about my sex life? "Sure. Lindie, meet Layla Krause." Not reaching for his lover as he turned toward her was a challenge. "Layla, Lindie Stockwell."

Layla touched her fingers to her earring, producing a faint clink of metal against metal, before she extended her hand. "Nice to meet you."

"You too." The interest in Lindie's gaze morphed to scrutiny as her eyebrows scrunched together and then shot upward. "We've met before! You bought apples the other day at the farmers' market. If I'd known who you were... Do you want a mug of warm cider? Come with me, and we can chat."

"That sounds wonderful." Layla's hand dropped to her side and into her pocket as she stepped toward their host. "I made apple butter with them this morning."

"Yummy. Are you interested in selling it? Do you make any other butters, jellies, or jams? I bet my customers would buy every jar."

Lindie tucked her arm through Layla's as they crossed to the stove, like they were life-long co-conspirators. When they turned to face one another, their profiles mirrored each other. Then they looked back toward Erik.

Their striking resemblance—from high cheekbones and pert noses to slightly pointed chins and matching intelligent eyes—put a thought in his head that made sense of the sudden appearance of a woman from Erik's past, Blaine's out-of-the-blue interest in renting the Cape Cod, and a handful of other details that had seemed unimportant until all the pieces fit together. If Layla hadn't cut off her hair, the two women could be mistaken for sisters.

My money says they are *sisters.* Blaine had probably arranged the family reunion, with the convenient benefit of a fix-up for his best friend. His wife was clearly in on the secret, given her invitation to dinner and the not-so-subtle glances she'd been aiming at her look-alike.

The only question that remained was whether Layla knew about the connection. If she didn't, she would probably figure it out tonight. How could she not, when looking at Lindie had to be like seeing her own reflection?

"Hey, Erik." Russ greeted him with a handshake and a tired smile. "How's it going?"

"Good. You? I hear you're thinking of relocating."

"Doing okay." His friend shrugged. "Ready to move on to something new."

"The mid-life itch. Look what it did to Blaine." Erik sipped his cider and grinned when an oaky hint of Scotch coated his taste buds. "I have to admit Lindie isn't so bad, though. Spiked punch makes up for her occasional prickliness."

"My wife is strong-willed and blunt, not prickly. There's a difference." A glance across the kitchen accompanied Blaine's lowered voice. "And she's mellowed a lot since the wedding."

Russ snorted. "So have you."

"Maybe. I like being married this time."

"Did you know I asked Sasha to marry me on the anniversary of the day we met for the last six years? She finally says yes and leaves two weeks later." After a long gulp from his mug, Russ sighed. "If I'm ever dumb enough to fall in love again, the woman's doing the proposing. And no more living together without a marriage certificate."

Blaine's hoot of laughter drew questioning looks from Lindie and her near twin. "Sorry, but you sound like an overprotective parent. Next, you'll be quoting that adage about free milk and buying the cow."

"Nah, more like no woman's getting my kielbasa without buying the pig." Russ's real smile finally showed itself. "Damn, I've missed hanging out with you guys."

Erik raised his mug and waited for both men to join him. "To good friends."

With his drink lifted, Blaine nodded. "Good friends."

Russ clinked his cup against theirs. "To excellent friends and starting over."

The combination of cider and Scotch warmed Erik's insides from his throat to his stomach. *Starting over.*

Or was he trying to relive the past?

If not for the recurring vision of Layla naked and on the verge of an exquisite orgasm, Erik might've continued past the gravel drive to his dream house. His earlier offer to cancel their deal had been more about his own doubts than guilt from pressuring her to let him make her forget her grief. As much as he wanted to believe he could engage in a purely sexual relationship, an in-depth analysis of their previous association on the drive to his condo and then his mom's house had uncovered some things he'd never acknowledged before.

The Cape Cod dared him to admit the truth—that working his ass off in law school and in every job since then had been the most effective way to bury the feelings he'd developed for her all those years ago. Walking away from her had allowed them both to do what they needed to do without jeopardizing their future careers, but it hadn't changed his connection to her. Deep down, their differences meant nothing because she inspired him, let him be the man he was afraid to be. The uptight version of him she disliked was subconscious protection against the possibility that she considered him temporary, disposable, only worthy of an exceptional fuck.

Lights glowed in several of the windows, inviting him to play house with her while he had the chance. All he had to do was open the garage door, park, and walk inside like he belonged there. Blaine and

Russ had made it clear they thought he and Layla were destined for each other and a happily-ever-after.

What if they were right?

He stopped in front of the door on the left and counted the rectangles below the narrow row of windows at the top. *What if they're wrong?*

His phone lit up in the cup holder beside him, its brightness invading his hiding spot.

"First date was a success! Quit overthinking." Blaine's message vanished into darkness, but his observation was a light at the end of the tunnel.

"It's what I do. Great timing, by the way." Erik pushed the button to open the garage door, hoping the light inside wasn't from a train about to flatten him. The safety net of dating women who didn't challenge him to live outside his comfort zone was gone, and the risk of falling head over heels was all too real.

He parked his car next to Layla's and stuffed his phone in the duffle containing an unopened box of condoms, three changes of clothes, and his shaving kit. Worst-case scenario, he was back where he started in his search for love, albeit with a few deep wounds and some nasty scars. Best-case scenario wasn't something he was ready to speculate on.

The garage door inched downward with the push of a button and he readied his key to unlock the door into the kitchen. Half a dozen empty moving boxes blocked his path, but he pushed through them and followed the resonant strains of Boston to the hall. With the end of the guitar intro, a female voice belted out the lyrics to "Hitch a Ride" along with the band. Her slightly off-key singing didn't inhibit the pure enjoyment that came through the words.

It embodied her disposition and attitude. She always showed her true self.

He took the stairs two at a time, his overnight bag flopping against his hip until he reached the landing. A flash of color whirled past the doorway to the master bedroom. As he moved closer, Layla danced into view, her long skirt swirling around her bare feet and her dangly earrings swinging back and forth.

He dropped the bag where he stood and closed the distance between them. The uncertainty vanished as soon as she was in his arms, still swaying to the music. She eased her hands to the back of his neck and up into his hair as she matched the movement of his feet. Each motion carried them closer to the bed, to the connection that had hooked him. The prospect of falling no longer worried him. She would fit into his life as effortlessly as their bodies fit together. All he had to do was let it happen.

CHAPTER 6

The sweet-and-spicy scent of apples and cinnamon teased her nose as Layla snuggled deeper into the toasty covers. It blended with another smell, this one on the pillows and from her memory.

Erik. She slid her palm across the sheet in search of warm skin and firm muscle, but his side was cool and empty. *Where—*

"G'morning." The mattress shifted and the aroma grew stronger. Then soft lips caressed her bare shoulder. "Ready for breakfast?"

"Mm-hm." A yawn escaped, and she wiggled closer to the dip in the bed without opening her eyes. Her fingertips met what had to be his slightly hairy thigh and snug-fitting cotton boxer briefs. "You're wearing too many clothes again."

His low chuckle tickled her belly. "I need food before we go another round."

She pried her eyes open. "You don't have to go to work?"

"My first meeting isn't until one, so I decided to take the morning off." He leaned against the headboard and moved a plate from the nightstand to his lap. "Apple butter pancakes with apple butter syrup. Want a bite?"

"That sounds amazing." She forced her sleepy muscles into action, cuddling against her surprisingly laidback lover. "When was the last time you played hooky so you could get laid?"

His laughter shook the bed and transformed the mostly naked, messy-haired, beard-stubbled man into an even more handsome version of himself. He poked a bite of pancake and held it to her lips. "Never. No, I take that back. Once when I was in college, I skipped a study session for a final exam to hook up with an incredibly sexy girl with long dark hair and the ability to distract me from anything."

She took the offered bite, pleased to have that kind of power over his self-discipline when the rest of her life was beyond her control. "Oh my God, this is so good. You brought some for yourself, didn't you?"

He grinned and handed her the plate. "Yeah. I remember your appetite."

"We burned a lot of calories last night." She dug into the stack, determined to take advantage of every minute she had with him this morning.

"There's more in the fridge. I made a whole batch." Even with his own serving on his lap, he seemed more interested in watching her than eating. "I can make breakfast again tomorrow if you want me to."

"Does that include another overnight stay? Because I don't need a big breakfast if I haven't gotten the exercise to keep it from going straight to my hips." Trying to hold in a groan of culinary appreciation proved fruitless.

He lifted her chin and pressed his lips to hers in a chaste but breath-stealing kiss. "Your hips are safe. I promised to be here for you whenever you need me. That includes as many nights as you want."

Will the real Erik Fielding please stand up? "You should plan on staying unless I say otherwise. It'll save us the trouble of a misunderstanding."

"Okay." He finally turned his attention to his pancakes, still no less calm, at ease, and not his usual self than when he'd awakened her.

Unwilling to ruin their comfortable exchange, she focused on the treat in front of her. If he could transform something as simple as apple butter into a restaurant-worthy entrée with the kitchen utensils and supplies she'd unpacked last night, she couldn't wait to see what he served during the rest of their time together. His skills went beyond the bedroom and a law office.

He set aside his empty dish a few minutes later and turned back with a mug in each hand. "Apple-hibiscus-cardamom tea. It was in the pantry. I had to Google how to make it. I'm used to tea bags, not the loose stuff."

Tears pricked at her eyes and her throat tightened. "It was my mom's favorite."

He frowned. "I'm sorry. I didn't mean to—"

"It's okay. I like thinking about her, even if not having her here anymore makes me sad. She'd want me to enjoy it and remember all the tea parties we had when I was little. So, thank you." She eased a mug from his grip. "We should drink it before it gets cold."

"You're a lot stronger than I was." He stroked the modest amount of hair that had grown back in the last two and a half weeks. His light touch moved from her scalp to the nape of her neck, soothing the fresh twinge of pain. "I was hurt and angry and distraught."

"You had no warning. One day you woke up, and your dad wasn't there anymore. Your world changed overnight." She took a sip of her tea and then set it on the other nightstand. When she turned toward him, his mug was gone too. "I had to be strong for her. I think I knew in my heart she was going to die. Even though I tried hard not to accept what was happening, I had time to start grieving. Life doesn't care about being fair."

"I learned that the hard way. You took care of her until the end, didn't you?" It was more statement than question, as if he truly understood how close she'd been to her mom. He wrapped her in a hug, the kind she'd given him when each hookup session ended and they said farewell until the next time.

Resting her head on his shoulder, she nodded. Tears trickled down her cheek, as much for his loss as her own. "I slept beside her for the two weeks before she died so she wouldn't be alone if she decided it was time. The last night, I woke up because I couldn't hear her breathing, but she'd found the strength to hold my hand at the end."

"I'm glad. Remembering her goodbye seems like a good thing.

How about if I make the pain go away for a while instead of making you forget?"

She lifted her hand to his jaw as she met his gaze. Understanding, desire, and something else she couldn't quite define shone in his eyes. He knew what she was going through, just as she'd sensed his anguish.

The first touch of his mouth on hers brought solace to the ache and sparked heat from the flame that never seemed to go out. He eased her onto the mattress, covering her body with his comfortable weight as he danced with her tongue the way he'd danced with her last night. Every motion was slow and sweeping, as if they had all the time in the world.

If only.

She smothered the thought in her hunger for him, surveying the broad expanse of his upper back and arching her pelvis into his hard length. If not for the underwear he wore, the temptation to guide him inside her without protection might have proven too strong.

He rolled to the middle of the bed, stopping when she straddled his hips. As he continued his lazy exploration of her mouth, his hands closed on her ass and held her pussy against his cloth-covered cock. With each of his gentle back-and-forth nudges, the coarse hair on his chest teased her nipples, a perfect accompaniment to the friction against her clit.

Ripples of pleasure spread through her body, carrying her away from the sorrow that would never completely disappear. She burrowed her fingers in his messy hair and tried to rock her hips faster. *Take me there.*

His hold tightened, keeping the slow and steady rhythm he'd set with his hands and his tongue. Gratification and frustration built in equal measure with each motion. She hovered on the edge of an orgasm, a fraction of a second from coming, but unable to cross the threshold into bliss. Every glide promised deliverance, but his patience brought it at a pace that rivaled cold molasses.

She whimpered into his mouth, ready to beg if she had to.

His tongue withdrew, and he nibbled his way to her ear. "Tell me what you want."

Another leisurely glide stole the breath she tried to take. How many times had she made the same request when their roles had been reversed? "Make me come. Fuck me."

He guided her up to her knees, breaking contact and creating a new sense of loss. With a minor shift of his boxer briefs, his cock popped out of the front flap, already sheathed in a condom. A second later, he slid inside her, going deeper and deeper as he pulled her downward. He collided with her G-spot at the same moment his thumb found her clit.

The tension inside her splintered, bringing a moment of relief before another climb. She cried out, and the next wave washed over her with another controlled collision. He continued his welcome assault, drawing out and adding to the sex-induced high. Each thrust sent her soaring, farther from the real world, until release radiated through every inch of her body.

Her muscles melted as he filled her again, this time fuller than the last. Then he tensed beneath her, his gaze still connected to hers. His lips parted, softening his determined expression, and he let out a long groan.

She leaned forward, too limp to sit up any longer. His arms closed around her, gathering her to his heaving chest and capturing her in a safe place she hadn't counted on a week ago. She closed her eyes, pulled toward sleep but not willing to give up the limited time she had with him. Sooner or later, they'd part ways, and the memories would have to last forever.

The lazy caress of his hand along her spine did little to soothe the spasms coursing from her inner muscles to her abdominals and the pang that came from knowing what had to be. Each aftershock was a reminder of the intensity he'd drawn from her. Their explosive chemistry seemed to grow stronger instead of weakening, fading, or dousing the flames altogether.

When their breathing returned to normal, he cupped her cheek with his other hand. "What are your plans for this morning? I can help you unpack if you want."

"No more unpacking until after I make a batch of cranberry-sage jam. My mom and I always made it for Thanksgiving. That and squash butter. Apple butter was for Halloween."

His sigh feathered through the buzz-cut hair on her head. "Damn. I did it again. I'm sorry."

She turned toward his hand and kissed his palm. "You didn't do anything wrong. I promised myself I wouldn't forget the traditions we had just because she's gone. She taught me to make butters and jams, so I found all her recipes and I'm going to make one every day until I run out. My earliest memories are of standing on the stepstool to help her stir whatever was in the jam pot. It's grief therapy."

"I know what you mean. Before I started law school, I helped my mom go through my dad's stuff. You got me through the worst part of grieving, but seeing the fishing gear he'd accumulated over the years made me remember the good times he and I had together when I was growing up. I think I finally started letting go of the anger then. I can take off if you need to do this by yourself."

"I appreciate your willingness to give me space, but you don't have to go." She laid her hand over his and linked their fingers. "Actually, I don't *want* you to go. It's nice being able to talk to someone about her, somebody who understands my loss. Thank you."

"You're welcome. Any time." The steady beat of his heart in her ear was the only sound for several minutes, the perfect accompaniment for the circular caresses over her shoulder blades and lower back. "I don't want to move, but I should get rid of the condom. Do you want to shower first?"

"We can shower after our jam session. It's usually a sticky job." She levered up and waggled her eyebrows at him. "You know, from taste-testing."

His wicked grin sent her tummy somersaulting. "I think I'm going to like making jam."

"Cranberries can stain your clothes, so you probably shouldn't bother getting dressed, either." Holding the base of the condom in place, she swung her leg over his hips and hoped this Erik stuck around until he had to leave for his meeting.

His fingers trailed along her calf as she climbed off the bed. "I'd never cooked in just my underwear until I made breakfast this morning."

"It's about time you broadened your horizons." She snagged an oversized T-shirt from the dresser on her way to the bathroom. "Back in a sec."

When she opened the door a few minutes later, he stood at the headboard with a pillow poised to mirror the fluffed-and-propped one on the opposite side. Both plates and mugs were gone from the night-stands. His grimace became a sheepish smile. "I couldn't help myself. Habit."

"I can live with a made bed and dirty dishes taken to the kitchen."

He slipped his hand around hers. "Good. I'll load the dishwasher and reheat our tea while you get out everything we need."

"Sounds like a plan." She led him out of the bedroom and down the stairs. If that was the worst of his uptight behavior, she wouldn't complain at all about him sleeping over every night for the next month.

His immediate attention to his self-proclaimed duties spoke of a man who never shirked his responsibilities and spent more time in the kitchen than eating carryout. He loaded the dishwasher and put both mugs in the microwave while she set out the recipe and gathered ingredients. "What's first?"

"Why don't you get the orange zest and sage ready? I'll rinse the cranberries and juice the orange." Glad she'd tackled the kitchen boxes while he took care of his errands last night, she pulled a zester from the utensil drawer and pointed to the block of knives. "Cutting boards are in the bottom cupboard next to the oven."

"Okay."

With two bags of cranberries draining in the sink, she juiced the orange into a saucepan and appreciated the graceful movements of his wrist and bicep as he sharpened the knife.

After a rinse and wipe of the blade, he chopped the sage leaves into a fine mince. His ass flexed beneath the layer of snug cotton when he loaded the knife and turned to transfer the prepped herb to a glass bowl. "If you're going to keep checking out my butt, you better run upstairs for a condom."

She tried and failed to hold in a laugh. "But it's so perfect. All tight and muscular."

His eyebrows rose and his lips twitched into a smile. "Glad you like it."

Unable to resist, she closed the few steps between them and glided her palm along the firm curve of his bottom. "Very much. You know, we could—"

A knock on the French doors leading to the back deck made her stomach drop to the floor.

Erik whipped the dishtowel from the counter and held it in front of the expanding lump in his underwear. "You have a visitor."

Lindie stood on the other side of the glass, holding a bag in one hand and waving with the other. Her muffled greeting carried through the double panes. "Good morning!"

God, my sister just caught me mostly naked with her husband's best friend. Way to make a hell of an impression. Layla fought the urge to tug the hem of her shirt farther down her thighs and opened the door. "Good morning. Come on in."

"I had some extra pears and you said you like leeks and bok choy, so I thought I'd bring them over." Stepping inside, Lindie aimed a grin in Erik's direction. "Hey, Fielding. How's it hanging? I always pegged you for a tightie-whities kind of guy."

CHAPTER 7

Erik kept his ass backed into the corner by the sink and his now-limp cock covered with the towel as Lindie yammered on about this afternoon's farmers' market. *Yeah, yeah, yeah. It's time for you to leave.*

"Why don't you come with me, Layla?" Blaine's wife stood with her fist around the handle, but she made no move to open the door. "I don't have much to sell today, so we can check out the other booths when I'm done."

Her shorthaired doppelganger clutched the bags of leeks, bok choy, and pears to her chest, probably trying to hide the fact that she wasn't wearing a bra. "Um, sure. What time?"

"Great! I'll pick you up at twelve thirty-five. Oh, and we should be home by about four thirty, quarter 'til five. You know, in case you have dinner plans." Cold air swept into the kitchen as Lindie swung open the door. She winked and stepped outside with a bearing so similar to Layla's, it fully supported his crazy thought last night that they could be sisters. "As you were."

His lover's cheeks flushed nearly the color of the cranberries when the door clicked closed. "I'm no prude, but she could've watched us having sex and we never would've known."

"And she probably would've applauded when we were done." He gestured toward the expanse of glass with his elbow, careful not to move the towel. "Would you mind closing the curtains?"

Shifting the bag to one arm, she shuffled sideways to the drapery pull. A single long tug cut them off from the real world again. "I got the impression last night that she either doesn't recognize personal boundaries or chooses to ignore them. Not that there's anything malicious about it. Just interesting. Psychology degree talking."

"No, she isn't vindictive, but it's definitely intentional. She knows I told Blaine to marry her a couple days after he met her. That evidently gave her permission to stick her nose into my private life." He folded his makeshift shield and returned it to the counter. "Tell me how you ended up a lawyer while we finish the jam."

Her grimace promised an interesting tale, but she transferred the pears to the fruit basket on the table instead of beginning her story. When she straightened from putting the leeks and bok choy in the refrigerator a minute later, her expression hadn't changed. "I was envious of the relationship you had with your dad, and I decided the best way to make my father pay for what I missed out on was to hit him in the wallet. In order to do that, I had to either hire a lawyer or become one to collect the child support he should've been sending my mom for eighteen years. It meant extra time finishing my undergrad coursework, but I wanted to double major in psychology and pre-law."

No wonder she'd shoved her business card in his face after yesterday's condom mishap. "It must've been hard. The degrees. Growing up without a father. His lack of acknowledgment and responsibility. Did you—"

"No." She turned on the flame under the saucepan and then added a cinnamon stick, nutmeg, and allspice. "I need to add the sage and orange zest with the cranberries when this boils."

Her blunt implication that the subject was closed stung a little, but he finished his part of the prep work instead of risking a complete shutdown. They had amazing chemistry in bed, but he had no delusions about a picture-perfect future with her. She wasn't the kind of wife he'd been looking for, primarily because they argued as aggressively as they fucked each other. In fact, he wouldn't change anything about her to alter that dynamic.

For the first time since they'd gone their separate ways, a true spark of interest in a woman consumed him. He'd figure out how to make a long-term relationship with her work, even if it cost him his sanity.

He scraped the peel against the zester a few more times and then set both ingredients he'd been in charge of on the counter next to the stove. Steam billowed up from the pan, filling the air with the scent of Thanksgiving desserts. "Are you ready for the cranberries?"

Her nod was less than decisive, but he retrieved the strainer and added the fruit to the mix of water, juice, sugar, and spices. She stirred as he poured in the fruit. "My mom refused to tell me his name when I finished my law degree."

"It's not on your birth certificate?"

"No." Rage swirled around her, as evident in the static-charged air as her white-knuckled hold on the spoon. Their clashes were child's play compared to the wrath emanating from her now.

He set the strainer aside and leaned against the counter. "How long does it have to cook?"

"Until the berries pop and it starts to thicken. About ten or fifteen minutes since the cranberries were cold." She stopped her vigorous stirring and dropped the spoon into the sage bowl. The clang of metal against glass rang through kitchen. "That deadbeat piece of shit should've died…instead of her."

The break in her words and the tightness in her shoulders triggered a wave of guilt. He opened his arms, hoping she'd allow him to comfort her. "I'm sorry. It's none of my business. I shouldn't have asked."

She rested her forehead against his breastbone. "It's okay. I'm not mad at you. I hate the anger that's always in the pit of my stomach. The grief. The injustice. I never realized just how much I resented him for what he did—and didn't do—until my mom passed away. Keeping it all bottled up isn't healthy."

He enveloped her in a hug. Her warm breath feathered across his skin, triggering possessiveness and protectiveness as much as lust. "You deserve better than what you got."

"But I have to accept that he won't ever be what he should've been. You, on the other hand, are exactly what I need."

Not reading too much into her statement proved difficult, especially in light of his revelation during the drive back to her and his dream home last night. Overthinking would've been easier, but he let the simple pleasure of being with her banish the tendency to use logic in the context of their relationship. Even though he'd told another woman he loved her several years ago, those feelings paled in comparison to his physical and emotional attachment to Layla. She held a special place in his heart and his memories—and, with luck, his future.

Despite the differences in their personalities, he wanted her in his life. He needed her. She was the missing piece he'd never been able to find. It couldn't be any clearer, even after less than a day since their reunion.

His search had ended long ago.

I love you, Layla. I don't understand how it took me so long to realize it, but I do. "You can always depend on me."

"I know." She snaked her arms around his waist and nuzzled his chest. Her chilly fingers inched under the elastic band of his underwear, inciting goose bumps across his ass and lower back. "That's why you're going to stir the cranberries while I warm up my hands."

"Works for me." He didn't try to hide the hitch in his breath as she palmed his butt cheeks. Cranberry-scented steam rose from the pan with each circuit of the spoon, but it couldn't compare to the heat generated by their skin-to-skin bond. "I think I got the better end of the deal."

"I beg to differ." Her lips closed around his nipple, and a flick of her tongue sent fire racing through his veins, bringing him back to the state of readiness he'd been in before their interruption. "Keep stirring while I play."

He snuck his free hand under the hem of her shirt at her hip. Silky skin invited him to touch until every inch of her was etched into his soul. "What if I want to play?"

A trail of light kisses down his ribs to his belly button carried her out of his reach. Each soft press of her lips made his cock harder. "It's my turn. You're not stirring."

Her tongue licked a circle around his navel as she worked his boxers past his erection. Cool air mixed with her warm breath, making his balls tighten and his dick twitch. Only the possibility that she'd put an end to their arrangement kept him from turning off the stove and carrying her to the table for a thorough fucking. Or she'd tease him relentlessly for turning into a caveman.

How does she do that to me?

He turned part of his attention to the spoon. "You're distracting me."

"*This* is me distracting you." She sucked half his scrotum into her mouth and wrapped her fingers around the base of his cock.

A shudder ripped through his body, forcing an uncontrolled groan from his throat. "Holy hell, I surrender."

She smacked her lips as she released his testicle and looked up at him. Mischief glowed in her eyes and wide grin. "I never take prisoners. Keep stirring."

Trapped by his underwear around his knees and his cock in her firm grasp, he gave in to her demand. A slow exhale did little to help his concentration. "The berries are starting to pop."

"But you haven't. Turn the heat down to simmer." She closed her mouth over the swollen head and swallowed him inch by excruciating inch.

Fighting rubbery legs, he grabbed the control knob and twisted it to the right. Flames flared around the pot. He turned it back the other way, not caring if the fire went out. His instincts told him to hold on to her for dear life—because she needed an escape from the harsh realities of her life and he wanted her to know she could, without a doubt, depend on him for everything she needed.

He gave the jam a final stir, barely able to think with her lips and tongue on him. "'Pop' isn't even close to describing what happens when you do that."

"Mm." She dragged her teeth across the sensitive spot below his slit and gently squeezed his sac. With another slow descent, she smoothed her other hand around to his ass, through the cleft, and up his spine.

The blaze she left in her wake should've made him spontaneously combust. "God, that feels good."

Her exploration continued to his stomach and pecs as she tortured him with more licking and sucking. Every touch and caress threatened to push him past the point of no return, but she retreated at the last moment, leaving him hanging on the edge.

"Let me come, Layla. I want to come in your mouth." He gripped the counter behind him to keep from collapsing. "Please."

She met his gaze and ran her tongue up the pulsing vein to the head of his cock. Then she fluttered her tongue on the bit of loose skin at its base, drawing him to the edge again. Her hold on his balls tightened and she sucked him into her mouth.

Heat and pressure rushed up his length, promising a release like he hadn't experienced since the blow job she'd given him during their final hookup in her dorm room. He forced his eyes to remain locked on hers, even though they tried to close as energy shot through his muscles and blasted him into ecstasy. The feeling stole his voice and his breath, but she was there. She was the only thing that mattered.

His legs gave out, and she guided him to the floor. Her arms encircled him, holding him against her chest as she kissed his shoulder, his neck, his ear. "You let me have total control instead of fighting it. You've never done that before."

He inhaled the sweet-tart-savory scent that clung to her, truly comfortable with the dynamic of their relationship at that moment. "I think you need it more than I do right now."

Two raps on his door pulled Erik out of the erotic daydream that had filled his mind since he'd opened his email at least ten minutes ago. Making Layla come in the shower after they'd finished the cranberry-sage jam had been every bit as satisfying as the blow job she'd given him in the kitchen.

He checked the time as he closed his laptop. *Another hour before she's home.* "Come in."

The door swung open and Blaine stepped into the office, with Russ on his heels. "Got a few minutes?"

"Sure." Erik gestured to the chairs across from him. "Have a seat."

Blaine's grin widened as he sat. "Lindie told me she caught you and Layla mostly naked in the kitchen this morning. Did you set a date yet?"

Russ offered his hand across the desk and rolled his eyes. "Stockwell can be such a self-righteous ass sometimes, don't you think? I'm available if you need a best man."

Smacking away his friend's hand, Erik could only laugh. "I'll let you know. What brings you here, besides your childish need to harass me?"

"Harass?" Blaine looked sideways toward Russ. "Would I do that? I thought I was the one who reunited him with his future wife."

Novotny shrugged. "Maybe he'll be more appreciative that we're bringing him business."

Grateful for the change of subject, Erik latched onto it. "What kind of business?"

"I'm buying the brick ranch and thirty acres from Blaine. I can run a custom software and design company from home, maybe some tech support. We're thinking of putting in a lake near where the creek runs through the property. Computers and fishing—what more does a guy need?"

Stockwell snorted. "I don't know about you, but Fielding and I need—"

"Sex, sex, and more sex." Russ dropped into a chair and propped his left ankle on his right knee. "Seriously, the hormone cloud during dinner last night about choked me. You two are slaves to your dicks."

Blaine exhaled on his wedding ring and polished it on his pant leg. "Yep."

Sliding a notepad in front of his friends, Erik shook his head.

"Speak for yourself. Write down everything you've agreed to while I print out a real estate purchase agreement. My fee is unlimited privileges after the lake's done."

"I guess that means you're finally ready to buy the Cape Cod. You're welcome. Again."

"Thank you." This time Erik couldn't deny Blaine credit for bringing Layla back into his life. She was everything he needed, except the occasional fishing trip with his friends.

CHAPTER 8

"D amn it!" Layla jerked her fingers from the hot butternut squash peel and hurried to the sink to run cold water over the burn. It eased the sting on her thumb, but nothing could make the pain in her heart better.

She yanked the towel from the hook as she turned off the water. A patch of pink skin marked the spot her carelessness had caused. Making squash butter should've distracted her from the complications in her life instead of adding to them.

A knock on the French doors twisted the knot in her stomach tighter.

Lindie stood outside the glass with a bright smile again, like she'd done every few days for the last two weeks—since the morning she'd caught Erik in his underwear. Today she held up a plastic container as she waved. "Cookies!"

Hanging the towel over her shoulder and trying for an upbeat tone, Layla welcomed her secret half sister into the kitchen. "You didn't have to do that."

"Yes, I did. Blaine's gone all domestic on me since he started working from home so much. He's spoiling Leo and Cam something awful, but I do the same when he isn't watching." Lindie set the container on the table and wiggled out of her coat. She popped off the lid on her way to the counter. "Here, have an oatmeal-apricot bar. My ass does not need cookies, cake, and pie every day, especially with the boys' Halloween candy from last night in the house. He says he'll help me stay in shape, but, geez, I'm about sweeted out. What you making?"

The blend of oats, almonds, and dried apricots soothed some of the tension in Layla's churning belly. "Squash butter. My mom liked to substitute butternut squash for pumpkin."

Lindie picked up the recipe. "Sounds really good. You still miss her, don't you? How long has it been?"

"Yeah. A month." *Today.*

She replaced the handwritten index card and turned to face Layla. The smile was gone, and no obvious emotion showed in her bland expression. "I don't remember much about my mother, not that she's worth remembering. Or my father. They yelled a lot and always told me I was in the way and to be quiet. I spent more time in foster homes than with my parents."

Although the matter-of-fact statements didn't seem to bother her, she stared at Layla as if she was waiting for an admission, an acknowledgment of their biological connection.

She can't possibly know.

The next bite of cookie stuck in Layla's throat. She couldn't reveal the real reason for being in this house. She couldn't even offer a sympathetic hug to the only living relative she had left. The truth had to remain a secret so she could leave when the time came. "I'm sorry."

"Can't change the past." Lindie pushed up her sleeves and headed toward the sink, breaking eye contact too late to prevent a twinge of regret. After a quick hand washing, she tugged the towel from Layla's shoulder. "Do you mind if I stay and help? I'm caught up on my chores, the boys are at school, and Blaine's at a meeting. You'd think I'd appreciate having two hours to myself, but damned if I don't hate the quiet now when they're gone. What do you want me to do first?"

Saying no wasn't really an option, so Layla handed her visitor the spoon next to the squash. "You scoop. I'll mash. Careful, it's hot."

Lindie dug into the orange flesh and plopped a steaming spoonful onto the plate. "Hanging out with you is a lot more fun than sewing buttons back on my work shirts. What else do you make with squash? I've been thinking about putting together a cookbook to sell with my produce next year."

"That's a good idea. The usual. Pie, cookies, breads. And butter, obviously. Squash fries. You know, like sweet potato fries." Mashed goo oozed between the tines of the fork with every squish into the baked squash. "Cubed and roasted with olive oil and cinnamon. Gnocchi with sage and parmesan."

"Those sound tasty. I've only ever cut it in half and baked it." Another large glob landed on the plate. "Blaine said you're going to handle the paperwork so we can adopt the boys. Did he tell you he's their legal guardian because his sister and her husband were killed in a car accident? He made me a guardian too in case of emergency, but we decided they should have something permanent. They don't have to change their last name or call us Mom and Dad. I just want them to know we'll always take care of them, and not because they're a responsibility. You can't imagine how precious they are to us."

Layla bit the inside of her lip and wiped her sleeve across her cheek. She'd heard every sad story since she began practicing law, especially in custody and divorce cases. Why would this one bring her to tears?

"Anyway, thank you. Sometimes I wish my parents would've died instead of theirs, if they're still alive. Hell, I don't even know—or care. They're not my family." The barest hint of hurt, anger, and grief colored Lindie's words, although she probably meant for nothing to show. Scars like hers were too deep to heal completely, no matter how much time had passed.

Layla transferred the mound of mashed squash to the pot, but she had little memory of creating it. Only the ache in her heart had her attention. She couldn't ask her half sister to leave. Unfortunately, she wouldn't be able to hold in her secret much longer if their conversation continued on its current track, either. "I've asked one of my colleagues to handle some of the legwork since I'm not in the office. It'll happen faster that way. Can you get the cider out of the fridge?"

"Sure. I never thought about having kids, mostly because getting married was the last thing I wanted to do. It's hard sometimes, but I kind of like being a mother. And marriage is way better than I imagined." Her sister measured the cider and poured it over the squash in the pan.

Then Layla added cane sugar, cinnamon, and allspice to the mixture. "This has to cook for about half an hour. How about a cup of tea?"

"Sounds great. Do you think you'll get married? Maybe have a baby or two? You and Fielding… You've been spending a lot of time together. I know it's none of my business, but I'd love to get the scoop before Blaine does."

"We haven't talked about it." *Yet.* Layla's insides tangled even tighter as she filled the teakettle and put it on the stove to heat. That conversation wasn't one she was looking forward to, but it had to happen soon. She returned to the counter, hoping to hide her discomfort with the new every-bit-as-personal topic by readying the teapot, tea ball, and mugs. "What made you decide to become a farmer?"

A snort of laughter came from behind her. "Funny story. After saving every penny I could from working at a desk for fifteen years, physical labor sounded so appealing. Working in a garden, taking care of animals, going to bed with tired muscles instead of a tired soul. I thought I wanted to live the rest of my life away from people. It turns out I need Blaine to help me find the kind of peace I've been looking for. I think I'm helping him find it too."

Her plainspoken half sister had managed to reach a place of contentment. As much as she deserved the prize, a pang of envy sliced through Layla. No happily-ever-after waited for her.

A muffled chime broke the silence a second before the kettle whistled. She turned off the flame while Lindie checked her phone.

"Well, damn. I'm going to have to flake out on you. There's a water main break near Leo's school and Blaine says they're releasing the kids an hour early. He's knee-deep in a meeting, so I need to pick up Leo."

The news eased some of the tension in Layla's neck. "That's too bad. I enjoyed our visit."

"Me too." Shoving her arms into her coat sleeves, Lindie smiled. "Thanks for the chat. See you later."

Her visitor waved as she hopped off the deck and jogged toward home, sparking another stronger twinge of regret. Living almost next door to Lindie had backfired. Confirmation of her mother's suspicion could've happened from a distance, far enough away to prevent the attachment that had begun to develop—a yearning for family.

No longer in the mood to make squash butter or have a cup of tea, she returned the teakettle to the stove and shut off the flame under the jam pot. Tears threatened as she climbed the stairs and entered the master bedroom. The contents of the small box were still strewn on the bathroom counter, where she'd laid them shortly after Erik had kissed her goodbye and left for the office that morning. The test had confirmed what she'd already known.

She stuffed everything into the shopping bag and hid it in the box of tampons in the cabinet beneath the sink. The second test would provide the opportunity to end what she never should've begun again.

She shoved back the covers and crawled into bed. The one-month anniversary of her mom's death shouldn't have been the day she found out she carried her lover's child. Giving him up was devastating, but walking away from a baby they created together hadn't crossed her mind when he'd appeared on the stairway two weeks ago.

Nothing had gone as planned.

Curling up in the blankets for a short pity party won out over tackling her first and most important task—making sure Erik had plenty of reasons to walk away from her without looking back.

With what was left of her world about to shatter into a million pieces, Layla folded the scanned and emailed legal document. Signing it was a formality she could take care of during a trip to her office in a few days, although that particular detail wasn't one she would share. Any number of her colleagues would witness her signature, etching her decision in stone. Erik would likely hate her for it, but he'd thank her eventually—when he realized she had done what was in his best interest.

She slipped the papers into an envelope and stowed it in her computer bag before longing stole her good sense. Life was about choices, doing the right thing even if it hurt everyone involved on some level. The pain might dull to a manageable ache over time and then to a sad memory, but she would take it to her grave, along with the secret she had to keep from Lindie.

This wasn't supposed to happen, Mom. Why did you make me promise to come here?

Grief pursued Layla to the kitchen, gathering strength as she finished the squash butter and chopped celery, onions, and carrots for supper. Not even the aroma of homemade chicken soup would cure her despair, but comfort food might help her prepare for what had to be done and console her in the days to come.

The faint hum of the garage door opener added to her roiling emotions. She had to face the man she loved and do the impossible— pretend everything was fine.

Erik hung his keys next to hers on the hooks by the door and his coat on the back of the closest chair. A smile erased the tiredness in his eyes, making him look happier than she'd ever seen him. "Geez, what a long day. I'm so glad to be home. I missed you."

Something in the way he said "home" warned her the fallout from her plan would be much worse than she'd projected. He would never forgive her for the pain she would inflict, but hurting him now was more humane than hurting him later.

She placed the lid on the soup pot and met his gaze. "Hi."

"Are you feeling okay? You look exhau—" His smile dimmed and he rushed to gather her in his arms. "Damn. I didn't realize what today is. I'm so sorry I wasn't here for you."

The warmth of his breath against her cheek and the gentleness of his embrace touched the broken pieces of her heart and pricked her conscience. Tears flowed again, this time sparked by how much sorrow letting him and their child go would cause.

"You'll get through this. I know it's hard, but you're strong and you can lean on me whenever you need to." His hold tightened for a long moment and then he guided her toward the family room. "It's time to relax. Everything else can wait."

She settled into the snug nest he created on the couch, her head against his chest and his legs tangled with hers. The sense of rightness and security tempted her to abandon her plan, but she closed her eyes to cherish these last hours with him. Her reality wasn't going to change and she wouldn't burden him with it.

Each brush of his fingertips along her back and through the inch-long hair that had grown out since her mother's death brought a measure of joy with the pain. It chased away the terrible knowledge that tonight was all she had left to hoard memories of their unexpectedly deep and powerful connection. Tomorrow wasn't here yet.

~

"Layla, are you awake?"

She blinked to clear the fog from her brain, not sure whether she'd been on the edge of sleep or had dozed off. "Hm?"

"You should eat something."

The scent of chicken soup teased her from the haze. "It can't be done already. I started it just before you got here."

Erik's low chuckle should've vibrated through her skull, but it didn't. "That was four hours ago."

She pushed upward on her right elbow and let her surroundings come into focus. The lamp cast a ring of light across the bedroom floor. "Four hours?"

"You fell asleep on the couch, so I carried you up to bed. You evidently needed sleep. Now you need food." He helped her sit and wedged the pillow behind her back.

I lost four hours I could've spent memorizing him. She dropped her chin to hide the distress that had to be written all over her face. "I need you."

He lifted her left hand to his lips and kissed each fingertip. "I'm not going anywhere. Try to eat a little bit and then you can rest some more. I'll hold you all night."

Half a dozen tasteless bites seemed to pacify him, unlike her roiling stomach, and he finally switched off the light and climbed into bed beside her. The heat from his body seeped into her as he drew her close enough to feel his heartbeat. It matched her own, beat for beat, and she counted his even breaths long after he fell asleep.

He'd made love to her so many times, but having him simply love her through this, their final night together, was the way she would remember him.

CHAPTER 9

Movement beside him brought Erik out of his half-asleep state. He followed his lover as she rolled toward her side of the bed, slipping his arm around her waist to close the distance between them.

The ring he'd stashed in his coat pocket called to him. His plan to propose had been temporarily put on hold because of Layla's melancholy mood last night, but asking her to marry him over breakfast worked as well. They could spend the day together, making plans and making love.

She lifted his hand and wiggled away. "I need to go to the bathroom."

"Hurry back." He dragged her pillow to his nose and breathed in her scent as she closed the door.

Ten minutes passed, but the door remained closed.

After another five minutes, he dragged himself out of bed and to the bathroom. A knock yielded a long silence before she finally turned the knob and let him in. "Are you okay?"

Her gaze skipped from him to a spot near the sink. A plastic device rested next to an open box. Large block letters announced its contents. "There's a pink line."

He steadied himself with a hand on the counter. Two weeks ago, a positive premarital pregnancy test would've brought panic. Now it brought relief and joy. It had to be a sign he was finally about to achieve the marriage-and-family goal that had eluded him for years. "Marry me, Layla."

She was silent as she shook her head. The distress in her shuttered eyes and stiff posture had to mean she'd hoped for a different result. Thankfully, it wasn't necessarily a reflection of her feelings for him.

Still, his gut twisted. "That's not funny."

"I'm serious, Erik. I won't marry you." She tossed the stick into the trashcan and returned to the bedroom, her stiff gait not inviting him to follow.

Ignoring the brush-off, he trailed after her. "I get that you've seen a lot of troubled marriages and broken families in your line of work, but what we have is different. I love you, and I know you love me. All those years we were apart... I couldn't find someone to share my life with because I was looking back for you. It was always you I wanted. Damn it, I bought a ring yesterday and was going to propose last night, but you were upset about— God, you already knew what the test was going to say, didn't you?"

"Please don't." She shrugged her robe on over her nightgown and knotted the belt.

More than anything, he wanted to pull her into his arms and hold her, but he kept his distance. "Don't what? Love you? Make you happy? We don't have to be perfect. We just have to love each other and be thankful we're together."

"It isn't about whether or not we can make it work. We would." Her voice softened, breaking over the words. "There's a damn good chance I'm going to die from cancer, and I won't put you through that hell. Neither of you. I drew up a termination of parental rights document yesterday and...I signed it."

The statement stole his breath for a full minute. How could she think he was unwilling to confront the for-worse and in-sickness parts of the vows he wanted to take? "Then un-sign it. You don't get to make that decision for me. Every second I have with you is priceless to me, if it's one day or fifty years. Besides, I could drop dead tomorrow from a heart attack or get run over by a bus. Does that make you love me less? Does that justify abandoning you and a baby I helped create?"

"It's not the same."

Her unwillingness to even consider his perspective hurt almost as much as her eagerness to desert the miracle they'd made together.

He paced to the window seat and back. "Yeah, it is. And I sure as hell won't let any child of mine grow up thinking her mother doesn't want her. Ask Lindie how it feels to have parents who don't give a damn. She can tell you firsthand what it's like to feel unwanted. You *will* be involved in raising this baby, even if you refuse to be with me. I can't force you to marry me, but I'll be damned if you're walking away from our child."

"I'm not changing my mind. Don't make this harder than it already is." She crossed her arms in front of her, hugging herself instead of letting him do it.

"You want easy?" He swallowed against the panic clawing its way through his chest. "Marry me. Because I'm going to fight you if you don't."

Her chin rose. "You won't win."

"I'm not fighting for me. I lost as soon as you decided what I feel for you doesn't matter."

"How *dare* you judge me?" She turned her back to him. "Get out. And don't come back."

He gathered his clothes, too heartsick to listen to her meaningless excuses and explanations. At the doorway, he paused, focusing on the muted shadows in the stairway instead of revealing how much her disregard for his feelings cut through his soul. More than likely, she'd already noticed and simply didn't care. "I guess I'll see you in court."

E rik ended the call with the attorney he'd retained and hammered his fist against the desk. How could he have no rights?

He couldn't stop Layla from ending the pregnancy. He couldn't stop her from giving up their child. She could walk away with absolutely no thought to their baby or him, but he couldn't sign away his parental rights and get out of eighteen years of responsibility unless she accepted those terms or she chose to sign away her rights too. How was that fair?

Perspective made all the difference. Not that he would shirk his duty, but a man's refusal to pay child support made sense now. Hell, he'd used a fucking condom, and she hadn't done a damn thing to prevent conception. Yet, she had all the power.

He pushed out of his chair and paced to the window. His only option was to negotiate for a few minor concessions that wouldn't gain him anything in the long run, even if she'd initiated that first kiss and asked him if he had protection. The judge's first question would revolve around whether he was a willing participant.

He'd been willing all right, and that had been his mistake. Responsible behavior meant nothing when it produced a baby. Male consent meant even less in that context.

A knock sounded on his door, but he wished the intruder away. The click behind him assured him that his wishes had nothing to do with getting what he wanted.

"Hey, Erik. Got a minute? I need to talk to you about something." Blaine's cheery greeting chewed on his last nerve.

He pivoted toward his unwelcome visitor, only to find Blaine an arm's length away. An unrestrained urge brought his fist up to connect with his friend's jaw. "You son of a bitch."

Blaine stumbled backward, rubbing his chin as he blinked. "What the hell was that for?"

"You just couldn't mind your own damn business, could you? It's your fault she's here. Oh, don't even try to pretend you don't know what I'm talking about. All that background shit you gathered on Lindie while you put me out there to deal with her temper. Anybody can see Layla's her sister. Wasn't it handy you knew about us fucking like rabbits in college? You could introduce your wife to her secret half sister and butt into my pathetic love life at the same time." Some of his anger and frustration vented for the moment, Erik dropped into his chair. Helplessness and hopelessness remained.

Blaine worked his jaw back and forth several times as he settled across from him. "Yes, they're sisters. I was hoping you could mention to Layla that you suspected so she'd finally speak up to Lindie about it. Layla's known since right before her mom died. That's why she's here —to find the family her mom told her about. Lindie's getting impatient for Layla to bring it up. The other stuff... When I found out who the sister was, I figured you two might admit your feelings for each other this time. Finally be in the right place at the right time."

Only harsh laughter kept Erik from crying. He tossed the balled up page of notes at his worst best friend. "She has no feelings."

"What's this?" Blaine flattened the paper against the edge of the desk and was silent for a long minute. "She's pregnant?"

"What do you think?" A cold sweat spread across Erik's neck and shoulders, and his stomach threatened to reject the coffee he'd relied on to get him through the call. "I asked her to marry me. She said no and informed me that she signed a termination of parental rights document before she took the home pregnancy test. She doesn't want anything to do with me or the baby."

"Jesus. That's...not what I expected." Shaking his head, Blaine placed the wrinkled paper on the desk. "I'm sorry. I honestly thought you guys were meant to be together. Have you tried to—"

"I told her I love her and practically begged her to marry me. The attorney I talked to basically said I have no recourse. There's nothing left to do but wait until the baby's born and hope she changes her mind. Or that she doesn't change her mind and have an abortion." Erik cradled his head in his hands and blew out a slow exhale in an attempt to calm his dread. "I'm not holding my breath."

"So you're giving up? You got all in my face when Lindie told me to fuck off. Do you really think I'm going to do any less to you? Go big or go home. Remember that advice? Flowers, ring, on your knee, declaration of love."

Maybe he hadn't offered her all those things, but she'd had him on his knees from the moment she had flipped back that red hood and spoken his name. "I offered her a ring and all the love I have to give. Flowers sure as hell aren't going to change her mind."

"Then find a way to make it happen. If you can't appeal to her heart, piss her off. Emotion has a way of bringing out the honesty in people."

"Honesty isn't the problem. She thinks she's going to get cancer and die. She spouted some bullshit about not putting the baby and me through that."

"So she's dumping her kid? Her mom didn't send her away. You point that out, and she won't have an argument." Blaine rubbed his jaw and grinned. "Or she'll take a swing at you."

Erik leaned back in his chair and balled his fists again. "Glad to see this is so fucking amusing to you."

Blaine's frown warned him he wouldn't let another slug in the jaw slip by him. "My wife is her sister. Stubbornness is a dominant trait in both of them, so you better get used to holding your ground when it comes to important stuff like this."

"What ground? If I try to talk to her, she'll probably get a restraining order. She knows what options she has, and she won't hesitate to use her expertise. I may understand contracts inside and out, but she has the kind of knowledge that could destroy my life. She *is* destroying my life."

"Then preempt what you think she'll do. Meet with the lawyer, draw up a list of demands, and make her respond. Let her know you're serious about wanting her, not just the baby."

"I told her I've always wanted her. It started a hell of a long time before that condom broke. How can she not care?" Erik shoved his hands through his hair. The waves tangled around his fingers, reminding him he still hadn't gotten around to making an appointment for a haircut.

"Tell her again. And then again. Until she accepts it." The chair creaked as Blaine shifted in his seat. "You have the advantage of already knowing how you feel about her. The first time I asked Lindie to marry me, I was negotiating a shady business deal. We'd both get hot sex and I'd get my grandparents' farm back. I didn't offer her anything she wasn't already getting. Hell, I even tried using Leo and Cam to influence her decision. I was a dick for expecting her to say yes to a half-assed marriage proposal. And she was smart enough to refuse."

"You are a dick. And this isn't even close to the same circumstances."

A grating chuckle accompanied his friend's eye-roll. "You're so full of shit. You and Layla were already satisfying the itch before she signed the lease. I know what intense sexual attraction looks and feels like. Your complications might be a little different, but our women have the same aversion to commitment. You just have to wait out the resistance."

Erik shoved himself out of his chair and poured another cup of coffee. Scotch might've numbed the pain, but he needed his wits about him. "'Our women?' I don't own Layla, and Lindie would kick your ass if she heard you call her that."

"You might be surprised by what my wife likes nowadays, not that I think she's my personal property. Belonging to each other means trust, support, somebody we know we can rely on."

"Apparently, I'm only trustworthy, reliable, and financially well-off enough to raise a baby, not be there for its mother."

"Quit feeling sorry for yourself and do something constructive." Blaine leaned forward, sliding a notepad and pen toward Erik. "Let's make that list of demands. If she's asking you to sacrifice spending the rest of your life with her, what do you want from her in return?"

"For her to admit she loves me." The ache in Erik's heart spread to his whole body. "I want her to tell me I'm as important to her as she is to me."

"Nope. It has to be stuff she'll be uncomfortable with. Being with her when she's having the baby. Making her help you decorate the nursery. The things you should be doing together while she's pregnant. You have less than nine months to convince her to change her mind. Don't you think you ought to take advantage of every minute you can?"

Erik returned to his desk, fairly certain he'd keel over if he didn't sit. "I don't know anything about having a baby."

"Lucky for you, I'm here. I remember when Bree was pregnant

with Leo and Cam. There were doctor visits, Lamaze classes, baby showers, ultrasounds. Open your computer and do a search for prenatal care. We're going to list everything. When she sees what you expect, marriage will look like the easy way out. Besides, I have a secret weapon that's guaranteed to make her reconsider."

CHAPTER 10

L ayla pressed a hand to her belly and choked back the urge to gag
as she stirred the suddenly too-sweet mixture of pears, sugar,
vanilla beans, and cinnamon sticks. The cooking therapy she'd
employed since her mom's death wasn't helping her work through the
grief anymore—or the unexpected bout of what was probably morning
sickness that had struck at lunchtime. Plus, she'd have to give away all
her butters and jams to be sure the cupboards were bare before she
moved again, which would be sooner rather than later.

She shut off the flame under the pot and waffled between going
back to bed and hanging out in the bathroom. The doorbell chimed
before she managed to shuffle half the length of the hall. A twinge in
her gut accompanied a pang near her heart, reminding her that Erik
hadn't contacted her in the five days since he'd promised a legal battle.
He certainly wouldn't show up unannounced, at least not for another
attempt to convince her to marry him. She'd done a damn good job of
pushing him away.

Nobody's home.

She continued toward the stairs, glad she'd closed all the drapes
against the dreariness outside.

The bell rang again, somehow sounding more insistent this time.

A stealthy peek through the sidelight curtain settled her nerves and she opened the door far enough to greet the uniformed woman. "Can I help you?"

The middle-aged brunette offered a warm smile. "Good afternoon. Sorry to bother you. Ms. Layla Krause?"

"Yes, I'm Layla Krause." She wrapped her arms around her middle to ward off the brisk chill. Thankfully, the cool air eased her nausea.

"I have a delivery for you. Sign here please." Holding out an electronic device, she pointed to a place near the bottom.

Layla scribbled her signature on the dotted line. "I'm not expecting a package."

After a tap of the stylus on the screen, the woman tucked the device into her pocket. Then she slid an envelope from inside her coat and held it out. It slipped from her grasp a moment before Layla's fingertips closed around it. "Oops!"

Layla grabbed for the falling piece of mail, hoping to catch it before it landed on the wet porch. Luckily, the legal-sized packet dropped onto the threshold and teetered until she picked it up. When she straightened, the delivery person was climbing into a nondescript black car parked in the driveway. "Damn it. How could I be so stupid?"

Her nausea returned full force, prompted by what was obviously an official summons or legal notification. Her colleagues had used the tactic dozens of times to serve divorce papers and other instances where the recipient wouldn't willingly accept delivery. Experience and a law degree told her Erik couldn't legally challenge the choice to give up her parental rights, nor could he impose visitation on her. He could, however, complicate a simple transfer of custody when their child was born, making it even more devastating than it would be under the best of circumstances.

She tore open the flap with shaky hands and removed a sheaf of papers that promised to test her willpower against the tears she hadn't been able to control since he'd left. The cover sheet was printed on letterhead, the practice a prestigious name in Ohio family law circles. Erik had retained the finest counsel money could buy in the area, reinforcing the knowledge that he was determined to pursue every possible avenue to hell.

She skimmed the polite greeting and introduction, all too familiar with the importance of presenting a professional—and intimidating—face to the enemy.

"I have informed Mr. Fielding that he has no legal recourse should you choose to terminate the pregnancy or exercise voluntary termination of your parental rights. Rather than waste time and resources on a fruitless challenge of those rights, he has asked me to handle negotiation of terms under which the pregnancy, childbirth, and parenting will progress."

A flip of the page revealed an endless list of demands, but the words blurred with another onslaught of unwelcome queasiness.

"There you are. I went to the kitchen door, but then I heard a car out front." Lindie grasped Layla's arm and guided her into the foyer, closing the door behind them. "Layla, are you okay? You're whiter than Fielding's spiffiest dress shirt."

"I need to sit down." A study of the space around her yielded nothing but the steps where she and Erik had renewed their long-dormant attraction and conceived a child together.

Her unexpected visitor nudged her forward. "Come on. I'll help you into the kitchen."

The hall seemed longer than usual, and Layla inhaled and exhaled for the slow count of five to clear her spiraling vision. She shouldn't have agreed to come here, no matter what she'd promised her mom.

"Sit." Lindie hooked her foot around the closest chair and dragged it out from the table. "We need to talk."

Slumping into her seat, Layla pushed the handful of papers toward her visitor. "I don't know what he told you, but it doesn't change anything. My grandmother and my aunt died from the same disease that took my mom from me. In all probability, I'm going to die from it too, and I won't let Erik and our child suffer through that."

"What are you talking about?" Lindie's gaze dropped toward the documents. Then her eyes widened as she flipped through the pages.

"You're *pregnant*? And what's this nonsense about giving up parental rights and guaranteed visitation?"

Layla straightened her spine, letting resentment chase away the nausea. "It isn't nonsense. He's just upset because he doesn't understand how hard it is to watch someone you love die. I've been there. I won't do that to him."

The scrape of Lindie's chair on the tile echoed through the kitchen as she stood. With her hands perched on her hips, she stared down her nose at Layla. "Screw your martyr syndrome. Fielding might be too noble to do it, but I'm calling bullshit."

Rage bubbled in Layla's veins with the direct hit on her conscience. "I don't care what—"

"Shut up. You're going to listen anyway." Lindie's lower lip trembled, and she wrinkled her nose. "You want to talk about helplessness? I held my little sister in my arms while she died when I was five years old. She fell and hit her head, and I couldn't do anything to save her. She was three. Practically still a baby. I'm thankful for every minute we shared and *especially* that she didn't have to die alone."

A fresh stitch of pain smothered the anger.

Lindie paced to the counter before huffing out a noisy breath and swiping her forearm across her eyes. Her voice softened. "Did you know we have a sister who died?"

"No." Layla shook her head then buried her face in her hands as realization dawned. *What have I done?*

"But you *do* know you have a sister who lives up the road from you and her name is Lindie Brewster. Stockwell. Shit! Don't tell Blaine I did that. I'll never hear the end of it." Hands in her coat pockets, she paced back to the table. "Oh, and I'm guessing you didn't plan on sharing that information with your big sister."

"Half. You tricked me."

She moved her chair within a foot of Layla's and sat, putting them knee to knee. "I don't give a damn if it's a sixteenth. You. Are. My. Sister. Period. I'd never put a qualifier on my relationship to you or Leo and Cam, so you better not do it to me. Got it?"

A mix of guilt and embarrassment heated her neck and cheeks. "I should've gone back to bed. How did you find out?"

Lindie rubbed her palms on her jeans-covered thighs and rolled her shoulders, a sure sign that her answer was bound to be a complicated one. "Are you sure you want to know this stuff? I can't un-tell you later."

"I think it's already too late." The hunger for more details was a welcome distraction from her roiling stomach and emotions.

"Blaine did some research on me when he was trying to coerce me into selling the farm. His snooping found some things I knew nothing about. After a little more digging, he was able to tie your mom to our father. When he traced your mom back to you, you had just requested a leave of absence to take care of her and he used a mutual professional contact to make sure you knew about this house when she died. With my approval."

"You knew the whole time and didn't say anything?"

"We decided to let you make the first move since your choice of location hardly seemed coincidental, but you never did. That's what I came to talk about this afternoon. We took the long way around, and now I have a damn good argument for you to think about living instead of dying—besides the fact that you and Erik deserve to be happy and I'm going to be an aunt again." The determined set of Lindie's jaw warned Layla that long, hard battles were her specialty. "There's something else you should know. Blaine's pretty sure we have another sister."

"Another sister?" Layla's heart sank. Leaving behind Erik, their baby, and the sister she'd come to know would be difficult enough, but adding another sibling might break her will.

"Yeah." Lindie's wide grin morphed into a stern glower. "I didn't find you so the next time I see you is at your funeral. Fielding's not the only person who's going to be a pain in the ass if you try to leave."

Layla slumped in her chair, no less horrified today than five days ago by the way she'd treated the man she loved, even if she had his best interests at heart. She hadn't meant to fall in love, but having a connection to him again after so many years had given her a measure of peace and comfort. Her only consolation was he wouldn't be alone after she was gone.

Her sister shoved a single page at her, pointing to the laundry list of supposedly non-negotiable items. "He's demanding to attend every prenatal visit with you. Blood draws, exams, ultrasounds. Childbirth classes as your partner. Labor and delivery. For God's sake, it's every excuse he can think of to spend time with you. The poor man's trying to cram a lifetime into eight, maybe eight and a half months. Insisting on a picture of you and him with the baby is obviously because he thinks you're planning to make your getaway as soon as you get out of the hospital."

How could he have known the thought had crossed her mind? "What if you're wrong? What if he just wants to make my life miserable as payback for telling him I wouldn't marry him?"

Lindie drummed her fingers on the table, rattling the papers. "Fine, play devil's advocate and say he's being a prick. Men's egos get jacked out of shape by rejection. The problem with that cop-out is he's too concerned about what other people think of him to have an ego. Do you really believe Mr. Upright-and-Uptight wants to do all this to punish you?"

Unable to stand the censure in Lindie's stony expression, Layla lowered her gaze to the list. The final item stood out among the other demands, its larger type fitting. A fresh batch of tears stung her eyes.

"Love our child." Erik's simple request wasn't selfish or vengeful. It epitomized the kind of man he was and banished any notion that he meant to cause her pain.

"By the way, Fielding is a good guy. I only tease him because he's the reason Blaine didn't give up on me. And he puts up with me because he understands what real love is, even when he thought he'd never find it."

Layla pressed her lips together and drew a shuddering breath. *I can do this.* "Okay, how do I get him to talk to me—without his lawyer?"

With a wicked laugh, Lindie wrapped her arms around Layla, enclosing her in a cozy hug. Then she tugged her to her feet. "Leave that to me, dear sister. I'll text you once I have the plan set up. In the meantime, go take a nap. You look like you haven't slept for the better part of a week."

Grateful for her sister's easy acceptance of the ruse, Layla followed her to the stairway. Halfway to the master bedroom, she cast a glance over her shoulder at the woman she'd deceived, hoping her sister didn't trail after her. The packed boxes in the bedroom next to hers would be a dead giveaway. "I appreciate your help."

Ignoring the rap on his office door, Erik scrolled to the last paragraph of the contract he'd promised to review by the end of the day. His next appointment wasn't due to arrive for fifteen minutes and Mrs. Resnick had orders not to disturb him. Only one person had the balls to violate his privacy.

I don't want to talk about it. There's nothing I can do.

The door swung inward.

He focused on the words filling the computer screen, hoping Blaine would get the hint. "Next time, I'm locking the damn door."

"I learned to pick locks when I was six."

His stomach lurched at the sound of Lindie's voice. She had bigger balls than his best friend, and he'd underestimated her again. "Why am I not surprised? I'm busy. If you need a contract drawn up, make an appointment."

"Mrs. Resnick said you're free until five." She shrugged off her jacket and hung it on the back of the chair across from him. Then she dropped into the seat, hooking her leg over the arm, clearly determined to make his shitty day worse. "The bruise on Blaine's jaw is green and yellow today."

"So? He deserved it."

"Maybe, but it sure has messed with his ability to perform oral sex. I like oral sex."

He turned his attention back to his laptop to avoid letting her see how uncomfortable that information made him. "You'll have to forgive me for not giving a damn."

"It's okay. We've found other ways to be creative." Her laughter shredded the last of his patience.

Glaring in her direction, he pushed away from his desk. "If you're here to irritate me, it worked. You can leave now."

"Although getting a rise out of you always brightens my day, that's not why I'm here. It's about Layla. She wants out of the contract. Oh, and the scruffy, bad-boy beard looks good on you. Too bad it clashes with your personality."

He shoved his hands in his pockets and wandered to the window, ignoring her jibe and hoping to maintain the aloof front he'd tried to master since he'd been ordered to leave what should've become his happily-ever-after. "She'll forfeit the security deposit if there's damage to the house, which is at your discretion, and whatever rent's remaining for the rest of this lease period." *Eleven days.* "Otherwise, since it's an open-ended contract, you have no legal grounds to sue for a termination. Blaine asked for a month-to-month lease with the next month's rent due by the eighteenth to continue the agreement. Simple, straightforward, and no long-term commitment."

The last words summed up exactly what Layla had expected from him as well. Given the choice, he'd take a financial loss over the wounds she'd inflicted.

All trace of humor in Lindie's voice vanished. "Not that contract."

"Then what contract?"

"Maybe contract isn't the right word. The legal stuff between you and her. The custody agreement."

"We don't have a custody agreement. My attorney delivered a letter about negotiating terms today. She hasn't agreed to any of my requests. The only thing she's signed is the termination of parental rights document." Panic surged through him, aggravating the knot in his stomach. He whirled around to face his visitor. "She's not thinking of…" *Ending the pregnancy? Keeping our child from me?*

Lindie's silence and grim expression spoke louder than any response she might have made.

He yanked his coat from the stand on his way out the door and shoved his arm into the sleeve as he passed Mrs. Resnick's desk. "Will you cancel my five o'clock appointment? Oh, and tell Mr. Warren I said the buyout contract looks good."

His receptionist frowned at him. "Is everything okay?"

"No." He struggled into the other half of his coat and shoved the outer door open with his shoulder. "I won't be back."

"Never?"

"I'm pretty sure he means just today, Mrs. R." Lindie waved at him from his office doorway, shooing him like she did her chickens. "Go, go, go."

His coat flapped in the icy wind as he jogged to his car, and a flurry of snowflakes swirled onto the driver's seat before he could duck inside. Under normal circumstances, he might have complained how bad his day had been, but it could get worse—a lot worse. His gut pushed him to hurry, to avoid losing his only connection to the woman he'd fallen in love with half his life ago.

He merged into the nearly bumper-to-bumper traffic and willed time to slow. Red and blue lights flashed in his rearview mirror, ripping away the last of his optimism. The telltale *thump, thump, thump* of a mostly flat tire followed him to the edge of the highway. He turned off the engine and lowered his head to the steering wheel.

A tap on the passenger-side window broke the relative silence and Erik straightened. With a press of a button, the glass whizzed downward, letting in the wintry weather.

The officer reflected in the side mirror leaned down to look at him through the opening. Her friendly smile wasn't a greeting he'd expect from someone about to write up a violation. "I was going to warn you about the low tire, but I'm guessing you already figured that out. I radioed the Safety Patrol to help you change the flat. Safer than trying to do it yourself during rush hour."

"Thanks. I appreciate it." Of course, the way his luck had gone lately meant the spare had no doubt sprung a leak too.

"You're welcome. They should be here in about five minutes. Lucky guy. It's usually at least fifteen or twenty. Drive safely and enjoy your evening." She waved and then headed back to the patrol car.

Lucky? Not by a long shot. Should he be grateful for not getting a ticket, even though he hadn't done anything wrong?

The overcast sky gave the illusion of dusk, adding to his dismal mood. An endless line of taillights glowed red in front of him and headlights illuminated falling snow in the rearview mirror. Flashing yellow lights broke up the monotony in the distance, but his window of opportunity to stop Layla's plans was probably closing faster than he could get to her.

CHAPTER 11

Dusk became night by the time Erik made the turn into the Cape Cod's driveway. His whole body ached and the tension in his neck had given way to a full-blown headache more than half an hour ago—before the guy had finally arrived to change his tire. At any other time, prioritizing a four-car fender bender over a flat tire would've been well within the realm of acceptability, but it hadn't happened at any other time.

Not a single light glowed in the windows to welcome him. The house appeared deserted, much more so than on the rainy day he'd met its tenant for a tour. It was a distinct possibility, considering Layla had changed her mind. She could've packed up her belongings and moved back to the house she'd lived in next to her mother. Hell, she could've taken an overnight bag and gone anywhere to avoid letting him be part of her life, their child's life.

He stopped in the front of the garage, reluctant to use the opener still hooked on the driver's side visor. The house keys on his key ring urged him to exploit whatever means he had at his disposal to put forth a last-ditch effort. Entering without knocking seemed intrusive, but what did he have to lose? Hadn't he already lost everything that mattered most?

The garage door rose with the tap of the button and he held his breath while his headlights illuminated the area behind it. An empty cavern awaited him. The void drained every bit of optimism from his soul, leaving wounds far worse than the ones he'd experienced when his dad had died.

Her car was missing, as were the broken-down moving boxes she'd stored on the shelves lining the back wall. Only the snow shovel that had been hanging from a hook near the kitchen entrance prior to her arrival remained.

She was gone, and all hope of having a family with her was gone too.

He didn't pull forward into "his" side, but he didn't shift into reverse, either. Going back to the office or to his house held no appeal. Nothing held any appeal, not drinking himself into a stupor for listening to his best friend's idiotic advice or punching Blaine in the jaw again for suggesting he antagonize Layla into marrying him. The pain and the emptiness would still be there. Numbness, or even shock, would've been a welcome alternative to the bitterness eating him from the inside out. Losing her to cancer couldn't possibly hurt any worse, but she hadn't given him that choice.

Lights flickered through the trees lining the driveway, reflecting in the rearview mirror. The car didn't slow or turn toward the house. The momentary flutter of hope died and he forced himself to press on the gas pedal. He could stay here for the night, with no one the wiser. Wallowing in the memories they'd made together and searching the rooms for a hint of her presence might get him through the first hours of knowing he would never see her again. Eventually, years of experience of going through the motions would kick in, maybe enough to convince everybody, except himself, he was okay.

Life would go on, whether he wanted it to or not.

The garage door closed out the world before he worked up the energy to retrieve his bag from the backseat and cross to the steps leading to the kitchen. The contents of his palm were cast in shadows, but he found the right key easily. It was next to the key fob for his car, where he'd put it the day Layla had invited him to spend every night with her.

Although almost utter blackness surrounded him when he shut the interior door behind him, he had no trouble picturing her at the stove stirring a batch of fruit butter or jam. Sweet and savory aromas lingered in his mind, scents that had clung to her skin and filled his senses as he made love to her.

Using the wall to guide him, he lumbered toward the foyer. Light would only force him to see an obvious truth, to accept what he should've seen all along. She'd never intended to stay—under any circumstances. The house that was supposed to have been theirs was devoid of everything but his fantasies, his memories, and the barely discernible outlines of corners and doorways.

He continued to the stairway, determined to find his way in the dark. The toe of his shoe hit the bottom step as his knuckles made contact with the oak newel post. Closing his eyes, he ascended the stairs, passing through the ghost lovers blocking his path. That moment would haunt him for the rest of his life.

The railing curved beneath his fingers, indicating he'd reached the second floor. Not ready to enter the room he'd shared with Layla, he walked past the master suite to the bedroom he'd chosen for the son or daughter he would never know. The dream was over. When he left the Cape Cod this time, he wouldn't return.

He bit his lower lip to distract himself from the stab of pain and entered the room. A narrow swath from the security light outside the house angled across the floor, illuminating a row of boxes along the closest wall. The ache flared again, and he let the duffle bag slide from his shoulder. The muffled thud on the floor seemed like a door slamming closed in his face, without the requisite window appearing. The world he'd created in his mind shattered.

I'm too late.

Retracing his steps, he trudged to the master bedroom. The mound of blankets near the center of the bed supported his guess that she'd made a quick getaway and didn't care what kind of disaster she left behind. They promised a final night surrounded by her presence. Hours of imagining her in his arms wouldn't bring her back, but the sweet torture of breathing in her delectable scent was better than having to give up all of her.

God, I love you, Layla. How could you do this to me? He crossed to the bed and lifted a pillow to his nose. Pears, cinnamon, and vanilla filled his senses, blending with the unique perfume of her soap, shampoo, and skin.

A sob struggled against the tightness in his throat, amplifying the emotions he'd mostly held in check during his desperate search for a solution. *How am I going to get through the rest of my life without you?*

Burying his face in the pillow, he let his grief out without holding back. If he'd learned anything from her, it was to recognize and admit how deep his feelings went. Hiding from the truth had gotten him nowhere and cost him everything. He should've spoken his mind when he'd had the opportunity.

Several chimes rang out in quick succession, invading the silence and sending his pulse racing. As he located the source of the sounds and the sudden light on the opposite nightstand, the blankets shifted and a form rose from the bed. It reached toward the cell phone a moment before the screen dimmed.

A heavy sigh came from the shadowy silhouette he'd know anywhere. "Looks like *I* underestimated you too."

~

L ayla blinked her puffy eyes and reread the series of text messages.

"My plan went off without a hitch!"

"Oh, and I borrowed your car after you fell asleep so you can't run away. *insert evil cackle*"

"Don't bother denying you planned to."

"Fielding is coming to see you. Let yourself be happy."

"That's an order."

"Love you, sis." The sentiment and a row of colored hearts seemed at odds with Lindie's brusque nature, but she apparently loved with as much gusto as she did everything else.

Although Layla was tempted to ignore her sister's interference, she couldn't smother the desire to follow the advice. "I don't know how to be happy, not when I'm going to cause him so much pain."

"Going to? You already have." The softly spoken indictment sliced open her conscience and she whirled toward the voice behind her.

Erik stood the width of the bed away. He was barely visible, but she didn't need to see his stiff expression to know it was there. The elusive man with the easy smile and sense of humor was clearly gone again, stuffed back inside by his old self—with a lot of help from her.

He switched on the lamp beside him, proving her wrong. Hurt and something he'd never shown her before radiated from his unshaven face. "Do you love me?"

The question was harsh and accusing. Anger clung to it, demanding an honest answer.

"Tell me." The light reflected off a drop of moisture on his cheek, revealing another far deeper emotion she hadn't expected from him. "I deserve to know."

She planted her feet on the cool floor to counter the sensation of free-falling and nodded. "Yes, I love you, but—"

"No buts." His hold on the pillow he clutched to his chest loosened, and he tossed it on the jumble of blankets. "I want you to prove it to me. Give me all the love you have for as long as you have, with no conditions. For once in my life, I'm going to be selfish, and I expect you to be selfish too. Take what you want instead of sacrificing us for a cause that isn't even noble."

"Not noble?" She crossed her arms in front of her, ready to defend her right to protect him. "I'm doing this for you."

"Baloney. This is all about you." He paced to the dresser and back without breaking eye contact. "Part of it's survivor's guilt. Or some variation of it."

"Oh, so now you have a degree in psychology?"

"No, but I spent most of the last week trying to figure out why you think I'm better off without you. I came up with quite a few questions and a lot of reasons your decision doesn't make sense."

"Really?" She perched her fists on her hips. How dare he analyze her motives? "Such as?"

A spark of confidence in his eyes warned her she had a much stronger adversary in this argument than any legal negotiation she'd ever engaged in. "Did your mother give up her parental rights so you wouldn't have to suffer through her death decades in the future? Did she send you away when she found out she might die from the disease that took your grandmother from her? And your aunt? Or maybe you want to repeat your father's mistakes."

She clutched at the blankets to keep from heaving the unlit lamp at him. "Don't you even compare what I'm doing to what he did. It isn't the same, not by a long shot." *It isn't. It can't be. Can it?*

His gaze didn't waver, adding strength to his case and weakening her defenses. "That's for you to decide, I suppose. Why did your mom make you agree to come here? Was it because she wanted you to know you have a sister? So you wouldn't be alone? And why the hell didn't you tell anyone who you are?"

The depth of his knowledge about the situation registered as she followed his progress in another lap past the end of the bed and back.

"I was protecting…" Every step made another piece of her reasoning crumble.

"Protecting who? Yourself, so you wouldn't have to watch us love and lose you?"

Panic overpowered defensive anger. "That's none of your business."

"Maybe, but I was at least ninety-five percent certain you and Lindie were sisters the first time I saw you together. We all knew. Blaine finally admitted it last week when I confronted him about setting up the whole damn scenario, our reunion included. Did you know your mom was in on it too?"

"She couldn't have been. She wouldn't have kept that from me.

Meeting Lindie was the reason she made me promise to come here. I don't want either of you to watch me die. I can't stay and…" The words her mom had said before she'd gone to sleep the last time resonated in Layla's head. *The only regrets you should have when you're dying are the things you wish you hadn't done. Don't have regrets about what you didn't do.*" She dropped her gaze to the floor and drew in a shaky breath. "Oh my God, somehow she knew about you. About us."

"I think everybody knew what was happening between us back then. Except us." He dug a small box from the inside pocket of his overcoat and snapped open the lid as he closed the distance between them. Resolve had crowded out the anger and resentment in his gait and his tone. He stopped less than an arm's length from her, setting off an itch to reach for him and beg him to forget the horrible things she'd said. "See this ring? I bought it because I accepted my feelings for you, and being imperfect with you is better than being without you. Loving you is the riskiest thing I've ever done, but I can't help myself. You're part of me. You have been for a long time and that isn't going to change, no matter what you say or do to try to change my mind."

Lamplight glinted off the trio of diamonds, shining like the beacon he had been the day she'd arrived to heal from the loss of her mother and to meet her sister. He was light and hope in her most difficult time, as she'd been for him.

Regrets. Her only true regret in life was refusing his proposal the morning after the plastic stick had confirmed what she'd already known. She might've convinced herself that connecting with him again had been her last grasp at happiness before she accepted her fate, but letting go wasn't the answer.

"I'll do everything I can to make you happy if you tell me your secrets, Layla. Confide in me. Trust me with your heart, not just your grief." He dropped to one knee as he slipped his hand around hers. Then he slid the ring onto her finger. "Marry me because you love me. Because you're greedy and you won't settle for less than what you've wanted for as long as I have."

The gold band was warm against her skin, fitting like it belonged where he'd put it, the same way he fit inside her when they made love. She had the chance to erase regret and to follow her mother's advice instead of her father's example. "My mom was afraid she'd make another mistake, so she devoted her life to making sure I was happy. She never tried to find someone to fulfill her own needs. I didn't understand her sacrifice until I met you. You were smart and talented and focused, and my job was to help you through your grief. I couldn't hold you back by telling you I loved you."

He stood and gathered her in his arms, shielding her from the lingering doubts. The tension was gone from his body and his voice. "I held myself back. I may not have admitted it to anyone, myself included, but I loved you then. I can't let you go again. And it has nothing to do with accidentally making a baby. Sharing that with you sweetens an already irresistible deal. I should've promised you a commitment when it happened, not just accepted responsibility for a chance event. I'm sorry for implying you weren't important to me."

"I didn't handle the situation well, either." His love surrounded her, insulating her from what-had-been and the what-ifs, and revealing the what-can-be future they could have. She yearned to be greedy, to mold her own future and hoard as much happiness as they could find.

"Besides, I like taking a break from being uptight when I'm with you."

She pressed her ear to his chest, needing his steady heartbeat for reassurance that he was here with her and she wasn't dreaming. "I've always enjoyed being able to bring out your repressed animal."

He lifted her chin and met her gaze. Love and hunger shone in his eyes. "Then marry me. I'm going to keep asking until you say yes."

Her throat too tight to speak, she could only manage a nod.

He brushed his lips against hers in a gentle kiss. "God, I missed you. We have so much time to make up for. The last five days. The past eighteen years."

She pushed his coat off his shoulders and rose on her tiptoes to whisper in his ear. "Show me how much you missed me."

The overcoat dropped to the floor as he released her, but his mouth covered hers in a far more possessive move than his embrace. His tongue slipped through her lips and dared her to wrest control from him. Then he cupped her ass, drawing her against his erection.

Layers of clothing separated them, keeping her from taking what she wanted, but it wasn't insurmountable. She worked her hand between their bodies, in search of the button and zipper that would free him. Her fingers connected with the first obstacle, and she twisted the button from its hole. The zipper slid downward with an easy pull when he broke the kiss for a breath. She shoved at his pants and boxer briefs, desperate to rediscover the bond they'd always shared.

He bunched her nightgown at her waist and eased her underwear past her hips. The cool air on her bottom did nothing to temper the heat surging through her veins. Then he lifted her onto his lap as he sat on the edge of the bed. His cock rested against her opening, but he made no move to enter her. "Show me how much you want to spend your life with me."

She cradled his scruff-covered jaw in her palms and let gravity guide her down his length. For the first time, no barriers—physical or emotional—separated them, and it magnified the pleasure of having him inside her. Every inch of him filled her, caressed her, brought peace and contentment.

He kissed her again as he wrapped himself around her in the same way her body cocooned his. The motion carried her another inch lower, triggering a rush of tingles over her skin. The sensation was worth living for. *He* was worth living for.

She rocked her hips forward and back, taking him deep and then almost releasing him before she welcomed him all the way inside her again. He filled her completely with every smooth glide, and his erection seemed to swell to match the love in her heart and soul for him.

His mouth left hers, but his panting breaths warmed her neck as he nuzzled her cheek. "I want you. All of you. Forever."

The admission, his honesty, that leap of faith drew her to the edge of paradise. She could jump and not think about where she landed, because he would always catch her. "I'm yours."

He tensed beneath her and groaned against her neck as a flood of wet heat urged her to join him. The world exploded around her, sending her soaring, and he was with her, never letting go.

Minutes passed, and still he held her as the pieces fit together again around them. Some had changed, some hadn't. Some were missing, but they would help each other create those pieces.

His sex-softened lips nibbled a path along her jaw. "And I'm yours."

REELING HER IN

CHAPTER 1

R uss Novotny flipped on his signal, downshifted, and made the turn into Reel Time Bait and Stock without braking. The back end of his Mustang fishtailed as he gunned the engine, the packed snow providing his entertainment for the day. It sure beat thinking about spending his first Valentine's Day in the better part of a decade without a woman. Running his own IT business, fishing, and his new car were his only loves now, and that suited him fine.

The parking lot was empty and a CLOSED sign hung in the window below a crooked GONE FISHING plaque, but he grabbed his computer bag and followed the shoveled sidewalk to the front door. The security pad light changed from red to green when he entered the last digit of the code his new client had said to use.

After a couple vigorous stomps on the rug, he walked to the counter. Lights shone from the office on the other side, but the quiet suggested it was empty. Although he didn't necessarily need her presence to install software and set up her integrated network, he wasn't overly comfortable working in a place where he hadn't met the business owner face-to-face, even if they'd exchanged emails for almost three months and become friends of a sort.

"Hello? Dr. Terrell? It's Russ Novotny from Software Innovations and Repository Engineering."

"Damn it!" The curse came from somewhere beyond the wide hallway that ended at a partially closed door. Gurgling and splashing carried through the narrow opening. "Argh!"

He rapped his knuckles on the counter as he rounded the end of it. "Lee Anne? It's Russ from SIREN. Are you okay? Do you need help with something?"

"Well, shit." Incoherent muttering nearly drowned out the squeak of his wet boots on the floor. "I'm fine, but I could use a hand. You don't happen to have a pair of needle-nosed pliers on you, do you?"

"Two, actually. One in my work kit and one in the tackle box in my car." Following her voice, he passed the office on his way down the hall. The distinctive odor of chlorine grew stronger with every step. "What do you need them for?"

"Not to remove a fish hook, unfortunately."

He eased the door open, stalling mid step when a lap pool with churning water stretched out several yards in front of him.

At its closest edge, a woman held onto the side, with only her head and neck visible. Long, dark hair fanned out behind her on the surface of the roiling water. "Would you mind handing me the pliers and turning around?"

He dropped to one knee and unzipped his computer bag, unable to hide a chuckle. "Are you naked?"

"I wish." Color flushed her cheeks, but she raised her chin. The movement drew his attention to her bare shoulders. "No, I'm not naked."

Pliers in hand, he approached the edge of the pool. A flash of iridescent blue-green swept through the water below her waist. *Not naked, but that swimsuit doesn't cover much.* "Then why do I have to turn around?"

"Because I said so." The grim line of her full lips warned him not to defy her request. Her coffee-brown eyes, however, invited him to watch her, drink in her beauty, worship her.

No way in hell am I falling for that. So what if she seemed nice in her emails.

He set the tool within her reach and returned to the hallway, resigned to being a gentleman like always. Getting involved with a woman, and especially a client, wasn't on his to-do list. A rebound relationship would bring nothing but a week or two of fun and months of wondering what he'd done wrong when she dumped him. Sasha had dished out enough reasons to last him at least half a dozen relationships.

Grunting and growling mixed with another round of splashes. "This isn't working at all. Mr. Novotny? Russ. Would you come here please? And don't you dare laugh."

"Why would I laugh?" Curiosity urged him back through the entrance, but the woman lying on her belly at the side of the pool kept his feet from moving any farther.

Shimmering scales covered her from flared hips to an elegant gossamer tail. Wet hair clung to her skin, half hiding the matching seashells on her breasts as she rose on her elbows.

Every semi-dormant male hormone in his body awakened. "You're a mermaid."

"Only if I can't get this zipper unstuck." She twisted to her left and tugged at the fabric hugging the delectable curve of her ass and the shapely outline of her trapped legs. "I think a thread's stuck in the teeth, but I'd have to be a contortionist to grab ahold of it with the pliers and not strain a muscle."

Undress her? Surely, fate wasn't that cruel, not after he'd worked so hard to make a fresh start.

He set his bag in the doorway and hoped his coat covered the hard-on growing behind the fly of his jeans. Four hesitant steps brought him within touching distance of her. "Let me see what I can do."

She rolled toward him, giving him another look at the full breasts barely restrained by the shells. "Try not to damage the fabric. This thing cost me an arm and a leg."

"Don't you mean two legs?"

Her laughter echoed through the high-ceilinged room. "I like your sense of humor."

At least somebody does. Sasha clearly hadn't, given the massive list of grievances in her *Dear John* letter.

Pliers in hand, he knelt beside his mermaid client. "I always imagined the Sirens from Greek mythology looking a lot like you. Where'd you find the fish-tail costume?"

"An online shop. It was a birthday present to myself. A fan of *The Odyssey* and *The Quest of the Golden Fleece*, are you? Is that why you use SIREN as the acronym for your company?"

"Yep." *And to remind myself that women have the power to smash my heart on the rocks if I give it to them.* Careful not to make contact with her skin, he tugged on the zipper pull, but it didn't budge. Another try in the opposite direction yielded the same result. "I don't see any threads on the outside."

She shifted until her backside rested against his leg. "Then check inside."

Her invitation added to his uncomfortable erection and the instinct to run like hell. "Are you sure?"

"Well, I can't exactly get rid of my fluke without you, can I? Run your finger along the inner teeth." The frilly tail waved forward and back, tempting him to smooth his hand over her gorgeous scales. "You might have a better angle to reach inside if you get down here next to me. But you should probably take off your coat so it doesn't get wet."

He swallowed to keep from choking on his own spit as he rose from his squatting position. Taking off his coat meant he had to take control of his cock, no matter how turned on he was by Sirens of the sea.

"Is there a problem?"

"No." He shrugged off his ski jacket and tossed it toward his computer bag. Considering her predicament, she probably wouldn't notice what was going on below his belt anyway. "Do you have a towel handy?"

"On the rack by the spa. Could you hurry? My feet are getting tingly."

The distance hardly gave him adequate time to deflate his dick, but draping a couple towels over his arm on the return trip provided some cover. He tossed one toward her tail and spread the other on the wet tile next to her. Then he stretched out with his front to her back, leaving plenty of space between his hard-on and her shimmering ass. "I'm going to slide my hand in right under the zipper."

"Ready." She jerked as soon as his fingertips met the skin at her waist, and goose bumps popped up along her back and forearm. "Go ahead. Your hand's kind of cold, but I'll live."

"Sorry." He rubbed his hands together to create some friction. "Maybe I should try folding down the top edge a little instead."

A nod accompanied her brisk exhale. "Okay."

The fabric gave little resistance when he rolled it downward an inch. A bright green string zigzagged through several teeth in the blue-green zipper. "I think I found the problem. Try to hold still."

More goose bumps rose on her toned bicep. "Damn, I should've turned up the heat in here. Of course, I didn't plan on spending twenty minutes as a beached mythological sea creature."

He eased the tip of the pliers beneath the thread. The end disappeared into the teeth and reappeared closer to the top a second later. "Almost there. You swim a lot?"

"Yeah. I was on the swim team in high school and college, and I'm going to give private lessons to supplement my income during the bait-and-stock operation's off-season."

"Sounds like a solid business plan." Another careful pull released the green string from the last of the teeth. "Got it. Let me see if I can unzip you."

The fastener slid freely, revealing inch after inch of beautiful skin along her hip and the outside of her upper thigh. Not even a narrow strip of elastic interrupted the expanse. *Eight bits equals a byte. A kilobyte is a thousand twenty-four bytes. A megabyte is a thousand twenty-four bytes, which is a thousand four hundred twenty-four shy of a million fifty thousand. That's—*

"I think I'm going to need some help taking it off." She pushed at the waistband, but it barely moved. "Can you stand by my feet and pull at the waist so it comes off mostly inside out?"

"I'm pretty sure you're not wearing anything under there." He rolled away from her and stood, renewing the hopeless fight with his erection.

"So? Haven't you ever seen a naked woman before? And there's no way in Hades I'm getting out of this thing without help." Her breasts heaved toward him as she shifted to her back and levered up on her elbows.

Two backward steps put him against a row of lockers. "Well, yeah, but... We have a contract and I'm trying to be professional."

A wicked grin lit up her face and her gaze drifted to somewhere lower than his chest. "That lump in your pants says otherwise. We're adults and neither of us has any power over the other. You'll still set up my content management system and I'll still pay you with bass, bluegill, and redear and a consult for your lake. That's our agreement. Hell, I'll throw in a mix of beneficial plants to help with oxygenation and algae control if you get me out of this thing. Sex is a totally separate deal, if we decide to do that."

Even though getting propositioned by a mermaid ranked in his top two fantasies, ground rules seemed safer than diving in headfirst. "You should know I'm not up for anything serious right now. I got out of a long-term commitment last summer and I'm not doing that again anytime soon." *If ever.*

She flipped her fluke and licked her lips. "I'm only interested in casual sex, so no worries. Is your divorce final? I don't sleep with married men."

This time, the reminder of his lack of marriage triggered disgust instead of disappointment. "Divorce? Ha. She finally said she'd marry me after seven years and six proposals. Then she dumped me two weeks later with a note on the fridge while I was away on a business trip."

Her grimace scrunched up her nose. "Geesh. That's tacky. She must've been a real winner. I've been divorced for a little over a year."

"I should've listened to my friends. They didn't like her. Why'd you get divorced?"

"He hit me. Once. I kneed him in the balls on my way out the door, called the cops, and hired a lawyer the next day." Her expression revealed nothing—not anger, fear, pain, or remorse. "You should be thankful you weren't married. Divorce is an expensive pain in the ass. Much worse than being stuck in spandex and silicone."

Standing on either side of her calves, he tried to focus on the glistening pattern encasing her body instead of the horrific experience she'd shared with him. "Your ex is a worthless piece of shit."

"Yep, and I'd rather have you undress me than talk about him anymore." She lowered her shoulders to the floor and raised her hips. "You fill out a pair of jeans very well. That isn't a rolled-up sock in there, is it?"

"Nope." He grasped the fabric clinging to her skin and eased it toward him. Her belly button peeked at him, but he worked the scales past her ass rather than surrendering to the urge to swirl his tongue around the tiny pool filled with water. Miles of smooth skin reminded him how many months had passed since he'd had sex with something other than his hand.

He grasped a bigger fold of fabric and tugged a little harder. Without the most curvaceous part of her body holding the tail in place, it easily slipped free of her thighs as he took a few backward steps, revealing a neatly trimmed triangle of tight curls and a pair of toned legs. "I have one condom in my wall—"

Churning water swallowed him at the same moment the absence of something solid under his right foot registered. He exhaled and let his weight carry him to the bottom of the pool. A light push sent him back to the bubbling surface and floating toward the opposite end.

Laughter rang through the mostly empty space and a spectacular vision of naked beauty greeted him as he turned toward the sound. The shell bra was gone, along with the fluke.

More amused and horny than embarrassed, he hefted himself out of the water and onto the wall. Water dribbled along his temples and dripped from his month-old beard. "You must really be a mermaid. A human female would've warned me I was about to fall in. Well, some of them."

She shrugged and sauntered toward him, dragging the towels behind her. The hypnotic sway of her hips and breasts almost made him wish he'd succumbed to a watery death. "It looks like I'm going to have to help *you* undress now. I can't do much about your boots, but you can use my washer and dryer after we find something to do with that condom. I have a brand new box if we need more."

Okay, fate, I give up. "That's a distinct possibility." He swung his feet out of the pool and set to work untangling his soaked bootlaces.

"Leave the boots." She stopped in front of him, giving him a thorough preview of unrestrained sexual appetite even Dionysus would envy. "Can you get your wallet out of your pocket? The only things I need right now are that condom and your cock."

CHAPTER 2

The flicker of attraction Lee Anne had experienced when she'd searched the internet for Russ Novotny's bio and professional profile was nothing compared to the intense desire to get naked with him right this minute. His once-smooth jaw now sported a well-groomed beard that added a level of unbelievable sexiness to the mystery in his gray-green eyes. He wasn't like any other computer geek she'd ever known.

"You'll probably want to put this under your head." She folded a towel into a makeshift pillow and handed it to him. "I like being on top. Do you have a problem with that?"

He dropped the towel on his lap and opened his wallet. A few dark patches mottled the brown leather, but it seemed none the worse for wear after its dip in the pool. The foil packet he pulled from the cash slot showed no signs of having gone for a swim. "Top, bottom, upside down. I don't care as long as it's good for both of us."

"Right answer." She snagged the condom from his grasp and gave him a gentle shove in the chest. "My turn to check your zipper."

After a quick swipe of the towel across his face, he tucked it behind his head and stretched out on the tile. "Button fly. No chance of a troublemaking thread. And I haven't gotten around to doing laundry since last week, so I had to go commando today."

A delicious shiver skittered up her spine. "You really know how to sweet-talk a woman."

His eyebrows dipped toward his nose and a frown marred his handsome face. He rose to his elbows, looking ready to push to his feet and stomp to the nearest exit.

"I meant that as a compliment. Fewer clothes means faster sex." She worked the top button of his jeans free and then made her way down the fly. Each flash of skin supported his claim of nakedness beneath the body-hugging denim. "For the record, I'm not your ex-girlfriend, -fiancée, or whatever you want to call the spineless manipulator. I say exactly what I mean, and I expect you to do the same."

The corners of his mouth curved upward the tiniest bit. "A friend of mine called her that too. Nice to meet somebody else who doesn't like games."

"Oh, I like games, just not those kind." She freed his hard-on and stroked its length down and up, pleased to see their conversation hadn't affected its interest in getting laid. Silky pink skin covered a boner worth bragging to her sisters about—after she introduced herself to them. "Sexual positions roulette is one of my favorites."

He groaned and grasped her wrist. "Jesus, woman. Put on the condom and fuck me already."

A jolt of panic tried to make her pull away, but she smothered the reaction. He deserved better than to be automatically lumped in with the likes of her ex. *I hope you're enjoying your stay in jail, you bastard.*

Russ froze for less than a second before he released her, obviously sensing her discomfort. "We make a hell of a pair, don't we? I can't take a compliment at face value and you're scared to death I'm going to hit you. Maybe this isn't such a good idea."

She straddled his legs and leaned forward until they were almost nose-to-nose. With the slight contact with his flannel shirt, a ripple of pleasure zipped from her nipples to her vaginal muscles, bringing her back to the here and now. "I'm not scared of anything, damn it, and I know you want sex as much as I do, so shut off your brain and kiss me."

He touched his lips to hers with a light caress, clearly testing the waters before he dove in for a taste. His tongue glided inside her mouth, somewhere between tentative and passionate, drawing her into the kind of sensual exploration she hadn't experienced in a very long time. Every careful movement promised a wonderful ride to satisfaction—not too fast, not too slow—with an attentive lover. Despite his admission about not wanting a relationship, he seemed intent on ensuring the encounter was better than a mindless quickie with a near stranger.

A palm closed on her left butt cheek and he exerted a hint of pressure, enough to make the thick seam along the crotch of his jeans graze her labia. The minimal contact sparked a contraction in her clit and lower belly that took her breath away. His calloused fingers climbed her vertebrae from her tailbone to the base of her neck, mimicking the same steady pace of his tongue. It was intoxicating, maddening, divine.

She blindly tore open the foil package and slid the condom from its wrapper, unwilling to sacrifice a second of the rolling waves of desire their imminent physical connection created. His hands moved with her as she lifted her hips to finish her preparations, their gentle weight letting her move like she was suspended in water.

A low, rumbling moan vibrated through her jaw when she unrolled the latex down his hard length. His cock grew against her grasp as she lined up the head with her opening, but he didn't arch upward or guide her downward. The decision was hers. She had total control over what happened next. All she had to do was trust her instincts.

I want this. I want him.

With shaking quads, she lowered her body onto his, taking him inside her with excruciating slowness. The unhurried glide down his larger-than-average girth scattered her thoughts and reminded her of the intense pleasure a real dick could offer. His fingertips danced along her skin, urging her to match the rhythm of her hips to the movement of his tongue. All of their motions seemed synchronized and fluid, like his body had been created for joining with hers.

This is how sex is supposed to be. Desperate for a breath, she broke the connection with his mouth and arched toward the ceiling.

His lips closed over her nipple as he lifted his head from the towel. Then he lapped at the sensitive tip, sending a riot of sensation from her breast to her uterus. He rocked his hips into hers and his cock caressed a spot deep inside her, triggering several successive tremors.

Fighting the sudden loss of muscle control, she clutched his shoulders and pulled him straight up, away from her breast and in line with her upper body. The action propelled him deeper and prompted a long moment of breathlessness. "There. Right there. Fuck me, Russ."

He groaned and tightened his hold on her ass enough to guide her up and down his length but without his fingers digging into her flesh. His erection swelled inside her walls, filling her and stroking her sweet spot with every thrust. Shallow puffs of air bathed her bare skin in warmth and humidity. The mix of his gentleness and determination to give them both pleasure carried her to the edge of release, but his steady invasion and retreat threatened to leave her hanging until she lost her mind.

His beard tickled her collarbone as he buried his face in her neck. Then he stiffened and let out a long, low growl. The animalistic sound inspired a sudden burst of euphoria that sent her freefalling through the bliss of a never-ending orgasm and into an ocean of pure hedonistic gratification. Aftershocks rippled through her middle, one after another, dragging her under again and again before she reached the surface.

She finally managed a breath, but the soft touch of his lips below her ear and an almost immeasurable caress over her clit stole it. Another orgasm shattered what was left of her thoughts, tossing her into the once-again rushing tide. Cries echoed in her head, and she drowned in unexpected pleasure.

Russ caught her as she slumped against him, his thrumming pulse matching hers. It slowed after several minutes, but he didn't loosen the hold he'd wrapped her in and his fingers threaded through her hair.

The soothing massage along her scalp almost lulled her to sleep. She rubbed her cheek against his furry jaw instead. "Damn."

His fingers stopped their hypnotic motion. "Is that good?"

She nuzzled his beard and sighed. "Very good. That surprise at the end… Wow. Usually, when a guy is done, he's done."

"I was experimenting." He leaned into her touch. "Besides, why wouldn't I want to feel you come again?"

"Experimenting, huh? I think I'd call it an innovation—and a tremendous success."

His muscles tensed beneath her jaw. "It never worked before."

She frowned as she leaned away from him. "Just because your ex didn't like it, doesn't mean all women won't. And what guy in his right mind wouldn't want as many pussy hugs as he can get? She really messed with your ego, didn't she?"

He scraped his fingers through his damp hair and seemed to study the colored tiles at the edge of the pool. "The breakup letter had a list of everything she'd never liked about me. Some pretty specific details about sex were at the top of the list. She said she faked orgasms most of the time."

"Her loss, if she wasn't lying. Did she complain about the size of your cock too?"

A blush crept up his neck and cheeks, and he didn't meet her gaze.

Anger on his behalf burned in the pit of her stomach. "It's not like you can help you have a Moby dick."

His bark of laughter made his deflating erection twitch inside her. "*Moby dick?*"

She sucked in a shaky breath to calm the contraction in her uterus. "I like whales. If she wanted a minnow, why did she stick around for seven years?"

"Evidently, she liked a rent-free place to live. She was pissed when I didn't give her half the money from the sale of my house and made her buy my car instead of just signing it over to her."

"Why would she need to buy your car? Didn't she have one of her own?"

"She took mine when she left and expected me to keep making the payments. Her fifteen-year-old junker was still in the garage." His eyes held sadness when he finally looked toward her. "How did I miss seeing the kind of person she is?"

Lee Anne pushed to her feet, hoping her rubbery legs didn't fail her. The loss of connection brought an empty ache, but she extended her hand to help him up instead of psychoanalyzing the simple physical attraction. "Love blinds us. We see what we want to see. I think I got off a lot easier than you did. One smack, and it was over."

With his impressive latex-encased cock still escaping his jeans, Russ draped a towel around her shoulders. "I would've willingly suffered through a hundred years of Sasha's disapproval to stop that piece of shit from hitting you once."

"I'm pretty sure his balls hurt worse than my jaw, and he gets to be somebody's bitch in jail. We're even." She led him toward the other end of the pool. "Grab your bag. We'll go put on dry clothes and you can work on installing software while I do laundry and throw together some lunch. Do you like grilled cheese and tomato soup?"

"One of my favorites." The *squish, squish, squish* from his boots as he walked warned her they'd take days to dry. "Even? If he flinches every time he sees a woman's knee, maybe."

"I doubt it. He was a repeat offender. That's why he's serving his full sentence. I refuse to let him put me in a different kind of prison." She adjusted her extravagant costume on the tile and turned off the jets in the pool while he put the pliers back in his bag, slipped the strap over his shoulder, and picked up his coat.

A nod was his only response, but the fire in his eyes told her how appalled he was by her ex's behavior. The anger would eat him alive if he didn't let it go. She'd learned that lesson quickly.

She gestured to the side door. "This way."

He followed her into her adjoining apartment, still quiet as he took two hesitant steps toward the kitchen and laid his belongings on the table. The stiffness in his movements made her want to promise him she was fine. "I feel like I should be protecting you, but I don't think you need me."

"It's sweet of you to say so, but he just caught me at a bad time. I won't be fooled again. Undress while I look for something to corral Moby. Then we can throw your clothes in the washer." Not waiting for an answer, she padded to the bedroom. Being completely honest with him now seemed like the best course of action, so she fished clean underwear, yoga pants, and a long-sleeved tee from the laundry basket as she sorted through her thoughts. "My parents passed away right before I met him."

"I'm sorry. Your mom *and* your dad at the same time? That must've been rough." A noisy *clunk* suggested he'd successfully removed one boot.

Envy suffocated the stitch of pain in her heart. "They were in their eighties. Married fifty-six years. The doctors said my dad had a stroke the night my mom died from pneumonia complications, but I think it was a broken heart."

"That's really sad. But romantic too." Another *clunk* carried to the bedroom. "Wait a minute. They must've been close to fifty when you were born. How old are you?"

"Thirty-eight." She pulled her shirt over the waistband of her pants and returned to the kitchen with her robe folded over her arm. Seeing his reaction to the next revelation was too compelling to pass up. "My parents were forty-six and forty-eight when they adopted me. I've been searching for my birth family for the last six months."

His dark eyebrows drew together above his nose as he looked up from tugging his hands free of the drenched sweatshirt sleeves. Then they jumped toward his forehead. "Did you find them?"

She laid the robe across the back of the couch and forced herself not to move as he stared at her. If he couldn't see the resemblance, he had to be blind. "The private investigator I hired did. My biological mother has a husband who doesn't know about me, and she'd rather not relive what happened with my biological father, which is understandable and I don't blame her. Daddy dearest is gone, but I have two sisters."

"Lindie and Layla." The names were barely out of his mouth before he dragged the sopping wet sweatshirt back over his head and fastened his jeans. "I'm not sure how I didn't see it sooner. The hair, the eyes, the chin. Isn't it damn convenient and coincidental that I happen to know both of them. I guess lust blinds too."

The bite of his sarcasm stung. "Russ, I—"

"Save your apology. The sperm whale got to fuck a mermaid—on Valentine's Day, no less. He's happy, so I'm happy." He slung the computer bag onto his shoulder and turned toward the door. "I think it's best if you find some other sap to—"

"Damn it, there's no reason for you to be defensive. I chose you weeks before I knew who they were." She winced at her choice of words, but it was the truth. She had *chosen* him, almost entirely for his expert skill set. The zap of attraction his picture had sparked had been a reminder that she could be normal, that she wasn't damaged goods. So what if it had influenced her decision a tiny bit? "When the PI gave me the report and I found out you're a close friend of their husbands, I decided telling you everything up front was the right thing to do. Disclosure. Transparency. No chance of a conflict of interest. Whatever you want to call it. I sure as hell didn't expect to have sex with you ten minutes after we finally met."

"Neither did I." His fingers flexed and unflexed on the doorknob. "Because of the adoption records being sealed, they haven't been able to find out your name. They'll want to know."

"They already do. I didn't want you to have to keep it a secret or feel responsible for introducing me to them. I called Lindie this morning. She couldn't come to the phone, but her husband invited me to supper tonight." An army of tadpoles wiggled and fluttered in Lee Anne's belly, as much from excitement as anxiety about meeting her sisters.

His gaze flicked to hers, disappointment obvious in his expression. "They're having a party to celebrate adopting Blaine's nephews. I was planning to go."

"Then go. I'm not stopping you." The implication that he couldn't possibly eat dinner at his friend's house because she would be there was ridiculous. Did he think she couldn't be civil in public to a man she hadn't expected to sleep with? "And I expect you to honor our contract. You're the best at all the computer stuff I need done, and I don't want some amateur wasting my money and my time. If we have sex again, fine. If not, that's fine too."

He shifted from his drippy-socked left foot to the right. "Are you always this...direct?"

"Life's too short to be anything else. You're staying. It'd be a damn shame if my rescuer ended up with hypothermia." She patted the robe. "Put this on when you're done undressing."

CHAPTER 3

Russ tugged at the hem of Lee Anne's robe, trying in vain to cover his knees as he clicked through element after element of his creation. Hers wasn't the biggest project he'd had since opening the virtual doors of SIREN, but the Reel Time Bait and Stock account had given him the opportunity to build something from the ground up. Updating programs and adding to existing software was tedious, with too many restrictions and limitations. A new business offered him more options and the freedom to use his talents to invent instead of fix.

"Knock-knock." Lee Anne stood framed in the doorway to her office, her long hair now pulled back in a ponytail. "Ready for a break?"

A vision of her stretched out under him while he fucked her again formed in his mind, catching him off-guard. *Okay, brain, back to business.* "In a minute. I want to check the feed the security company hardwired in. I've recommended this system to other clients, but better to find any glitches now than to have them show up when you're in the middle of serving customers or being robbed."

"That's why I picked you. You're thorough and conscientious." She leaned over his shoulder as he entered the password to access the surveillance system.

A waterfall of dark waves swung down and brushed against his neck, scenting the air with roses. She'd evidently showered while he worked.

He exhaled to dilute the power of her seductive perfume. "This'll just take a second."

A dozen views from different parts of the buildings and surrounding grounds filled the screen—some completely dark, some barely discernible, and some clear as day. A blue jay flew through the lower right image of the parking lot, setting off the record function in the motion detector. Twenty seconds later, the activity light shut off.

She straightened, giving him a reprieve from her smell and the silky caress of her hair. "Looks like it's working."

"I need to check one more thing." He returned to the main menu and clicked the Retrieve button. Rather than choosing a date and time, he set the program to play the last active recording of two minutes or more from any of the twelve cameras. If the clip of his arrival appeared, the installation of his software package hadn't affected the security component.

Lights flickered on in the dark rectangle, illuminating the lap pool, spa, and most of the area from the hallway that led to Lee Anne's office, the door to her apartment, and the rear exit. The shell bra covered her breasts and the scaly blue-green fluke in her arms hid the fact that she was naked from the waist down as she walked to the pool.

"Oh my God." Lee Anne grasped his shoulders and leaned toward the computer screen.

"There's a camera in the pool room?" He tried to click Pause, but his hands refused to obey.

"Yeah. I want to be able to watch the swim lessons to see if my students are making progress." Her grip pulled the front edges of the robe apart at his chest. "Fast forward to the good part. You can copy the video onto the desktop or a flash drive, right? Because I'm guessing our sex tape is hotter than any porn I've ever seen. Never mind. I'll do it."

Frozen in place, he could only watch when she reached over him and hit the fast-forward icon. The mermaid zipped back and forth in the pool, her motions resembling the jerky movements of silent movies. Then he was there, peeling off her costume.

The clip slowed to normal speed as he fell in the churning water. Every moment of their encounter had been captured by the surveillance equipment, revealing far more sexual chemistry than he'd experienced with the woman who had stolen seven years of his life. The uninhibited display suggested Sasha's accusations about his inability to please a woman sexually were out of line.

Lee Anne sighed as the couple in the video rose from the tile flooring. "Holy moly, that was easily the best sex I've ever watched. Well, *had* too, but that's stating the obvious. How about we go another round before lunch? Maybe oral. I think the condoms I have might be too small."

Finally regaining control of his body, Russ turned the desk chair and pulled her onto his lap. "I'm deleting this recording from the video history."

Her lips curved into a wicked grin. "Are you afraid I'll upload it to YouTube?"

He brought up the erase option and clicked to confirm his selection. "I'm more concerned that Lindie'll find it when she comes to the shop. She's been talking about putting in a surveillance system to figure out how one of her chickens keeps breaking out of its pen. Given the opportunity, she'll go snooping around on your computer to see how yours works."

"You think she'll want to get to know me?"

"Are you kidding? She's been pestering Blaine about finding you for months. Layla told her about a legal loophole and looked into using it, but the red tape has dragged out, even with her specializing in family law. They're hoping they have a sister who's as interested in being a family as they are." With visual evidence of his sex life removed from immediate access, he deposited Lee Anne on her feet and stood. "Since that seems to be the case, I want to talk about something else that's on my mind."

She switched off the lights as they exited her office. "What might that be, Mr. Novotny? Getting laid again?"

"Indirectly, yeah." The robe flapped against his thighs, generating a cool draft across his naked balls and semi-erect cock on the walk through the darkened pool room. "We have a good working relationship and neither of us has expectations beyond…"

"Mutually enjoyable sex?" A few steps from her apartment door, she raised her eyebrows at him and snickered.

He shrugged. "That's probably as good a description as any. Anyway, what do think about going through Sasha's list with me and providing an assessment of it?"

"You mean like telling you whether I agree or disagree with her criticisms?" Barely slowing, she ushered him into the living room and toward what was likely her bedroom.

Although admitting he needed some help rebuilding his confidence was slightly embarrassing, he nodded. "Exactly. Eventually, I'd like to date again, so some feedback about my good and bad traits would be helpful. Kind of an evaluation. Then I can work on the stuff you both dislike."

"I'm all for self-improvement, but do it because you want to be a better person, not to please somebody else. Remember what I said about the size of your dick? You are who you are. Unless you're an asshole, I see no reason to change. And from what I know of you, you're the least asshole-ish guy I've ever met." She stopped beside her unmade bed and dropped to her knees in front of him. "Did she whine that Moby was too big for her to give you blow jobs?"

She loosened the robe's tie with one hand and slipped the other under the robe to cradle his balls, turning his *yes* into a choking gasp. Then warm fingers closed around his girth.

Tilting his head back, he fought the need to rock his hips forward. The moan clawing its way up his throat broke free.

Seeming to know what he wanted, she moved her hand down to the base and up again. "Blow jobs aren't just about deep-throating."

Her lips closed on his cock, sending his eyes rolling back in his head and his heart hammering in his chest. She licked along the slit and then fluttered her tongue across the loose skin below it, setting off more fireworks. Her fingers massaged his testicles as she sucked a few more inches into the welcoming heat of her mouth.

He widened his stance to maintain his balance, but she nudged him until the backs of his knees hit the mattress. Momentum pushed him onto the rumpled blankets without interrupting the torturous combination of her hands, lips, and tongue.

Careful not to force himself deeper, he slid her hair free of the ponytail and combed his fingers in the silky waves. "Damn. The only thing better than this is being inside you."

"Mmm." Her hum vibrated through his length. The she released him, bringing a moment of frustration before she kissed a path to the base and sucked his left ball into her mouth.

Sensation rushed through his nerve endings, setting fire to his skin with a surge of goose bumps. "God, you're gonna make me come."

Her husky laugh added fuel to the flames. She slowly eased him from her mouth and rubbed her cheek against his aching cock. "That's the idea. You do want a real blow job, don't you, Russ?"

The sexy way she spoke his name intensified the building pressure where her thumb continued its smooth up-and-down motion over the sensitive spot she'd teased with her tongue.

"What do you want? Tell me so I can give it to you."

Had Sasha ever asked him what he wanted? She certainly hadn't offered to give him anything that didn't involve some benefit to her.

Lee Anne traced the bulging vein up his erection and licked a drop of fluid from his slit. "Let go. Be selfish. I want to make you feel good."

How long had he waited for those words?

He loosened his hands from her hair, almost certain he'd been holding her back more than wanting to pull her closer. "I want you to make me come in your mouth. Blow me. Body and mind."

"With pleasure." She smiled up at him and then swallowed half his dick while she gave his balls a gentle squeeze.

His eyes tried to drift closed, but he focused on the woman between his legs and the feel of her hands, lips, and tongue. Every lick, suck, and embrace drew him toward what he wanted most at that moment.

His muscles tensed of their own accord, signaling an impending orgasm.

She hummed again, her true enjoyment of what she was doing to him apparent in the sound. That knowledge liberated him, revealed the awareness that mutual satisfaction didn't have to be simultaneous. It allowed him to let go.

The tension spread to every inch of his body as she laved and pumped his cock. Heat rushed up his length, suddenly relieving the pressure. Light exploded in his vision and rapture propelled him into a world without gravity. Clouds softened the harsh reality he'd dealt with the last five months.

"Lay back." She guided him onto the bed and lay on her side next to him, her tongue sneaking out to sweep a dribble of creamy fluid from her lower lip. Her dark eyes glowed as if she'd experienced an orgasm as exceptional as his. "I'm looking forward to disproving more criticisms."

Faint ringing of chimes cut through the haze, but he didn't try to speak or move his relaxed limbs.

She pushed up on her elbow. "Your clothes are dry."

When she levered toward a sitting position, he rolled her on top of him with an arm around her waist. As soon as the floating sensation dissipated a little more, he planned to enjoy thanking her for her generosity. "They can wait."

"Oh?" Amusement lit up her face.

"Mm-hm. I've been told I salivate too much during oral sex. You need to tell me if it's true."

Her smile widened. "Are you sure it's not just you feeling guilty for getting off when I didn't?"

He cupped her cheek and touched his lips to hers. "No guilt. I've always wondered what it would be like to go down on a mermaid."

Her uninhibited laughter shook him and the bed. "Well, I can hardly deny you the chance to find out, especially since you helped me escape my fluke."

"But now you have pants on." He shimmied his fingers inside her stretchy pants and immediately encountered a strip of lace covering a narrow band of skin above her ass. "Take them off. Shirt too. But leave on the thong and your bra. I want to take those off."

She wiggled against his hand until it was out of her pants. Then she pushed to her feet between his knees. "I like a man who isn't afraid to say what he wants."

"And has a big dick?" He sat up and scooted to the pile of pillows at the head of the bed for a better view.

"Of course." She grasped the hem of her shirt and yanked it over her head. Her hair fell across her shoulders, half hiding the see-through black cups cradling her breasts. "You're staring like you've never seen them before."

"I like lace. It's sexy and feminine, and your nipples are looking at me." The few minutes he'd had to touch and taste them by the pool hadn't been long enough.

"They want your mouth and your hands on them, like this." She rubbed her thumbs across the pebbled tips and treated him to another of those seductive hums.

His spent cock twitched, even though he had no intention of risking a condom failure because the only available protection was too small. "Finish your striptease, and I'll give them lots of attention."

With her back to him, she slid the form-fitting pants past her hips and bent to remove them. Two strips of lace hid almost nothing—the deepest part of the valley between her rounded butt cheeks and not any of her gorgeous ass.

He fought a wayward groan and lost.

"Like what you see?" She twisted toward him and dragged a finger up the line of delicate lace. "I thought you might be a leg man since you have a thing for mermaids."

A zing of electricity pulsed through his balls. "I like everything about a woman's body. Legs, ass, breasts. Hair, feet, shoulders. The soft skin along her inner thigh, her neck, and the curve of her lower back. It all begs to be worshipped."

She climbed onto the bed and crawled toward him on her hands and knees, with mischief and anticipation written in her elfin features. "Not her pussy?"

"That too."

When she was within touching range, he tucked several strands of stray hair behind her ear and guided her to his lap. The front clasp of her bra tempted him to unhook it, but he lowered his mouth to one taut peak for a nibble instead.

She gasped and arched against him, her hands holding his head in place as he sucked her nipple through the thin layer. Her breath caught again and her abdominal muscles shuddered. "Mm. I'm pretty sure you could make me come doing that and nothing else."

He kissed the pale stretch of skin between her breasts and ran his fingertips up the inside of her thigh. A quick caress over the damp lace covering her pussy suggested he wouldn't have to play for long before she came that way, either. "Not if I can help it. I'm acting out a fantasy, remember?"

"Act away." Her breathy voice encouraged him to indulge himself, to explore her body to his heart's content.

Starting at her earlobe, he licked a path along her jawline to her chin. A few nibbles led him to her lips for a slow and sensual tangle of tongues, earning him a soft sigh as she leaned into him. His stomach growled, but he dropped light kisses on her eyelids and the tip of her nose before moving on. Lace stopped his progress across her collarbone, and he followed it downward to the gentle turn leading him toward the swell of her breast.

Ignoring another rumble in his belly, he traced the upper border with his tongue and eased the strap from her shoulder.

She drew in a shaky breath. "You're hungry."

A flick and twist of the center clasp resulted in a swift separation of the cups and left the lace clinging to the full mounds trying to escape. "For you. Food can wait."

With a wiggle, she freed her breasts and ground the front of her thong against his cock. "Then eat me."

Her invitation tested his patience, but filling his hands with her flesh, pressing them together, and lapping at both her nipples in a single swipe seemed to make her forget her rush to the finish line. When her groans changed to needy mewls, he released her breasts and lifted her ass from his lap. Several careful sweeps of his beard across her abdomen brought her protests to a quick end.

Nudging the front of her underwear away from his target, he snuck beneath the scrap of lace. The sweet scent of her desire and the tart-and-salty essence of her pussy filled his senses, urging him to bring her the greatest pleasure he could give a woman.

He dipped his tongue into her opening and then glided through her wetness toward her clit. She cried out when he found the swollen bud, hinting at how close she was to an orgasm. He backed off and slid his middle finger into her slick channel.

"Oh God, in my ass too." She grabbed his wrist and led his finger to her puckered anus. The creamy coating let him slide inside her up to his first knuckle with no effort. "Both places."

Her eagerness to experiment brought new life to his cock, but he inserted his thumb in her vagina instead of his erection. He wouldn't be focused solely on her satisfaction if he had a stake in the game.

She rocked on his hand as he sucked her clit between his teeth and fluttered back and forth. Her muscles flexed around his finger and thumb while he alternately licked and suckled. A glance at her face revealed total abandonment as she lifted her chin toward the ceiling. Her uninhibited groans gave way to high-pitched cries. Contractions rippled through her ass and pussy into his hand and mouth, signaling an incredible release or a damn good faked orgasm.

Her legs shook, prompting him to withdraw his fingers and ease her down onto his lap again. She went limp in his arms and panted against his chest. "Wet. Hell...yes. Not from...drool."

CHAPTER 4

Lee Anne zipped her ski jacket and pocketed her keys. The moment she'd been looking forward to for months had finally arrived. "Ready?"

"Yeah. Thanks again for getting my running shoes out of the trunk." Adjusting the strap of his computer bag, Russ closed the front door and offered his arm. "Are *you* ready?"

"Yep. And you're welcome again." She slipped her hand into the crook of his elbow and walked with him to the yellow and black car in her parking lot. His steps matched hers, even though his legs were longer. "Nice wheels."

"That's what a forty-year-old single man buys when his almost-paid-off family sedan goes missing with his ex-girlfriend. Now I have a business-associates-with-benefits deal to go with it. The ultimate mid-life crisis." Although he grinned through the words, bitterness and hurt shone in his eyes.

"I still want to see that list." She reached for the passenger door handle, but he beat her to it. "If the spineless manipulator said you're not a gentlemen, she needs to have her head examined."

"It's about the only thing she didn't criticize." After a moment's hesitation, he handed his bag to her. "The black folder in the expand-able pocket inside."

Watching him round the hood of the car, she sank into the leather seat and buckled her seat belt, aware of how much trust he'd placed in her. She could honestly assure him at least some of the faults were bullshit, but letting her read the breakup letter for a seven-year rela-tionship had to lay bare the most vulnerable parts of his heart, ego, and self-esteem.

He settled into the driver's seat and started the engine. "How am I supposed to distract you from being nervous if you don't read the letter?"

"I'm not nervous." She pulled a parchment envelope from the black folder. "Okay, I'm a little nervous. And we're friends with benefits, not just business associates."

The smile he aimed at her this time was genuine. "You're right. Friends. Now read the letter so you can tell me how wrong everything is."

The dainty handwriting on the envelope reminded her of birds, pretty but prone to flightiness. "Russell. Did she always call you that? I thought you liked being called Russ."

"She did. I do." He didn't sound pleased about it. "I used to think it was cute."

"Strike one—not calling you by the name you prefer. Anybody ever call you Rusty?" Lee Anne unfolded the lined paper and hoped he didn't expect her to read the dumping portion of the letter aloud.

"My mom and dad until I was in college. My grandparents still do. It's a family thing."

"Unless you tell me different, you're Russ to me." Appalled that his ex hadn't had the decency to give him the heave-ho in person, she skipped past the first few paragraphs to the numbered list of griev-ances. "Wow. Do you mind if I call this woman a bitch? 'Your penis is too large for any normal woman's vagina.' I think she meant average because, while I'm normal, I don't consider myself average. In either case, I'd like to see scientific data to support her statement. Your penis is perfect and I'll happily let it visit my vagina any time it likes."

His choked laughter filled the enclosed space. That he could even smile after spending seven years with someone so critical was a wonder. "I need to remember that."

"Yes, you do." Finding her place on the page, she rolled her eyes at the next complaint. "'Or mouth.' Now I know I have a big mouth in the figurative sense, but seriously? She doesn't know how to give a decent blow job and she's blaming you for it. Am I right?"

He flipped on his turn signal and slowed at the upcoming cross-road. "Probably. You're much more creative than she was."

"Remember that too. Number three. 'Oral sex with you is disgusting. You slobber all over me.' Yeah, she's a bitch." She shook her head at the insult. "Your drool is *not* what made me wet."

"I know. She wasn't very adventurous, so most of the ways I tried to show her I loved her didn't go well."

"I'm going to be brutally honest here. She's a two-faced leech and she treated you like crap. You're a nice guy who deserves better than someone like her."

"I can't disagree. I'm sorry she wasn't truthful with me from the beginning, but not that she dumped me. At least, not anymore." He glanced at her as he downshifted on the snow-covered country road. "Look what happened. I'm running my own business, which is something I always thought about doing. I've had sex with a mermaid, which is something I've always *dreamed* about doing. Up ahead on the right is Erik and Layla's house. I live in the brick ranch on thirty acres after that, and Lindie and Blaine live on the other side of me. I'm practically within casting distance of my two closest friends."

"And my sisters." The paper shook in her grasp as a bad case of nerves set in with the realization of the impending introductions. "Blaine guessed who I was this morning on the phone and said he wanted to surprise Lindie. What if—"

"It'll be fine. I promise." Russ turned into a driveway next to a sign for Brewster's Roosters and stopped the car. His hand closed over hers, relieving the sudden chill in her fingers. "She might threaten to make Blaine sleep in the barn for not telling her you called, but she'll be so excited to finally meet you. Layla'll probably cry, even though she's going to be thrilled too. She's been a little emotional lately. Erik says it's normal for pregnant women."

The seat belt kept Lee Anne from clutching at his sleeve and demanding to know every detail about her sisters. "I didn't know she was expecting."

"Yeah. Your family is growing."

Family. How had he known the right word to say? That having a blood connection had become vitally important to her?

He gave her hand a gentle squeeze. "Ready? I'll be right there if you need moral support."

Unable to speak through her own emotions, she nodded. She'd been right about him being a good guy. His computer expertise was worth every penny he'd quoted her and sex with him was exceptional, but his friendship was priceless.

"Take some deep breaths and try to relax." He put the car in gear and continued down the lane. "They're going to love you."

The setting sun shone on the pale gray two-story house, giving it a welcoming glow. The feeling of family emanated from it, especially with a lopsided snowman greeting visitors at the bottom of the porch steps. It was a home, something she hadn't known since her parents had moved into an assisted-living facility three years ago. Her apartments and the bungalow she'd owned had never had that feeling. She'd slept, eaten, and sometimes worked there, but they didn't provide the same sense of security or comfort.

"We're a few minutes early, so Lindie's probably still out at one of the henhouses or planning this year's garden. If she sees the car, she'll think it's just me, and Blaine's plan to surprise her should work. Same with Layla since she isn't here yet. Blaine's parents and Erik's mom will be here too." He parked beside a delivery truck emblazoned with the Brewster's Roosters logo and removed the keys from the ignition. "You know, this is the best Valentine's Day I've had since I was a kid. Old friends, new friends, family. No pressure to be anything I'm not."

"You can always be yourself with me." She refolded the letter and tucked it back in its envelope as he played gentleman again.

His easy gait around the front of the car seemed to indicate their discussion had helped him as much as it had her. Taking his extended hand, she focused on not falling on her ass in the driveway instead of worrying about her sisters' reactions. It was beyond her control.

"Hang on a sec. I forgot to grab the present." He reopened the passenger door and reached inside. A minute later, he emerged with a flat package more than half as long as he was tall. The bright red wrapping paper sported a jumble of silver curling ribbon in one corner. "Not the greatest wrap job, but it's the thought that counts. And considering you're here today, this is the perfect gift."

"You did better than I can. I'm guessing it's a picture of some sort from the shape." She walked with him past the snowman and up the front porch stairs, glad for such normal conversation.

"It's one of those collage frames. In the center is a picture I took of Blaine and Lindie with the boys on Christmas Eve." After stomping the snow from his shoes, he rapped his knuckles on the screen door. "Lindie's going to want to add a picture of her newest sister."

The front door swung inward, revealing a man with a smear of what looked like pink frosting across his cheek. His eyes widened as he met her gaze. "Holy cow. I think the DNA test is only a formality. Your facial structure and the hair. You... Wow."

Russ cleared his throat. "Aren't you going to invite us in?"

Holding open the screen door, their host gestured for them to enter. "Sorry, it's uncanny how much you look like Lindie. Layla too, now that her hair's grown out some. Hey, Russ. Did you get here at the same time?"

"We rode together." Russ laid the gift on the coffee table and then took off his coat. "Lee Anne's a client of mine. Reel Time Bait and Stock, the new aquaculture business on the way to the interstate. We figured out we were going to the same party while I was installing her software today."

While the story wasn't exactly false, she was impressed by his quick thinking. It would save them both a lot of unnecessary explaining.

Blaine scratched his cheek, flaking off a bit of the pink smear. "Ah, the supplier you lined up to stock the lake. So you know the good news then? I tried calling to give you a heads-up, but you didn't answer your phone."

With his jacket hanging on his forearm, Russ nodded. "Yeah. Lee Anne, meet Blaine Stockwell. Blaine, Lee Anne Terrell."

"Good to meet you, Lee Anne. You couldn't have picked a better guy to handle your tech stuff." Blaine's stare was a bit unnerving, but his friendly smile put her at ease. "I can't believe you're here. We've been trying to find you for months. I hope you like loud family gatherings, because there's going to be a hell of a celebration when Lindie and Layla see you."

She breathed an inward sigh of relief, even though her tumbling insides still needed a tranquilizer. "Nice to meet you too."

Boisterous children's laughter carried from somewhere down the hallway.

"I better go see what the boys are up to." Blaine shook his head, but he looked amused rather than frustrated or angry. "There's probably frosting everywhere but on the cookies. And we don't stand on ceremony here. Hang your coat on a hook by the door and follow the noise to the kitchen when you're ready to join the fun."

Watching him walk away, she let Russ help her with her coat. "I always wondered what it would be like to have a big family. I guess I'm about to find out."

He rubbed his thumbs up and down her neck once before he eased the jacket down her arms. His firm but soothing touch was as comforting as it was sensuous. "You're tense. If you need a few minutes of downtime during the party, come find me. We can sneak off for a tour of the house or go for a walk outside."

She barely suppressed a moan. "If we sneak off, it'll be for a quickie. I'm about ready to melt, and all you did was rub my neck a little."

"Too many people here. We'll swing by my house after the party and I can give you a back rub." His low voice caressed her spine and promised much more than a simple massage. "Come on, before you wake up Moby. I'd rather not have my friends sticking their noses in my sex life."

She snickered as he hung their coats and picked up the present. "It probably wouldn't make a positive impression on my new family, either."

"Ha! They'd just tease you until you turned as red as a lobster. The kitchen is this way."

Giggles met them as they entered the large farmhouse-style kitchen. A pair of young boys wearing oversized threadbare work shirts sat at the table on the opposite side of the room. The sleeves were rolled up to their elbows, and pink and white spatters dotted the faded blue fabric from collar to hem. Heart-shaped cookies covered the area in front of them.

The younger boy waved a paintbrush in Russ's and her direction. "Happy Valentine's Day, Uncle Russ! I know a secret. Is that a present for me?" His mouth formed a perfect O as his gaze met hers. "Are you Aunt Lindie's sister? You look like her. I don't have a sister, but I have a brother."

Blaine's quick grab for the boy's wrist came a moment after a drip of icing landed on the floor. "Okay, I think we're done. Brushes in the bowls and hand me your paint shirts."

With a frown at his sibling, the older brother did as he was told. "You're awful at keeping secrets, Cam. Hi, Uncle Russ. Hi, Aunt Lee Anne."

Russ set the gift on the butcher-block island in the center of the room and walked to the table. He ruffled Cam's hair before he helped him out of the messy shirt. "Happy Valentine's Day, guys. The present's for all of you. It's kind of fragile, so we'll have to be careful with it. Go wash up and then we'll talk about secrets."

Both children ran toward another hallway across from the table, presumably to a bathroom. The grin the two men shared spoke of deep affection for the boys and the importance of them in their lives.

Russ tossed the shirt at Blaine. "Since you told Leo and Cam about Lee Anne, Lindie's obviously not here. What time will she be home?"

Heading the same direction as the boys, Blaine chuckled. "About five minutes. Between Erik's mom and my mom, they've kept Lindie and Layla busy all afternoon."

Five minutes. Lee Anne closed her eyes and exhaled as her brother-in-law disappeared into the hall.

"You okay?" Russ's whispered question caressed her jittery nerves.

A *clunk* from the vicinity of the front door brought her eyes wide open and her heart almost leaped out of her chest. Then a disembodied male voice relieved her panic. "Hey, Russ, can you give me a hand?"

"Be right there." Russ gestured toward the living room with his head. "Erik, Layla's husband. You want to go meet him or wait here?"

"Go. If I stay here, I might sneak out the back door. This is a lot harder than I thought it was going to be."

He draped his arm around her shoulders and led her out of the kitchen. "It'll be over soon, and everything will be better than you expected."

"God, I hope you're right." More than anything, she wanted to believe him. If not for his connection to her sisters, she would've been on her own for this family introduction.

"I am." As he released her, he grinned at the slack-jawed man staring at her from the rug by the front door. "The resemblance is pretty remarkable, isn't it? Lee Anne, this is Erik Fielding. Erik, meet your new sister-in-law, Lee Anne Terrell."

Erik closed his mouth, opened it as if to speak, and closed it again.

Shoving her nervousness aside, she stepped forward to greet her other brother-in-law. "Nice to meet you, Erik."

"Resemblance?" He shook his head. "That's an understatement. Lee Anne. All your names start with L. Layla's going to cry when she sees you."

Russ laughed and slapped his friend on the back. "I think he's in shock. Buddy, the correct response is 'Good to meet you, Lee Anne.'"

"Good to meet you, Lee Anne." Although the poleaxed expression had cleared, Erik Fielding didn't look happy. "Seeing her cry rips me apart."

A herd of footsteps thundered up behind her, announcing the presence of the boys and Blaine. Cam's excited voice rose over the din. "They're almost here! Aunt Lee Anne has to hide so we can yell 'Surprise!'"

Blaine shuffled her away from Russ and to the far side of the coffee table. "Stand here. Erik, we're going to stand in front of her until everybody's inside. Leo, your job is to open and close the door. Cam, get ready to throw the confetti. Straight up to the ceiling, remember? Russ, you're on picture duty."

Organized chaos ensued, but Russ's thumbs-up helped her focus on something other than the wiggly tadpoles quickly metamorphosing into hopping frogs in her belly. Blaine moved in front of her, blocking her view.

I will not throw up. I will not throw up. I will not—

"I see Grandma and Grandpa's car." The slightly calmer cadence of Leo's announcement did little to slow her erratic pulse. "And there's Aunt Layla's."

An eternity seemed to pass before the door clicked open.

"Ready?" Thankfully, Blaine's whisper seemed directed at everyone rather than only her, because the answer teetered toward *no*. Lively conversation filled the room for several long seconds before the door clunked shut. "One. Two. Three. Surprise!"

Blaine and Erik stepped away with the exclamation, giving Lee Anne a clear line of sight to the two women standing less than ten feet from her. Confetti drifted into the space between them, slowly falling to the floor.

The eyes staring back at her were familiar, like the ones she saw in the mirror. No matter that she'd looked at her sisters' images at least a hundred times, seeing them in person stole her breath.

The longer-haired woman, Lindie, raised her hand to her lips. "Oh my God."

Layla glanced toward Lindie and squealed as she grabbed her hand. "It's her!"

Then they hurried to Lee Anne, dispelling her doubts and worries. Arms closed around her and laughter rang in her ears.

Home.

CHAPTER 5

*B*usiness before pleasure.

 With a condom in his wallet and the remainder of the six-packet strip in his computer bag, Russ punched in the code on the security pad. His plan was to get two or three hours of work done *before* he lured Lee Anne to her bedroom for his mermaid fix, even though their post-party hookup had been derailed by a later-than-expected evening and bringing her straight home.

Man can't live on sex alone. Go back to sleep, Moby.

The doorknob slipped from his fingers as he turned it and his client greeted him with a sheepish half smile. "Sorry I fell asleep on you last night. Stress, even the good kind, is definitely more exhausting than swimming laps for an hour."

He stepped inside and closed the door against the cold, pleased by her unexpected and unnecessary apology. It was a distinct improvement over his life with Sasha. "Nothing to be sorry for. It's not every day you meet your family. Besides, the occasional cold shower helps me stay humble."

Her giggle-snort was far from ladylike, but damned if it wasn't cute. "Yeah, you have a real problem with that overblown ego of yours,

Mr. Novotny. Make yourself comfortable while I grab a cup of caffeine. Want some?"

"Sure." He followed her to her office, the rich aroma of coffee with a backbone teasing his nose as he rounded the checkout counter. "Did you sleep well?"

"Like a proverbial log. That back rub hit the spot." She stopped at the coffee pot and flipped over two mugs. "Thanks for yesterday. Knowing I had support made all the difference in the world."

"Any time. The friends-with-benefits gig includes the friend part too, not just sex." With his belongings on the desk, he powered on her computer and removed his coat. "Not that I mind getting laid."

"You have to be the most unpretentious man I've ever met." Although she sounded amused, more than a hint of something else colored her compliment. "Sugar or half and half?"

"Black's fine." He pulled a binder with his company logo on it from his workbag and opened it to the first tab. "I like honesty. I've decided it's more important than hiding from the truth."

"I agree." She handed him a steaming mug.

"Thanks. Have a seat and we'll jump into your training." The irresistible scent of her hair surrounded him as she sat next to him in the office chair, testing his willpower. A sip of hot coffee cleared his senses enough to focus on the task at hand. "Damn, that's good. We're going to start with the intro section of the manual I made for you so you can familiarize yourself with the software capabilities and how to navigate the different elements. There's a help function built into the program, but some people prefer a hard copy, so I provide both."

"Because you're the best at what you do." She lifted the mug to her lips and met his gaze, clearly daring him to refute her statement.

He couldn't disagree that he had a knack for writing user-friendly programs and related better than most programmers to end users and their limited understanding of software. "Yes, I'm very good at meeting clients' specific needs and expectations. It's the one thing about myself I've never doubted. Anyway, I'll walk you through the basics now and leave you to play around with the pricing and inventory features while I work on your website and server this afternoon."

"Sounds like an efficient plan." She typed in the password and tapped Enter. "I hope lunch includes dessert."

The twitch in his balls was easier to hide than his grin. "I was thinking we'd take a fifteen- or twenty-minute break about ten o'clock. Sitting at a computer for two hours at a time is my limit."

With one hand on the mouse and one on the keyboard, she raised her eyebrows expectantly. "Then show me what to click on first. The stopwatch is running."

❧

"So when I log a sale or check in a delivery, it automatically feeds the information to my sales and inventory records *and* the spreadsheet for my accountant?" The wonder in Lee Anne's voice reminded Russ why he preferred working with small business owners.

"Pretty cool, isn't it? I had a request for that combination of features a few years ago, but the company I worked for wanted to price the product too high to make it attractive. You were my guinea pig. If you need a recommendation, I know two CPAs who'd probably be happy to handle preparing your taxes." He emptied his second cup of coffee and set it on the desk.

Her all-knowing look was accompanied by a snicker. "They wouldn't happen to be Lindie and Blaine, would they?"

"Yes, actually. How'd you know?"

"The private investigator did a thorough job." She leaned back in the chair and stretched her arms over her head.

"Ready for a break?"

A seductive smirk spread across her face as she tapped her wrist. "What do you think?"

"It's only two minutes after ten. You might want to—"

"No." She jumped out of the chair and grabbed him by the hand. "I want to take advantage of my benefits."

Her enthusiasm was refreshing, encouraging him to follow her down the hall, past the pool, and into her apartment.

The door barely clicked closed behind them before she tugged her hooded sweatshirt over her head and threw it toward the couch. Her bra landed at his feet in the doorway to her bedroom. She kicked off her shoes and attacked the button closure of her jeans. "You brought a condom, didn't you?"

Trying to catch up with her state of undress, he yanked off his shirt. Then he tossed his wallet on the nightstand. "Six. One in there and five in my computer bag."

"Smart man." The remainder of her clothes flew past the end of the bed. Before he managed to remove his second shoe, she crawled across the mattress toward the pillows. Her bottom moved back and forth in time with her breasts. She flopped onto her back with her knees spread wide, giving him an unobstructed view of her pussy. "Your choice of position this time."

He finally shoved his pants past his feet, mulling over diving between her legs or fucking her from behind. As he retrieved and donned the condom, another option surfaced in his brain. He stroked his latex-covered cock. "Back over here."

"I can see the wheels turning in that creative mind of yours." She bounced to the edge of the bed and grinned up at him. "Now what?"

"Stand up." As she rose, he threaded his fingers into her hair. "I want to kiss you first."

Her tongue snuck out to wet her lips and her hand came up to his jaw. The motion dragged her nipples across his chest. "I like kissing you. Your beard feels nice against my chin."

He leaned into her touch, savoring the physical contact. "All of you feels nice against me."

She met him halfway to a kiss, a soft caress of her lips on his and then a slant of his mouth over hers. She welcomed him inside with a decisive glide along his tongue as she pressed her lower belly against his cock and her breasts into his ribs. Her pulse beat strong and steady where his thumb rested lightly on her neck. Nothing about her was weak or tentative.

A needy moan vibrated through his skull, but he had no idea whether it was his or hers. The lust she inspired was all that mattered.

He dove past her lips again, tasting her a last time before he finally dragged in a breath and turned her in his arms. "I want to look at your ass and play with your clit while I fuck you."

She bent forward until her forearms rested on the blankets. Then she met his gaze over her shoulder as she widened her stance. "Hearing a horny sex-starved geek talk like a player is a major turn-on. You should probably get to it."

"Maybe I better check to make sure it's true." Curving himself around her, he slicked his middle finger along the folds hiding her clitoris and cupped her breast with the palm of his other hand. As he made the return trip through her folds, he eased his finger inside her. "Mm-hm. I think you're right. Your nipple's hard and you're definitely wet enough for a visit from a whale."

Her breathing changed to gasps and shuddering exhales, and her body tightened around the digit he'd slipped in a little farther. "Told you so."

He withdrew and brought his finger to his mouth to lick off her essence. "Mm. Tasty."

She wiggled her bottom until his erection lay nestled in the cleft between her butt cheeks. "I'm a big believer in helping karma with payback, just so you know."

After a laugh and a quick kiss on her spine, he straightened and guided his cock to her opening. As he rocked forward, she arched back, putting him balls deep in her snug pussy. Every bit of air exited his lungs and he fought against the impulse to wham-bam her until they both collapsed.

Her muscles tugged and squeezed him, and uninhibited groans filled the room. "Fuck me, Russ."

Fuck control. Grasping her hip, he found her clit again and set a pace sure to bring them both gratification that exceeded their expectations. Her cries, one after another, urged him on, adding to the gift of being welcomed and embraced by her body. Contractions gripped his cock over and over as pressure built in his balls. Every thrust carried him to a place where he could drown in carnal decadence, allowing him as much pleasure as he gave.

The dam released, sending heat rushing through his dick and letting loose a hoarse yell from his throat. His limbs shook, all control swept away by the flood of unequaled bliss. He wrapped his arms around her and brought her down on top of him as he toppled onto his back on the bed. His mind swam in the post-orgasmic surf, still dazed by her ability to push aside his doubts and make him feel wanted.

She melted into him, her muscles lax and her head lolling into the crook of his neck. Miles of silky hair spread over his chest and shoulders, bathing him in her mythical beauty. Her shaky exhale mirrored his exhilaration and momentary exhaustion. "Holy mackerel. And, yes…that's *damn* good."

"Mm-hm." He laid his hand on her belly as his heart rate slowed. Aftershocks quivered through her middle for several minutes and her breathing gradually returned to normal.

Content that he'd met her sexual needs, he closed his eyes and let Lee Anne's slow, even breathing fill his mind. God, he missed holding a woman as he fell asleep, awoke in the dead of night, and stirred from sleep in the morning. Why couldn't he have met her before they'd been damaged by people who didn't give a shit about their feelings?

She shifted until she lay beside him, her ear over his heart and her palm resting on his right pec. "Stop thinking about her."

He discarded the thought of denying her assertion as soon as it popped in his head. "What makes you think I'm thinking about Sasha?"

"Your upper body is tense instead being relaxed." Her fingertips sank into the tight muscle. "You always stiffen up when you talk about her, and not in the aroused way."

"I'm pretty sure I couldn't get it up for her if I wanted to anymore. It's amazing what a few harsh words can do."

"I seem to recall there were more than a few, but you don't have to let her have that power over you. You can't change the past and it's time to dump the baggage she saddled you with. They're her issues, not yours." She rose on her elbow and cradled his jaw with the hand that had found his tension. "We're going to finish going through that list before we do any more work. Then we'll burn the letter so you can forget that chapter of your life."

He placed his hand over hers. "You're ruthless—in a good way."

Her voice softened, as did her expression. "I've had to be, or I wouldn't have been able to move on after the mistake I made."

Anger flared in his gut. "It wasn't your mistake. He violated your trust. He violated *you*. That's not your fault."

She nuzzled his beard and then rolled away. As she stood, she extended her arm. "Come on. We need to tackle our issues head on and be done with it."

The determination in her pursed lips and dipping eyebrows prodded him upward to grasp her outstretched hand. "That list is pretty long. You better make another pot of coffee and plan to spend the rest of the day taking turns on the psychologist's couch."

"Nah. We'll have your ego happy and healthy again by lunchtime." With her ass in the air, she dug through the pile of clothes on the floor and tossed his pants on the bed. "There's probably no point in putting anything else on until you're ready to leave for dinner with the guys."

"Taking full advantage of the benefits package?" He straightened his khakis as she slipped her shirt over her head without donning a bra.

"Damn right." She stepped into the thong and then slung her jeans over her shoulder on the walk toward the master bath. "Help yourself to the other bathroom."

Still a little dazed from his explosive orgasm, he made a quick trip to the half bath to get rid of the condom. By the time he returned from her office with the letter and another condom, she was sitting on the couch with a legal-sized envelope on her lap. The frown lines etched in her forehead warned him she fully intended to face down her own demons—and that it wasn't going to be a pleasant experience for either of them.

His stomach as unsettled as his nerves, he handed her the letter and sat beside her. "Is that the paperwork from your divorce?"

"No." The curt answer held no anger, but some other profound emotion came through the softness of her voice. "I took pictures of my face after he hit me. Right after I left and a few days later, when the bruises showed. I deleted them from my phone and my computer. It's time to get rid of the prints."

A wave of nausea threatened to rebel against the bowl of cold cereal he'd eaten for breakfast.

She blew out a noisy sigh. "I'll never forget how I looked and I don't think anyone else needs to see his handiwork. The people's reactions to the exhibit photographs in the courtroom were enough."

He nodded since no words could come close to accurately describing the sick feeling in his entire being or the shocking desire to pound the hell out of her abuser. The petty insults Sasha had dished out were nothing compared to what Lee Anne had endured. His ego was insignificant.

"Hey, I see what's going on in your head. No comparing what we've each gone through." She set aside both envelopes and wrapped her arms around him. "I'm going to make you feel better about what happened to you, not what happened to me. I'm okay."

Pulling her onto his lap, he buried his face in her neck and held her closer. The tightness in his throat prevented a response, but nothing he could say or do would take away what she'd gone through.

She rubbed circles over his shoulder blades and kissed his ear. "This is why I had to let it go. If you don't, the obsession will eat you alive. When we burn those pictures, I want you to remember that I was lucky. I wasn't in a position where I had to put someone else at risk by fighting back and leaving."

As right as she was, the knowledge didn't make letting go any easier. He wanted to hide her away and protect her, keep her safe and prove to her that he was different, that he'd take care of her.

The scent of her hair surrounded him again, soothing the urge to destroy something, and the shift in his focus brought another feeling to the forefront. It was every bit as scary as rage.

Well, hell. This is what it feels like to really fall in love.

CHAPTER 6

Lee Anne stuffed her keys in her coat pocket and hurried to the front door of the Cape Cod instead of rehashing the bewildering evolution of her feelings for Russ. Burning the bridges to their pasts shouldn't have given her heart permission to lose its sanity. At least she hadn't blurted out the feelings trying to assert themselves while she assured him all the other items in the letter were a load of malarkey.

As she reached for the doorbell, the door swung open. Layla stood framed in the doorway, a hand on her adorable rounded belly and the same wonderment in her expression Lee Anne suspected she also wore. "Come on in. Lindie texted a few minutes ago to say she's on her way over."

Unable to stop a grin, Lee Anne stepped into her sister's outstretched arms, grateful to have familial security and comfort wash over her. Her sister's protruding bump nudged her in the abdominals. "Oh! The baby! I felt her…him…move."

Layla giggled and released her. "That doctor's appointment I mentioned last night? It included an ultrasound. When Lindie gets here, I have some news to share."

"I'm here!" The voice came from another room and a door banged shut. "What news? Come put this bag on the counter so I can take my boots off."

Grasping Lee Anne by the hand, Layla turned toward the hallway leading from the foyer. "In case you didn't notice last night, our older sister is kind of bossy. The kitchen's this way."

Lee Anne chuckled and allowed herself a quick glance around the bright and airy space as they walked in the direction of Lindie's voice. Light streamed in an arched window above the front door and an oak railing off the entryway led up a wide set of stairs. "Your house is gorgeous. I love the carved banister."

"Thanks."

Lindie's snicker carried to the short hall. "Want to know a secret? Baby Fielding was conceived on those steps."

Layla sighed. "I never should've told her. Next, she'll be telling you about how she and Blaine met. He caught her using the spray from the garden hose to shower. And masturbate. In her backyard."

"How can I tell the story if you just gave away ninety-nine percent of the details?" Laughter welcomed them as they entered the spacious kitchen. Lindie held out a shopping bag while she unzipped her coat. "Homemade rolls. They need to rise one more time before they go in the oven. What else are we having for supper? And you, baby sister, have to share the craziest story about you and Russ having sex."

Heat rushed to Lee Anne's neck and cheeks. She shrugged off her jacket and hung it on the back of the closest chair to avoid meeting her sisters' gazes. "What makes you think Russ and I are more than friends?"

Lindie passed off the bag to Layla and snorted. "Very funny. Let's see. Maybe the fact that when I stopped to see if you wanted some eggs on my way home from deliveries earlier today, I saw him running around in nothing but a pair of jeans. You really should hang some blinds on your windows. The possibility that he forgot to put a shirt and shoes on before he went to your shop doesn't seem very likely, considering the weather. But I suppose he could've spilled coffee on them but not his pants."

Her other sister lifted a covered muffin tin out of the bag and set it on the counter. "He also spent practically the whole party watching you, like he was ready to whisk you away if you needed him to. Besides, he should start dating again. Or at least enjoying some female companionship."

Her boots now standing on the rug inside the French doors, Lindie removed her coat. "Your story must be really good to cause that shade of red. So spill, sis. Most interesting location, position, or situation."

With no chance of escape, Lee Anne straightened her spine and willed away the blush. "This is between the three of us? No telling Russ or your husbands I told you?"

Both women crossed their hearts with their index fingers.

"Okay. We've been emailing back and forth about a custom software package and my website design since before Thanksgiving, but we'd never met in person before yesterday. I think the chemistry surprised both of us, and we, um, had sex by my lap pool after he helped me get unstuck from my mermaid suit."

Lindie's jaw dropped. "A mermaid, huh? You definitely win. Best seduction ever. I do have to admit, though, I never thought Russ was a first-date sex kind of guy. He seems so…wholesome. Is it serious?"

"No." Wary of delving any deeper into the stupidly giddy feelings being with him evoked, Lee Anne turned to her silent sister. "What's the news? Did you find out if the baby's a boy or a girl?"

Layla's lips twitched, a clear indication that she recognized an obvious change of subject when she saw one. "Sort of. Good evasive maneuver, by the way."

Their older sister frowned. "What kind of answer is 'sort of'? And we'll get back to you and Russ."

"Let's make supper while we talk." Layla grasped their hands and led them toward the stove. "We're having loaded baked potato soup and peach cobbler. I'm craving carbs and peaches."

Lindie froze midstep. "Oh. My. God. It's twins, isn't it? That would be unbelievably awesome. Didn't I tell you your belly is growing a lot faster than Sahara's?"

Layla pointed to half a dozen red potatoes laid out on crinkled rectangles of foil on the counter. "I took the potatoes out of the oven right before you got here. They should be cool enough to handle now."

Leaning around her pregnant sister, Lindie met Lee Anne's gaze. "Sahara owns a diner about a half an hour from here and is one of my three-times-a-week egg deliveries. They have the same due date, but Sahara barely looks pregnant. You know that stage where you don't want ask how far along the woman is because she might not actually be expecting?"

"And you wonder why I don't take you to my prenatal appointments." Layla turned toward Lee Anne and winked. "She thinks she should know everything I do at the doctor's office, including if I pee in a cup."

"I have no desire to waddle like a duck for months, so that means I'm living the experience through you, dear sister."

The teasing made Lee Anne smile and she hooked her arms around both women, bringing them into a tight circle. "This is what I always imagined having sisters would be like. I'm so glad I found you."

"It's pretty amazing, isn't it?" Layla sniffled and her voice cracked as she spoke. "The doctor thinks we're having a boy. And a boy."

A squeak escaped with the joy that rushed through Lee Anne. "That's so exciting! Congratulations!"

Tears rolled down Lindie's cheeks as she opened her mouth and closed it again. "I knew it! I bet Fielding fainted."

Layla brought their group hug closer with a squeeze. "He cried because he was so ecstatic. Then he kissed me and he kissed my belly. And when we got home... I've never felt so loved in my life."

Lindie smirked and waggled her eyebrows. "I hope you guys went upstairs to celebrate. You never know when a peeping Tom will accidentally catch you mostly naked in the kitchen."

"You mean a peeping sister." The chastisement lost its effectiveness with another round of giggles. "Erik still insists on closing all the curtains before he undresses. And today's looking-through-the-window-and-seeing-Russ episode is justification."

"So sue me. I'm a little nosey. I'd do anything for my long-lost sisters." Lindie swiped her sleeve across her eyes. "I love you guys. You're the family I always wanted."

Fighting her own tears, Lee Anne swallowed against the tightness in her throat. "Me too, even though I loved my adoptive parents. Having a family again is indescribable."

Several long minutes of sniffles and hugs mirrored the needless introductions at yesterday's party. Nothing about the immediate connection with her sisters was awkward or uncomfortable. It seemed as natural as her attraction to Russ, with far fewer reservations.

Layla guided their hands to her tummy, where flutters and wiggles greeted Lee Anne's palm. "They're looking forward to meeting their aunts. Or they might be telling me they're hungry."

"If they're anything like their cousins, it's all about food." After a gentle pat on her sister's belly, Lindie rested her hands on her hips. "What do you want us to do first?"

"Let's get the cobbler ready to go in the oven. Then, while it's baking, the rolls can rise and we can make the soup. I'm thinking sautéed mushrooms, steamed broccoli, and fontina cheese for toppings." With a sigh and a shake of her head, Layla hurried past the end of the counter. "Back in a minute. Potty break. The peaches are in the pantry."

"If I ever mention wanting to have a baby, poke me in the bladder every five minutes for months on end." Lindie was halfway to the pantry when a chime sounded from somewhere near the refrigerator. "How much you want to bet that's a Fielding text? He was a nervous wreck about one baby. Two probably has him freaking out."

Lee Anne didn't doubt for a second that her brother-in-law was checking to make sure his wife was okay. The man had hardly left Layla's side at the party, his love for her evident in his actions as much as his words. To be honest, Lee Anne was a little envious of their relationship and the bond they shared.

Lindie's snicker urged her to join her sister for a sneak peek at Layla's cell. "Mr. Uptight is a squishy marshmallow. He sent three kisses and three hearts—one of each for the love of his life and their little bundles of joy. He also wants to know if we're here yet."

The sentiment warmed Lee Anne's heart. "That's so sweet."

"Isn't it? I should probably answer him." Several taps on the number grid unlocked the phone, hardly surprising given Lindie's tendency to take charge of everything. "Hmm, what shall I say? Oh, I know. Heart, heart, kiss, kiss. One for you and one for your super spermies. And send."

"Oh my God! I can't believe you actually sent that. I mean, I do, but… I hope I never get in an argument with you."

The message popped up on the screen, followed almost immediately by the dot-dot-dot bubble that indicated Erik was typing a response. *"Super spermies, huh? Is that the best you can do, Brewster? Take good care of my wife or else. Say hi to Lee Anne (the nice sister) for me."*

Lindie grinned and tapped in another text. *"I always take excellent care of my sisters. Kissies from the sissies. Keep the boys out of trouble or I'll get my bucket!"*

Lee Anne was almost afraid to ask what that threat meant. "I think I missed an inside joke."

"It's a reference to the time Blaine sent him out to the farm with a ridiculous offer to buy. He thought he could outsmart me, so I tossed an empty bucket toward him to scare him off. The way he tells it, I threw the bucket *at* him. It didn't even come close to hitting him, but I got the point across that I wasn't putting up with his bullsh— I mean bull hockey."

A groan came from behind them. "Another retelling of the bucket story? Are you tormenting my husband again?"

"Puh-lease. He enjoys sparring as much as I do. You only need to worry if we stop." Lindie puckered her lips and curved her hands into the shape of a heart. "He sends hearts and kisses to you and the babies."

As Layla reached for her phone, Lee Anne's cell buzzed in her sweatshirt pocket and Lindie jumped like she'd been shocked. Then she pulled her phone from the back pocket of her jeans.

A quick glance at the screen revealed a text from Russ. *"Hope you're having fun! See you tomorrow morning at 8. :)"*

Lee Anne bit the inside of her cheek to hold in a smile. Her stomach wobbled instead, betraying the feeling she wasn't ready to admit to herself, let alone anyone else.

"Everything okay?"

Both her sisters stared at her, but she had no idea which one had asked the question. *Act casual.* "Oh. Yeah. It was just Russ telling me when he'll be at the shop in the morning. More software training."

Layla tsked at her. "Not serious? You should see your face. You're a cross between glowing and terrified."

Their older sister flipped her ponytail past her shoulder as she sauntered toward the pantry. "According to Blaine, Russ looks as infatuated as you do and he didn't deny it when Leo asked if you were his girlfriend."

"We aren't dating. It's an itch and we're scratching. That's all." Lee Anne pilfered the quart jar of peaches from her sister and went in search of a bottle opener to pry off the lid.

"I told myself the same thing about Blaine. We got married eleven days after we met."

"Eleven days?" The first incorrect drawer shut a bit harder than Lee Anne intended, making her flinch. "I was married for eleven days. It's not an experience I care to repeat."

Layla set a casserole dish on the counter and added a stick of butter. A few seconds later, the microwave beeped as she pressed several buttons in quick succession. "Full disclosure. I was curious about you, so I did some research last night. Is your ex-husband the reason you left your faculty position? I mean, you were tenured and fully promoted. Something significant had to happen to walk away from that kind of job security."

The next drawer held a mix of utensils, including the item she needed. The canning lid gave a twangy *pop* a moment before the microwave beeped again. "I'd been thinking about starting a fish hatchery since my mom and dad died. Academics has become too much about competing for funding, pay raises, and lab space, and I couldn't picture myself spending another twenty years schmoozing with the right people. Even if I didn't have my own savings, I still would've left. I was the sole beneficiary of my parents' estate, and the divorce helped put things in perspective. There was no reason to wait."

Lindie measured flour, sugar, baking powder, and milk into the bowl. "Can't argue with that. I Googled you too and saw an article about his sentencing. You deserve an award for taking that bastard down."

Lee Anne returned the bottle opener to the drawer and grabbed a whisk from the crock on the counter. "I don't want an award. I was one of many and suffered the least."

"Abuse is abuse. It doesn't matter who got hit, belittled, or what-ever the most or least. We all have scars, and you probably prevented the abuse of someone else."

A hint of pain in Lindie's eyes reminded Lee Anne of the most horrifying part of the private investigator's report. They'd had another sibling, a sister who'd died when she was three because of parental negligence. Five-year-old Lindie had held Nina as she took her last breaths, probably leaving far deeper scars than the mostly superficial ones Lee Anne had.

"I hope so." She handed off the whisk, fairly certain Lindie needed a release of repressed anger more than she did, and joined their quiet sister at the cutting board she'd laid out on the counter.

Layla glanced sideways at her as she unwrapped the package of mushrooms. "Does Russ know about what happened?"

"Yes, but it doesn't mean I want a relationship. Or that he does." Although the words came out harsher than she intended, she stood behind them. Exploring romantic feelings for him wasn't worth the risk of losing him as a friend.

Lindie's grunt was loud and clear over the scraping of the batter bowl into the butter-laden baking dish. "Speaking from the voice of experience, you and Russ aren't fooling anybody but yourselves. You're not the first couple to deny what's staring you in the face, and you won't be the last. It runs in the family. Hand me the peaches and start mashing the potatoes. Hand masher is in the drawer where you found the bottle opener."

"Layla was right. You *are* bossy."

Her sister grinned. "Yep. And squishing spuds will make you a little less cranky about facing the inevitable."

CHAPTER 7

R uss shut off the engine and blew out a vigorous breath to calm his nerves. Three days had passed since he and Lee Anne had put the past to rest. Sex with her was beyond amazing and their friendship had developed into something he valued as much as his long-standing camaraderie with Fielding and Stockwell. She understood and respected him. However, he hadn't come to grips with his feelings until Erik and Blaine had treated him to breakfast and an intervention—their word, not his—bright and early this morning.

Falling in love with her had been so damn easy, even if accepting it had not.

I can do this.

He slung the strap of his computer bag over his shoulder as he climbed out of his car, all too aware that the end of the day marked the completion of the installation and training sessions of their agreement. Although her proximity allowed it, tech support wasn't usually an in-person service.

The door swung open when he stepped onto the sidewalk, and Lee Anne waited in the doorway. Instead of greeting him with the seductive, hungry look she'd had all week, her lips formed a grim line and her arms were crossed in front of her.

Following her inside, he closed the door behind him. "Everything okay? You didn't have a fight with Lindie or Layla, did you?"

She shook her head and rounded the service counter. "No, they've been great. But they... We need to talk, preferably before we pick up where we left off yesterday."

His gut spasmed and every bit of oxygen deserted his lungs. "Did I do something wrong?"

"No!" A growl accompanied her abrupt turn into the office. "Damn it, I knew I'd screw this up. Come in and sit down. Do you want a cup of coffee?"

He trailed after her, reasonably sure admitting his feelings was no longer the way to go. It would only complicate an already uncomfortable situation. "No thanks."

She flipped over a mug and picked up the carafe as he dropped into the chair, his coat still on and his bag hooked over his shoulder for armor. Then she returned the carafe to the warming plate without pouring. "There's no easy way to say this, so I guess I'll just..."

Rip off the Band-Aid? "Look, it's okay if you don't want to—"

"I— Wait. You think I'm breaking up— No, not breaking up. You think I'm saying I don't want to have sex with you anymore?" Her voice rose with every word and the color drained from the cheek he could see. Stepping away from the coffeemaker, she scraped her hands through her loose hair. "Is that what *you* want?"

"No."

"God, I told them I wasn't ready to tell you." She finally looked at him. Confusion and apprehension were written all over her face. "I don't want that, either."

Relief eased some of the tension in his neck at her admission, enough to dispel the possibility of her dumping him from his thoughts. *It's now or never.* "Good, because I'm pretty sure I love you. Not just as a friend. In love. I'm in love with you."

She blinked at him and the stiffness in her body dissipated, suggesting she might be receptive to the idea of more than a friends-with-benefits arrangement. "Okay. I mean... Here goes. My sisters said I'm in love with you too. I think they're right."

The stutter in his brain function made him second-guess the rushed words. "I'm not sure I heard that correctly."

She stepped closer and her voice softened. "I love you too."

"You have no idea how relieved I am to hear that." He guided her down to his lap and buried his face in her neck. With his eyes closed, her familiar scent filled his senses and soothed his soul. "I want to cook dinner for you tonight, like a real date."

"That sounds nice." She leaned into him and exhaled. "I didn't know if I could say it. Thanks for doing it first."

He kissed the soft skin beneath her ear. "You should thank your sisters' husbands. They threatened to tell you if I didn't."

"Lindie and Layla threatened me with the same thing over tea and scones this morning. Actually, Lindie more than Layla. I never really understood sibling dynamics until now. I know they mean well, just like Blaine and Erik, but I don't believe for a second they weren't working together. I think they conspired against us." Her mischievous giggle sent a wonderful shiver along his spine. "I'm tempted to send my sisters a text message saying I'll be out of touch for a couple days. That I'm going to Vegas for the weekend and turning my phone off."

He grinned against her hair. "That's devious. You're getting the hang of having siblings."

"Yeah." She leaned back and cradled his jaw in her hands. "I'm glad you've been here with me through meeting my family and starting a new life."

"I help out my friends when I can." A light kiss on her soft lips was all he allowed himself for the time being. "I've never been friends with a woman before we got romantically or sexually involved until you. It's a good change. How about if we work fast so we can finish early today?"

The buttery-sweet aroma of the cooling pound cake did little to distract Russ from a bad case of first-date jitters. He sighed and popped open a jar of Lindie's home-canned salsa to pour over the rice in the saucepan. Lee Anne might appreciate a good meal, but his cooking skills wouldn't make or break their relationship. All the characteristics Sasha hadn't given a damn about were at the top of his new girlfriend's list—kindness, trustworthiness, honesty.

He could handle those.

Focusing on a day at a time was the hard part, and not looking for hints that they were meant to be together for the next forty or fifty years. How could he avoid the pitfalls of imagining a future with her, especially when it formed so easily in his mind?

His phone buzzed and lit up on the counter beside him. Instead of text from his date, a winter-weather advisory flashed on the screen.

Fuck you, snowstorm.

He typed in a message to Lee Anne before second thoughts had a chance to take shape. *"Tomorrow's snow is arriving early. I'm worried about you driving home tonight. Bring a change of clothes and your toothbrush just in case? I'll leave the garage door open for you."*

An overnight stay wasn't the same as living together, and concern for her safety didn't make him a controlling jerk. He wanted the chance to explore his new perspective on their relationship, experience slow lovemaking and hours of conversation with her—the kind of intimacy and connection his college buddies had found with her sisters.

Overthinking was obviously one of his strongest attributes as well.

His cell vibrated in his hand this time.

"So I shouldn't plan on walking next door to stay the night? Not that L or L would let me in the door. LOL They were far too interested in my sex life the other night. Speaking of which, I need an appetizer before dinner. I'm suffering from withdrawal."

Finishing early had meant no hanky-panky during their abbreviated breaks for coffee, lunch, and the switch from software to website instruction. His dick hadn't been happy about it, either, but they would make up for it during their date. *"I think that can be arranged. :)"*

"Looking forward to it. Overnight bag is packed and I'm locking up. See you soon. Oh, and clothing is optional while I'm there." A winking smiley face appeared after her message.

Would she approve if he welcomed her wearing nothing but his barbecue apron?

Abandoning his half-prepared dinner for the moment, he added a log to the low-burning blaze in the fireplace, pleased with the romantic ambience. The fire provided the perfect amount of light for eating and making love, and half a strip of condoms rested beside the open bottle of Vinho Verde and a pair of stemless glasses. He stripped off his clothes in the bedroom and then returned to the kitchen. With the apron in place, he opened the garage door with the app on his phone. A draft chilled his bare backside and chest, but the convenience of not having to undress was worth goose bumps on his ass.

A few minutes later, the hum of the garage door and a knock sent his heart reeling with the thrill of seeing her, more like a sixteen-year-old kid than a man heading into middle age.

God, that's a good feeling.

After a quick adjustment of the apron, he turned the doorknob and took a step back. Wintry air pushed inside ahead of Lee Anne.

"Brr! The temperature's dropped at least ten degrees since you—" Her eyes widened and then her smile did the same. "Well, I wasn't expecting my personal chef to meet me at the door quite like this. I'm getting warmer already."

He cupped her cold-pinked cheeks in his palms and touched his lips to hers. They parted with a teasing lick to the seam, welcoming him inside. Her tongue sparred with his, heating the chilled parts of him and reassuring him he'd made the right choice to undress before her arrival. He came up for a breath and leaned his forehead against hers. "Hi."

"Hi." She looked up at him with heavy-lidded eyes. "I've been wanting to do that all day."

"We wouldn't have gotten done with your training." He clasped her gloved hand and led her toward the living room. "Come on. I have a fire going."

She slipped her hand free and lagged behind him. "I like the view from back here better."

Three consecutive *thunks* alerted him that she'd probably toed off her boots and let the overnight bag slip to the kitchen floor. The distinctive *zip* and rustle of her ski jacket followed. More than likely, she would be nearly as undressed as he was when they reached his supply of condoms.

A backward glance as he entered the living room caught her yanking her shirt over her head. No bra covered her breasts, slowing his pace and making his semi-erect cock stand at attention. He tugged on the tie at his waist, but he had to fumble with the strings again to make the apron fall.

"Suit up while I get rid of my jeans." Her husky and slightly breathless command urged him to the end table.

He detached a packet along the perforation and tore it open as she shoved the denim past her hips and down her legs. The flickering shadows across her body mesmerized him, distracting him from his task. She was everything he'd ever wanted in a lover—smart, sexy, sweet. "I'm a very lucky guy."

She stepped closer and took the latex circle from him. In an efficient motion, she rolled the condom onto his erection, but her firm touch sparked a tightening in his balls. "I'm a very lucky woman."

As he lifted her against him, she wrapped her legs around his waist, putting her pussy within inches of the head of his dick. Her nipples caressed his chest and her gasp encouraged him to skip foreplay. He flexed his ass, taking his cock on a smooth ride through her slick folds. "Ready?"

"Yes." Her response came a second before she thrust her tongue past his lips and rocked her hips high enough to put their bodies in precise alignment.

She glided onto his length, deeper and deeper until he was an extension of her and she was an extension of him. The connection went beyond flesh, the physical part expressing so much of his emotional bond to her. She contracted around him, gripping and clutching at him, until taking them to paradise was all that mattered.

Somehow, he found the armchair and sat without dropping her or bashing his knee on the coffee table. As he sank into the cushion, she descended farther onto him. The friction from the rough back-and-forth motion of her hips and the muffled groans mixed with the kiss stole what little control he might have had over the pressure building in his balls.

Seizing the only opportunity to make her come before he did, or at least simultaneously, he worked his hand between them and hoped his thumb found her clit. A shudder rippled through her as he made contact and she cried out, breaking their kiss and pulling him toward his own release.

With each squeeze, she swept him closer, and then heat shot through his cock. He groaned into her hair and let the orgasm wash him away. Exhilaration blended with the heaviness in his limbs, elevating and pulling him under at the same time. The eruption had passed too quickly, but her body continued to massage him, even after he drifted back to shore.

Grounded by the comfortable weight of her on his lap and chest, he slid a hand into her hair and explored her shoulder blades with the other. She fit in his arms and his life like no woman had before.

Soft lips and warm breath caressed his ear. "The appetizer gets five stars. What's next?"

"How about chips and guacamole with a glass of wine? And fish tacos, salsa rice, roasted butternut squash, and pound cake with raspberry sauce." He slowly descended her spine with his fingertips. "You're welcome to relax in front of the fire while I finish supper."

"I'm here to be with you, not just to enjoy sex and your cooking. I'd like to help, if you don't mind sharing your kitchen."

Happiness spread through his heart and soul. "Have I mentioned that I love you?"

Her low laugh rippled through him. "You might have. I'll love you more if you tell me where to find the closest bathroom."

Their easy post-sex exchange stayed with him as he led her to the master bath, grabbed boxer briefs from the pile of clothes he'd abandoned near his bed, and disposed of the condom in the half bath down the hall. He didn't have to pretend to be comfortable with her. He could be completely honest about anything and everything, and she would do the same for him. She had no ulterior motives.

The apron lay in a crumpled heap in the hall, so he tossed it into the laundry room on his way to the stove. As he turned on the flame under the saucepan, light footsteps sounded on the tile.

Then Lee Anne hugged him around his waist from behind, her arms and breasts now covered. "Something smells wonderful. What can I do to help?"

"That's the squash. It has about eight minutes to go in the oven." He guided her around to his side and kissed her temple. "Can you grab a cooling rack from the bottom cabinet next to the stove?"

She retrieved the rack and set it on the counter. "What else?"

Pleased with her sincere offer, he reviewed his mental list. "We need butter, shredded lettuce, grated cheese, tortillas, and the platter of fish from the fridge."

Her saucy salute and pivot gave him a peek at her naked ass below the hem of her shirt. "I saw you looking at my backside, mister. No more nookie until after food."

"I won't argue with that, but didn't you say clothing was optional?" He preheated the iron skillet on the front burner and pulled a wide metal spatula from the tool crock.

"I'm trying not to distract you." Her hem rose again as she set the bowls of lettuce and cheese on the counter.

"It isn't working, not that I mind. I like having you here."

She handed him the lightly seasoned fillets and a stick of butter, her teasing expression softening. "I like being here. Where'd you get the bass?"

"Clear Fork last summer. Really good fishing that weekend."

"One of the best public facilities in the state for largemouth. Need anything else from the fridge?"

The butter melted and sizzled in the hot skillet as he checked the rice. "I almost forgot. There's sauce too. Red taco sauce and green salsa. Whichever you want is fine with me."

"Ohh. Now I *know* you're a good cook." She held up the jar of Hatch green chile salsa. "This stuff is world-class."

The addition of the fish to the skillet created a flavorful cloud of steam. "I got addicted to it when I visited my older brother and his family in Albuquerque about ten years ago. Now he sends me a case of assorted Hatch products for Christmas every year."

"Do you have any other brothers or sisters?"

"No sisters. My younger brother lives just outside of Pittsburgh, about a mile from our mom and dad. I didn't visit as much as I wanted to for a while, but I'm working on changing that." He eased the spatula under a fillet and flipped it over. The golden brown contrasted with the opaque white of the other piece. After another careful flip, he lowered the flame and checked the rice again. The oven timer beeped as he replaced the lid. "Everything's ready."

After several trips between the kitchen and the living room, they finally settled on the floor in front of the fireplace. Conversation lapsed into relative silence as they ate, but the occasional brush of a hand and contented smile promised a night he would never forget.

A soft sigh nudged Russ from the edge of wakefulness, but the special woman next to him still dozed after a long night of making love. Her hair lay in a dark sweep across the bedspread, adding to his real-life siren fantasy.

The rightness of waking beside her ranked as high as starting his own business and moving to be near his friends. She was the woman he wanted to spend the rest of his life with, and he would willingly break his vow to never propose again to achieve it.

CHAPTER 8

Lee Anne bounded up the porch steps of her oldest sister's farmhouse and let herself in the front door. "Sorry I'm late!"

"You're not the only one." Layla's disembodied voice carried to the living room from beyond the hall. "Lindie just came inside about five seconds ago. Goldie escaped from her pen again and decided she didn't want to be caught."

"Poor Goldie. She's more puppy than chicken." A few vigorous stomps removed the packed snow from her boot treads. Shrugging out of her coat, she hurried to the kitchen. "Guess what. I got my delivery of tanks and aerators this morning. It was like Christmas!"

Lindie hung her coveralls and hat on the hook by the back door, wearing a thoughtful expression. "I remember when I got the kit for my first coop. After months of planning, I felt like I was finally accomplishing something."

Lee Anne added her coat to the hook and hugged her sisters in turn. "I can't wait for the weather to warm up so I can start hatching fish for the customers I have lined up."

Layla grinned. "Chickens. Fish. Next thing I know, you'll be trying to talk me into raising goats or alpacas."

"Nah. You'll be too busy raising babies." A pat on her sister's belly earned Lee Anne a noticeable kick. "Hey there, kiddo."

Their older sister cleared her throat. "Speaking of raising babies—"

Layla's mouth dropped open. "Oh my God! You're preg—"

"Good God, no! What's wrong with you, woman? I wouldn't go through pregnancy and childbirth if somebody paid me." Lindie's scowl said she'd deck anyone who made an offer. "Leo and Cam mentioned wanting a sister at least a dozen times since we got married. Finding out you're having a baby made it worse. And twin boys. When Blaine and I made it perfectly clear we're not doing the baby thing, they suggested we adopt a girl close to their age."

Excited by the prospect of a niece to go with four nephews, Lee Anne clasped her sister's hand. "So you're adopting?"

"Maybe at some point? We decided to start with foster parenting. It'll give us a chance to decide if we really want to do this." Lindie adjusted the place setting closest to her. "We're done with the paper-work and most of the home study and trainings. Anyway, I want you to know you're both on our reference list, so you'll probably be getting a call soon. They want to interview all family members."

There's that wonderful word again. Fairly certain her sister was a lot more nervous than she let on, Lee Anne slipped her arm around Lindie's waist. "You're a fantastic mother. Any little girl would be lucky to have you in her life. I hope it works out."

Layla sniffled and wiped at her cheek. "Ditto."

"Knock it off, you guys." Several rapid blinks accompanied Lindie's huffy sigh. "I hate crying."

Not bothering to hide a grin, Lee Anne joined her pregnant sister at the counter. "I'll carry lunch to the table while you supervise. Lindie, go wash your hands."

The order was rewarded with a half-hearted glare, but her oldest sister headed down the hall to the bathroom without a word.

Layla snickered. "You got away with telling her what to do once. Don't expect it to happen again. She appointed herself mother hen and guardian of the family, and she likes being in control."

"It's understandable after what she went through as a kid, but we're more alike than we are different. Butting heads is half the fun." Lee Anne moved the individual servings of fruit salad and a bag of home-made cloverleaf rolls to the table. "I'll carry the pot of soup if you'll put the container of cookies as far from me as possible. I've been eating too many sweets lately."

Lindie's hoot of laughter announced her return. "That's not what I call it, but to each her own. I guess your declaration went well since you spent the whole weekend with Russ."

"What makes you think that?" Heat crept up Lee Anne's neck, much to her disgust. She'd done nothing to be embarrassed about.

"Blaine saw you pull into his garage Friday shortly after the snow started. And I saw you leaving Sunday afternoon when I was finishing plowing the lane—after I plowed eight inches of pristine snow from his driveway."

Joining her sisters at the table, Lee Anne ladled a bowl of chicken soup for Layla. "Fine. I stayed with him."

Lindie made an exaggerated flourish with her right hand. "And…"

"Geesh, you were right, okay? I've never felt this way about anybody before, and he loves me too. We had an amazing weekend together." She filled her bossy sister's bowl and passed it to her. "Thanks for blackmailing me into telling him."

"Actually, it was Blaine's idea. For a man, he's pretty perceptive about things like love."

Layla's eye roll was almost audible. "Says the woman who thought he was in love with somebody else until he pointed out that it was her. Romanticism is wasted on you, sis."

"Well, he didn't have to be so cryptic. If you have something to say, don't beat around the bush about it." Lindie broke a roll into its three equal parts and sliced her knife through the butter. "Enough about me. I want to hear more about your adventures with Novotny. The quiet ones are always full of surprises."

Lee Anne stuffed a chunk of fresh strawberry in her mouth and shook her head. No way would her big sister be able to resist teasing Russ if she knew he'd opened the door in nothing but a bibless apron.

"He cooked for me. We cooked together. We had sex. It was awesome."

Obviously gearing up to fish for more details, Lindie buttered her roll and frowned when the doorbell rang. She pushed her chair away from the table. "Back in a minute."

As soon as their sister disappeared down the hall, Layla grinned. "A temporary reprieve."

"She's not getting a play by play, no matter how much she badgers me." Lee Anne focused on her lunch instead of fruitless hope that the subject would be gone and forgotten.

"Then you need to give her something else to think about."

"Like what?"

A cheery voice and footsteps announced the visitor who'd pulled their sister away from lunch. "Thank you for the offer, but I had a snack while I was driving. My unannounced inspection isn't going to be quite what it usually is."

"Oh?" Lindie's hesitation as she led her guest into the kitchen was the only thing that betrayed her anxiety. "Mrs. Pruitt, I'd like you to meet my sisters, Layla Fielding and Lee Anne Terrell. Guys, this is my caseworker, the person who'll be calling you."

After exchanging brief pleasantries, the blonde woman turned toward Lindie. "Do you mind if we sit down? I have some news."

Lindie grasped the top of the spindle-backed chair and paled, but she gestured at the seat adjacent to the one she'd vacated to answer the door. "Is everything okay? We didn't—"

"No worries, Mrs. Stockwell. It's fine. Everything's going smoothly. Actually, my supervisor is hoping you and your husband can complete your training this week. She called me on the drive here. I can't share details yet, but we may need you for a placement."

"A placement? A girl who needs us?" Hope replaced Lindie's shell-shocked look.

"Possibly."

Lee Anne abandoned her lunch to give her statue-still sister a hug. "I'm so happy for you."

"Me too." Layla crowded in, her belly leading the way.

"I'm so glad you guys are here with me for this." Lindie's shaky breaths hinted she was as emotionally moved as the day Lee Anne had been the unexpected surprise. "Now go sit down and eat so I can take care of business."

There's the big sister I know and love.

The woman unzipped her tote-sized purse and withdrew a notepad. "I'd like to do another quick walk-through to double-check a few things. I can show myself around or wait until you're done with lunch, whichever you prefer."

Swiping at her eyes, Lindie stepped away from the table. "I can't eat now. Maybe later, after I tell Blaine."

"Let's get started then." Mrs. Pruitt tapped the end of her pen on the notepad, extending the writing tip. "Mrs. Fielding and Dr. Terrell, I can conduct your interviews while I'm here—if you have time of course."

"I do." Layla responded in unison with Lee Anne, and she shared a smile with her pregnant sister.

The caseworker gave a nod as she followed Lindie toward the living room, looking relieved to have their eager cooperation. Everything seemed to be falling into place, finally bringing each of them the kind of happiness they needed in their lives.

Family. And Russ. I have what I was missing.

The computer screen went dark and Russ closed the laptop he'd been working from most of the day. Website updates had been a nice break from the complete design overhaul he'd done yesterday, and the mindless labor provided steady income from month to month. It had also given him an opportunity to think through the decision he'd made last night after he drove Lee Anne home from their movie and pizza date.

He set the computer on the end table and headed to the kitchen to check on supper. At the kitchen doorway, he closed his eyes and let the mouthwatering aroma of spinach lasagna blended with the sweet-and-spicy scent of warm cinnamon bread clear his head. It smelled like home and family and contentment. Hopefully, his plan would make Lee Anne forget they'd corresponded by email for less than three months and officially met only eight days ago. She was the key to making the aromatic impression a reality.

Fifteen minutes remained on the timer, allowing him time to set the mood for a romantic dinner and proposal. The fire he'd lit during his lunch break still burned in the fireplace, so he positioned a pair of candles on the coffee table and added glasses and a bottle of red a client had given him for designing his winery's website. Then he placed the blue velvet jeweler's box next to the wine glasses. Shadows hid it from immediate view, but she wouldn't miss it when he put a match to the tapers.

His phone buzzed on the end table and displayed a message from the love of his life. *"Be there in two minutes!"*

Lunch at Lindie's had evidently turned into an afternoon of the sisters compensating for decades of not knowing each other. The losses they'd experienced on the way to discovering their connection reminded him to be grateful for the relationships he had with his parents and brothers. He had no intention of taking his luck for granted.

A last inspection of the living room as he walked to the foyer assured him everything was in its place. He held the sheer curtain aside to watch for her arrival through the sidelight. Dusk cast a grayish hue on the snow, but headlights chased it away.

Calm spread through him when she stopped in front of the garage. He had no reason to be nervous. She loved him as much as he loved her, of that he was absolutely certain. Neither of them had doubts about the other's loyalty or commitment.

She paused at the snowman they'd built during her weekend stay, adjusting the stick-arm that had loosened before continuing along the shoveled sidewalk. Her bright smile widened and her pace quickened when she met his gaze through the narrow window.

This is perfect.

He barely noticed the cold when he opened the door for her. Then she was in his arms, greeting him with a playful kiss. Her soft lips were cool against his for only a fraction of a second.

She nibbled a path along the edge of his beard and hummed. "This day keeps getting better and better. Dinner smells divine too."

The faint beep of the oven timer derailed his plan to enjoy a more intimate kiss. "Lasagna's ready. Take off your coat and tell me about your day."

Her snowy boots landed on the rug and she hooked her coat on the stand as she walked beside him toward the kitchen. "My tanks and aerators were delivered this morning, and lunch with L and L was pretty spectacular. Did you know Lindie and Blaine are thinking about adopting? They're fostering first to see how it goes, but Lindie knows what those kids experience. She'll be a goner as soon as she lays eyes on any girl who reminds her of all she went through as a child. Anyway, I'm going to have a niece."

"You like being an aunt, don't you?" He donned the oven mitts and transferred the casserole dish to the cooling rack on the counter.

"Yeah. It's amazing to have this much family after having none for a year and a half." She leaned over the cinnamon bread and inhaled. "And I have you."

That's a sign if I ever saw one. "That, you do. The lasagna needs to sit for ten minutes before I cut it." He grasped her hand and led her to the living room.

"Ten minutes, huh?" The light from the fire reflected in her eyes. "Whatever will we do?"

Flame engulfed the match with a single stroke on the box. He held it to the closest wick and then the other. Candlelight invaded the shadows and illuminated the space around the wine bottle and glasses.

Recapturing her hand, he picked up the box and placed it in her palm. "I love you, Lee Anne, and I want to spend my life with you. Will you marry me?"

Her gaze dropped toward her open hand and she pressed her lips together. Several long moments passed before she looked up at him, but distress filled her expression instead of happiness. "I'll love you and live with you until the day I die, but I can't get married again. Marriage doesn't mean to me what it does to you. It scarred me."

Hadn't they burned her pictures and his letter so they could move on with their lives? Obviously, that symbolic gesture had healed only the most superficial wounds that influenced their choices. They'd been fooling themselves.

He couldn't move, even though he wanted to soothe her pain. The ache inside him hurt too much to allow him to comfort her. Was their love really this weak?

"I'm not him. I won't do what he did to you. You have to know I wouldn't. All I need is a piece of paper that says we belong to each other."

"I know you do, and I wish I could give you what you need." Her voice broke over the last word. Silent tears spilled over her dark lashes, speaking louder than anything she could say. "I'm not her, either. Haven't I shown you that?"

She had—over and over. Why wasn't that enough?

"Yes, but..." Hadn't he already compromised by asking her to marry him instead of following through on the oath he'd taken in front of Erik and Blaine last fall?

She wouldn't ask him to marry her, though—ever. Fighting for their future was impossible if she wouldn't meet him in the middle. Her past was an obstacle he couldn't overcome, just as she couldn't overcome his. The wounds weren't healed. They'd only scabbed over, ready to bleed again. They *would* bleed again too, every time they tried to pretend living only for the present would satisfy them.

He rested his forehead against hers, craving solace in her arms but unwilling to prolong the agony of fantasizing that they could find a way to be together. It would make losing her that much harder. Love and lust had blinded him to reality.

She backed away and set the box on the table, the steady stream of tears not slowing. "I love you. Please don't hate me for this."

Unable to speak past the tightness in his throat, he shook his head. He couldn't hate her for choosing self-preservation over his need to do the same. Watching her walk to the foyer finally forced a whisper. "Never."

At the door, with her coat draped over her arm, she turned toward him. The grief in her eyes matched the grief in his heart. "I can't ask you for anything more. Our friendship means the world to me. I don't want to lose that too. I wish…"

"I know." Every muscle in his body struggled against his brain, wanting to stop her from leaving. Touching her would lead to making love one last time, but it wouldn't ease the pain of having to let go. If anything, acknowledging the truth would become more difficult. "It isn't your fault."

"Or yours." A sob broke the sudden silence as she looked back at him and stepped outside. Then she closed the door behind her, leaving him alone.

He blew out the candles and dropped to the couch, too blindsided by what he should've seen coming to do anything but stare at the fire until only glowing red embers remained. His ex had used the excuse of not being ready to get married every time he proposed, but only his ego had taken a beating. Lee Anne's experience meant she would never be ready, giving him no alternatives. A hundred proposals wouldn't change her understandable aversion to marriage. He would never have another chance.

His phone vibrated on the end table and lit up the room for a brief moment. Crazy hope made him reach for it before logic and reality kicked in.

"What the hell happened with you and Lee Anne???" Lindie's name and number vanished as the screen went dark. Another buzz brought it back. *"She's upset and she won't tell me anything."*

More vibrations buzzed through his hand.

"What's going on, Novotny?"

"Did you have a fight? Fix it!"

"Lindie thinks you and LA had a fight. I told her you guys don't argue. Ever."

"Russ! Answer me!"

"Your dad had an acc—" The phone went dark again.

Accident? Panic distracted him from heartache as he stabbed at the home button to log in and finish reading the text.

"Your dad had an accident with the computer again. Would you please tell him not to push so many keys at once?" His mom's message ended with an annoyed-face emoticon.

Pushing to his feet, he tapped in the only answer he had right now. *"I can fix this. Mind if I visit for a couple days? I'll be there in three hours."*

After her smile and thumbs-up response, he powered off his cell and headed to his bedroom to pack.

CHAPTER 9

Lee Anne tugged her hat lower over her ears and trudged along the narrow path in the knee-deep snowdrift, needing a reprieve from her sisters' well-intentioned meddling. They didn't need to know the reason behind Russ's abrupt departure before supper or why he'd vanished for two days before that. She'd rehashed it a thousand times since Tuesday. A piece of paper didn't prove she loved Russ any more than the three diplomas packed in a box in her garage made her a biologist with a PhD. Hard work, dedication, and sacrifice had earned her the degrees. Those three things provided better odds for happily-ever-after than a marriage certificate.

Still, his past had paved the way to his viewpoint on living together as much as her past had soured her on marriage. She couldn't blame him for wanting that kind of commitment. If they'd met two or five or eight years ago, she probably would've considered getting married over living together. But they hadn't, and she couldn't. Love wasn't enough to overcome the obstacle between them unless one of them caved. A concession like that would likely put another bigger obstruction—resentment—in their way and destroy their friendship.

What's left of it.

She pushed open the heavy sliding door, glad for some physical labor to work out her frustration and heartache. Moonlight reflected off the snow, illuminating the inside of the barn and lighting her way to the woodpile.

The steady lift, turn, drop did nothing to improve her mood. Neither did the *clunk* of firewood in the metal wheelbarrow. As she laid the last split log in the one-wheeled cart, the crunch of boots on the crusty snow announced an intruder. Why couldn't her sisters mind their own damn business, at least where Russ was concerned?

"Want some help?" Blaine's voice brought relief.

Yeah, you can tell your wife to stop being so nosy. "I got it, thanks."

He chuckled. "You're as stubborn as Lindie."

She aimed a scowl at him as she grabbed the wooden handles. "Did she send you out here?"

"No." Crossing his arms, he stepped in front of her load. "I had a chat with Russ when he got back from his mom and dad's, and again tonight. He's miserable. You're miserable. The two of you—"

"Didn't ask for your advice." *So that's where he went.* Instead of banging her brother-in-law in the shins, she released her grip and mirrored his stance.

"I'm going to tell you a story. It's sad and ugly, but then it gets better. A lot better. I hope you'll listen and think about it."

He paused, giving her the opportunity to tell him to go to hell, but she smothered the urge. It wouldn't do any good. "I don't really have a choice, do I? You'll tell me anyway. Not that it'll make any difference."

His shrug suggested he was willing to give it a try. "I was married —and divorced—about thirteen years ago. My then-wife had an affair with a friend of mine. Instead of contacting a lawyer and letting it go, I told my friend's wife and convinced her to sleep with me for payback. Then there were two bitter divorces. I lost my self-respect and the friendship I'd had with my friend and his wife. They had a brutal custody battle over their kids, especially since my ex-wife was pregnant with his baby. I swore I'd never get married again."

"But you did." The words came out more sarcastic than she intended, but his choice to remarry was his own, not hers.

"Yes, I did. Did Lindie tell you she kicked me out of the house the first time I asked her to marry me?" Regret lingered in his expression, but he grinned. "I offered her a business deal—marry me so we could share the farm. Classy, huh? A few days too late, I realized that I loved her and I wanted a real marriage with her."

"So you told her and then you rode off into the sunset together on your trusty steed." She patted her hand on her lips to cover a fake yawn and impatiently shifted her weight from her left foot to her right. "How touching and completely unlike the situation between Russ and me."

"Actually, I had to show her she could believe what I said about loving her, which meant choosing her over having my name on the deed to my grandparents' farm…and fear. Lots of fear. Because of her parents' fucked-up relationship, she didn't plan on getting married, either. We had to trust ourselves and each other, and take a leap of faith to get to where we are now. You and Russ love each other, but neither of you wants to be the one to take the risk."

"And you're telling me I should be the bigger pers—"

"I'm not taking sides. I told Russ what I told you, and you guys have to figure out how to make it work, *if* you're even willing to try. I hope so, for both your sakes. Regrets live with you forever." He shoved his hands in his pockets and walked to the wide doorway. "We all know he went away for a couple days to run from something he can't escape and he left before supper tonight to keep you from being uncomfortable at a family dinner, not because a work emergency came up. Do what you want, but it's pretty clear any pretense of a just-friends relationship isn't going to work."

Slumping against the woodpile, she bit back the automatic retort that they'd eventually find a way to stay friends. The truth was they wouldn't. She hadn't wanted to face reality. Their feelings for each other had never been in question, but a solution required giving him her all or giving him up completely. In between wasn't possible.

When her brother-in-law was out of earshot, she drew back her foot to kick the wheelbarrow tire and then put it back on the dirt floor. A broken toe didn't sound any better than a broken heart. "Damn you, Blaine."

His advice hadn't made her decision any easier. In fact, the lack of guidance was exactly the kind of advice her dad had dispensed—a life-experience story and a short list of yes-or-no options. He'd always expected her to weigh the pros and cons herself, citing perspective as the factor for one person's advantage being another person's disadvantage. Of course, the choice of not making a decision was on the table as well, but she didn't like the potential consequences of that any better.

Abandoning her task, she marched to the barn door and slid it closed from the outside. The path through the snow guided her past the biggest chicken coop and to the fork that led to the house or to more fenced hen yards. Since her car keys were in her purse in the house, she continued along the trail that led her past the other coops and toward the house next door. Maybe by the time she arrived at Russ's homey brick ranch, she would have an answer to her dilemma.

A line of packed snow zigzagged from the edge of the woods near Lindie's dormant garden toward the open area beyond the trees. Dusk loomed, but the moon on the white ground lit her way along the quiet quarter-mile hike. As she neared the far tree line, the golden glow of Russ's kitchen lights reflected off the crystalline surface in large lopsided rectangles. Then headlights flashed on and off through the tree trunks, announcing the arrival of a visitor. The engine cut off a moment after she stepped into the open, but she didn't slow. Her business with Russ was too important to put off, whether he had company or not.

As Lee Anne crossed the side yard to the front corner of the house, a willowy blonde exited the car in the driveway and closed the door. The woman's coat billowed out behind her, revealing a belly resembling Layla's, made all the more obvious by her thin build.

Despair nearly halted Lee Anne in her tracks. *Sasha. And she's pregnant with—*

Common sense prevailed before she finished the thought. *Like hell she is. That manipulative bitch.*

If he'd had even an inkling that his ex could be pregnant, Russ would've taken immediate responsibility. Sasha had kept the news secret on purpose or expected him to raise another man's child. Either way, she was a liar and a user.

Lee Anne rounded the corner of the garage, giving her a clear view of the front door from her place in the shadows. She stepped close enough to eavesdrop on their conversation.

Within seconds of the blonde pushing the doorbell, Russ appeared in the doorway. "Oh, it's you. What are you doing here, Sasha?"

The blonde launched into a melodramatic bout of sobbing. "I wanted to tell you, but... And I was scared you might not take me back. The baby's due in a few months. I'm sorry I left. Please tell me it isn't too late."

His short bark of laughter held no humor. "Do you really think I'm going to fall for that? You started your period before I left for the conference in San Francisco. You know, when you dumped me with a note on the fridge? And we didn't have sex for weeks before that. Not that I'd take you back even if it was mine or if you were really having a baby. I'm in love with somebody else."

Sasha's head jerked up, illuminating an angry frown and flawless makeup. "*Somebody else?* But you can't be. Who is she?"

He glanced toward the driveway and met Lee Anne's gaze over the roof of the car. "A very special woman. She respects and appreciates me, and she'd never lie about being pregnant. I'll do whatever I need to do to make her happy."

How did he know I was here? Lee Anne pressed a gloved hand to her lips to stay silent. The conversation they had to have wouldn't be prudent in the present company.

His ex scowled and yanked a round pillow from under her shirt. "You can't do this to me! I'm broke!"

You slimy little lying leech.

"Then sell the car you tried to steal from me and the ring I let you keep." Russ's tone was unsympathetic. "And you could try not to get fired from your next job."

The pillow connected with his bicep once before he wrested it from the crazy woman who'd used him. She stamped her foot and growled. "I put up with you for seven years! You owe me!"

He heaved the pillow toward the car in the driveway. "No, *I* put up with *you* for seven years and I don't owe you a damn thing. Leave. And don't come back or I'm calling the cops."

Lee Anne ducked past the corner of the garage as the liar whirled toward her car. The sound of the front door closing was closely followed by the slam of a car door. She hurried to the back of the house to the whir of spinning tires on ice and sank onto the deck steps outside the kitchen.

Cold hadn't begun to seep through her jeans before the patio door opened behind her. Then footsteps announced Russ's presence. "You should come inside before you freeze."

Tadpoles wiggled up a storm in her stomach, but she stood. "You handled that better than I would've."

He gestured for her to go in ahead of him. "I couldn't have done it without you. Want some hot chocolate?"

I want you. She shook her head and bent to unfasten her boots. "No thanks. I didn't mean to make you uncomfortable earlier. You shouldn't have to give up spending time with your friends because of me."

"And you should be able to spend time with your family without worrying about me being uncomfortable." He kicked off his running shoes on the rug. "Let's go warm up by the fireplace."

"We're going to have to talk about it." Her throat tightened around the words. His fingers brushed hers when he took her coat and hat, reminding her of his careful touches while they made love. "We can't go on like this."

"I know." Nothing about his voice, his expression, or his body language hinted at the resolution he expected. He hung her belongings on the back of the closest dinette chair without elaborating.

She led the way to the living room, no more sure of what to say or do than on the hike from Lindie's house. Blaine had made the decision sound so simple, but it wasn't. She and Russ had complicated baggage and neither of them had managed to unpack enough to make permanent room for somebody else.

He added a log to the low-burning fire and then sat on the floor. "I lit it just before you got here, so it'll take a few minutes to get going."

Flames licked at the wood, sending flickering shadows bouncing around the nearly dark room. The ebb and flow matched her emotions.

Picking up a small notepad and pen, he patted the spot next to him. "Sit with me. I need your help making a list."

"What kind of list?" She knelt beside him, hoping he didn't ask her for a last night of sex before they cut bait and reeled in the line. Saying no would be impossible.

"All the reasons I refuse to live with a woman again." The pen was poised above the paper, ready to record supporting evidence to end their ties. He'd made his decision, clearly defying Blaine's advice.

Swallowing the ache in her throat, she focused on the blue and gold flames. "You're afraid she won't be committed to you. You think she can leave you easier. You don't want to make the same mistake twice."

He moved the pen across the page. "Any more?"

"Not that I can think of at the moment."

"Okay." He tore off the top page and handed it to her. "Read it. Does it say everything you told me?"

A scan of his neat handwriting confirmed the contents. "Yes."

He scooted to the hearth and removed the log grabber from the tool stand. "Put the list in the tongs."

The paper crinkled as she weaved it in the overlapping ends of the tool. "What are you going to do with it?"

"Burn it." Adjusting his hold, he slipped the cast-iron tongs past the center opening of the fireplace screen. Orange flames engulfed the paper, turning it to ash in a matter of seconds. He laid the tool on the hearth and stared at her for several seconds before speaking. "I know you're committed not just to me but to *us*. Marriage wouldn't keep you from leaving if you wanted or needed to, which is how it should be. And loving you will never be a mistake. Living without you is."

His softly spoken words took her breath away with their insight and sincerity. He'd chosen her over his fear of repeating the mistake he'd made with Sasha.

She reached for him, desperate to renew the physical closeness they'd sacrificed to save their friendship. "You mean…"

Linking his fingers with hers, he nodded. "I want you to move in.

There's plenty of room in the dressers and closet, and I made space in the bathroom for your stuff."

"But—"

"No buts. All that matters is we're together. That's more important than anything else." He lifted her hand to his lips and kissed each finger. His gentle caress was as seductive as the desire glittering in his eyes. The combination embodied everything she loved about him.

She hooked her free hand around the back of his neck and pulled him close enough to touch her lips to his. The glide of his tongue along hers triggered shivers through her body, like the first time he'd touched her. Each motion created a wave of sensation that spread to the tips of her fingers and toes.

Impatient to renew their intimate connection, she worked his fleece pullover up to his chest and pulled the tucked shirt beneath from his jeans. His back was solid and warm against her palms, making her wish a snap of her fingers could eliminate the clothing between them.

He groaned into her mouth and eased her sweatshirt up to her breasts. His breath was sultry against her neck as he broke off the kiss. "I missed this. I missed *you*."

She shoved the layers higher, savoring the coarseness of his chest hair and the tautness of his nipples against her fingertips. "Take off your clothes and I'll show you how much I missed you."

His low chuckle made the muscles ripple under his skin. "If I didn't know better, I'd say you only want me for my body."

Firelight emphasized his movements as he dragged both layers over his head. A minute later, his pants landed on the pile on the floor, leaving him naked and beautiful in front of her.

He withdrew a condom from the end table drawer. "Your turn."

Fighting the need to hurry, she peeled her sweatshirt and t-shirt upward, halting when her ponytail caught in the tangle of sleeves and hood. Calloused hands eased her hair free of the mess and slipped the fabric from her arms, another reminder of how lucky she was to have this man in her life. The rest of her clothes put up less of a struggle as she stripped down to her bare skin. "I'm not wearing clothes anymore when we're alone."

He released her messy ponytail and threaded his fingers in her hair. "Sounds like an excellent plan. Couch or rug? Top or bottom?"

She pressed her lips to his collarbone. "Rug. Top."

His crooked smile suggested he either liked or had correctly guessed her preferences. "On my back or sitting?"

"What do you think?"

"Sitting, so we can hold on to each other." He guided her to the floor and positioned her knees on either side of his thighs. "Like the first time."

She grabbed the foil package and tore it open. His cock twitched as she rolled the condom into place. "After this, we're moving on to the second position we tried."

He lifted her by the waist and lined up his dick with her opening. "Is oral included in positions? Or do you want fucked from behind?"

His memory of their encounters shouldn't have surprised her. He was an attentive and sensitive lover, worthy of her complete trust and devotion—and he had willingly given her the kind of commitment she'd asked for.

"How about if we write them on scraps of paper and draw them from a hat?" She draped her arms over his shoulders and let gravity take him inside her until every inch of him filled her.

They gasped in unison and then he kissed her ear, adding to the wonderful sensations buzzing through her body. "Sexual positions roulette?"

"Mm-hm." She rotated her hips in a leisurely circle, rubbing the head of his erection into her deepest hollow. The friction set off miniature fireworks and turned her muscles to rubber. "You feel so good."

His hand drifted to the middle of her back, bringing his chest in contact with her nipples. The smattering of coarse curls teased the tips and his mouth closed over hers. A slow dance of his tongue with hers echoed the tempo of his subtle thrusts, drawing her into a floating state of euphoria. He swelled inside her and his pulse beat a steady rhythm against her fingertips at his neck.

He was as close to going off as she was.

Using the last of her energy, she squeezed her inner muscles around him and rocked forward. The world splintered, amplified by his moan and a sweep of his finger over her clit. Her cry was swallowed by a kiss as he stiffened, and another louder groan signaled his release.

His hold on her tightened, keeping her safe and loved while she swam in utter bliss and learned how to breathe again. He was her life-line, the man she would spend the rest of her life with. They would buoy each other through it all.

She stroked her cheek against his beard, more than willing to give him what he needed. "No catch and release this time. You're a keeper. Will you marry me?"

EPILOGUE

"You need to wait a little bit longer to release the button." Russ grabbed the line and retrieved Cam's hook from the grass behind him. "Reel her in and we'll try again."

The boy cranked the handle to take up the slack. "I don't think we have time, Uncle Russ. Aunt Lindie's waving at us from the deck."

A glance at the house confirmed Cam's observation, but the uptick in Russ's pulse wasn't from nerves. "Go tell her we're ready."

The fishing rod landed on the ground at his feet, and Cam sprinted past Stockwell, Fielding, and the rest of the milling guests. "We're ready!"

Blaine trailed after him with Leo at his side, followed closely behind by Erik. His slower gait spoke of a man in need of sleep, but the look of complete happiness hadn't left his face since he'd announced the birth of his and Layla's sons in the hospital waiting room three and a half weeks ago.

At the back of the house, Leo and Cam lined up next to their pair of foster sisters with matching hair and eyes, giggling and picking at each other like they'd been siblings for years. Behind them, Layla handed off a baby to her husband and cradled the other in one arm. Then Lindie and Blaine took their places on either side of Lee Anne.

The procession crossed the yard to the wide mown path leading to the open-air tent set up beside the lake. Lee Anne's shimmering blue-green sundress fluttered in the light breeze, giving Russ a peek at the legs that had entwined with his every night for the past five months. A halo of wildflowers ringed the tucked and pinned pile of hair on her head, but her smile took his breath away.

Her gaze locked on his as her sister and brother-in-law joined the other guests near the tent and she continued to his side at the edge of the lake. Her smile widened to a grin when she gave him a head-to-toe assessment. She evidently approved of his khaki shorts, fishing vest over a button-down short-sleeved shirt, and sandals.

The judge unfolded the paper in her hands. "Ready?"

"Yes." Lee Anne's answer was quick and decisive.

"And you, Russ?" A hint of humor colored the other woman's voice.

He slipped his arm around Lee Anne's waist. "Absolutely."

"Excellent. Let's get started then." Adjusting her hold on the paper, the justice of the peace cleared her throat. "Russ and Lee Anne, today I join you legally in marriage, but your hearts are already bound to each other by love. Celebrate your love every day as you share life's ups and downs. Rely on each other, and remember that your commitment is stronger than the paper making you husband and wife. The gifts you give are a reminder of the strength you find together."

His thumb and forefinger closed around the ring in the small chest pocket of his vest. He slipped the simple gold-and-diamond band onto her finger and lifted her hand to his lips. "Like this circle, my love for you never ends. You are my wife, my lover, my best friend."

Lee Anne blinked at him, sending a single tear spilling over her lashes. Then she untied a safety-pinned ribbon bow over her heart and slid the gold band into her palm. The cool metal warmed on his finger as she slipped it past his knuckle. "Like your love for me, my love for you never ends. You are my husband, my lover, my best friend."

The judge tucked the paper into her skirt pocket. "Congratulations, Russ and Lee Anne. You are officially husband and wife. Bride, you may kiss your groom and, groom, you may kiss your bride."

Gathering the love of his life in his arms, he met her halfway for a mostly chaste kiss. It was still enough to wake Moby. "Any chance you'll wear your mermaid outfit to swim tonight?"

Mischief sparkled in her eyes. "Do you promise to catch me, Mr. Fisherman? I promise to let you."

When her fingers aren't attached to her keyboard, Mellanie Szereto enjoys hiking, Pilates, cooking, gardening, and researching for her stories. Many times, the research partners with her other hobbies, taking her from the Hocking Hills region in Ohio to the Colorado Rockies or the Adirondacks of New York. Sometimes, the trip is no farther than her garden for ingredients and her kitchen to test recipes for her latest steamy tale. Mellanie makes her home in rural Indiana with her husband of thirty-two years and their son. She is a 2016 recipient of the RWA Service Award, RWA Chapter Advisor, and a member of Romance Writers of America, Indiana Romance Writers of America, Contemporary Romance Writers, and Fantasy, Futuristic, and Paranormal Romance Writers.

Email: mellanie@mellanieszereto.com
Website: http://www.mellanieszereto.com
Newsletter: http://eepurl.com/cDEHXL
Facebook: http://www.facebook.com/authormellanieszereto
Amazon: https://www.amazon.com/author/mellanieszereto
BookBub: https://www.bookbub.com/authors/mellanie-szereto
Book+Main Bites: https://bookandmainbites.com/MellanieSzereto
Goodreads: http://www.goodreads.com/mellanie_szereto

If you enjoyed this book, please consider rating or leaving a review on the retailer's website and/or Goodreads. Thanks!